Whispering Oaks

The Curse

Meredith Isaac Anderson

The Cover

Photograph: The author

Whispering Oaks,
The Curse

To Brittany, who said to me,
"I'll bet you can't."

To Brent —

Read — Enjoy!

God Bless...

McMeredith Anders

"Uncle Mert"

Acknowledgements...

I would like to offer special thanks to those who encouraged me in this endeavor, especially Professor Nikki Hansen, retired Doctor and Head of the English Department from Weber State University in Ogden, Utah, my alma mater. I would be remiss not to mention my high school friend, Linda, a historian and author in her own right, who became my wife and best friend over forty-five years ago when I was a young sailor in Uncle Sam's Seventh Fleet.

Monica Keene, Jim Cotney, Sherry Anderson, Kristi Sandgren and Dean Cody, author of PLATINUM DNA, all gave me meaningful critical reviews.

The members of my League of Utah Writers Critique Group, Vicki Wheeler, Ceil DeYoung, Pam King, John Robinson, Gayanne Ramsden, Kathy Brown, Karen Peck and Bill Tandy; all of whom helped with rewrite after rewrite.

My grandchildren, Mattea Jeffs, Josie Sandgren and Nick Toban offered artistic talent while Phillip and Ruby Sandgren offered ideas and inspiration. My son Tony and daughter, Nikki who discovered my major inconsistencies in the original manuscript.

My granddaughter, Brittany Sandgren, who, during her formative years offered me a model.

Last but not least, my friend and neighbor, Jennifer Groberg who read the proof copy from cover to cover.

Whispering Oaks
The Curse

Contents

Chapter 1

Shamus

Brittany lay on her grandfather's hammock in the shade of the towering oak tree in the side yard of the farm house. The warm sun slipped between the leaves above, touching her here and there as a light breeze moved them. She had spent most of the morning on the riding lawn mower. She didn't finish, but she mowed enough to get a handle on how it was done.

She had enjoyed the mowing, but she was looking forward to the lunch her grandfather had promised her at Torgilson's General Store. He said Mrs. Torgilson had a grandson, a young fellow the entire community called Jinx, who worked at the soda fountain. Her grandfather, who the family calls Potsy, said he was pleasant looking, intelligent and fun loving. At least this was his impression of the lanky dark haired youngster.

A nap. That's what I need, she thought. She closed her eyes, her eyelids getting heavy. Now was the time for rest. *Nothing is sweeter than a nap before lunch.*

The two acres of lawn spread away from the house and along the rolling hill beside her, down to the pond. The sweet smell of honeysuckle permeated the air as she turned slightly, trying to find that comfortable spot she would enjoy.

1

She heard a rustle, just a slight noise in the dry leaves that lay on the ground at the base of the great oak near the head of the hammock. A few leaves, blown up there from the previous fall season, were crisp yellow, gold and brown. The slightest breeze caused them to crackle softly, like a roaring camp fire. It was a comforting sound as she was trying to relax in the warmth of the late morning.

Potsy had gone to the hardware store in the village. He said he was picking up cabinet door hardware for a special project he was building in his woodshop.

At first she was lulled by the movement of the dry leaves, just enjoying it, but when it continued after the breeze dropped off, her curiosity piqued. She rolled over half-asleep, her left eye peering through the mesh near the pillow at the top of the hammock.

What? She couldn't believe what she was seeing. There below the hammock at the base of the great oak stood a little man not as big as one of her brother's G. I. Joe figures. A floppy felt hat on his head, a strange shirt, looking like a maple leaf, adorned the front of his small body.

Her senses suddenly stirred to the level of *wide awake* as she rolled slowly to her left side, moving to the edge of the hammock. She kept her right eye closed as she moved her head to the outside of the hammock to get a clear view of the little man. He was frozen, looking like a tiny doll holding a large oak leaf in the air.

She was in a position to see him clearly now. She blinked and opened both eyes. The little man was *gone*. She blinked again and opened only her left eye.

In that wink of an eye, the little man had dropped the leaf and appeared to be in mid-stride, running toward the great oak tree. He was frozen now, appearing like a picture of an athlete in a text book, one foot on the ground and the other in the air behind him. His entire body leaning forward, arms raised slightly.

Brittany slid from the hammock onto the grass, all the time keeping a single eye on the figure. She was close enough now, to pick him up. She reached carefully for the small figure.

"Brittany! Don't you dare touch him!" A thick Irish brogue re-sounded from her left.

The command was clear and heavy.

That's not Potsy's voice, she thought.

The tone was that of a big man, gruff and a little frightening. She wanted to look around to see who was giving her orders, but she had lost sight of the little man once and she wasn't going to take a chance on losing view of him again.

"Brittany! You touch him and I'll come over there and smack you upside your head with my shillelagh!" The voice growled. "You'll have a headache that'll last you two weeks."

Brittany gritted her teeth and withdrew her hand. She didn't want to be struck in the head by a big stick. The man talking was obviously standing over and behind her.

"So, you can see this little guy too?" She asked.

"Of course I can see him, you dolt. How do you think I knew you were holding him?"

"Holding him? I'm not holding him. I haven't laid a hand on him. He's just standing there. I don't want to hurt him. I just want to talk to him."

"Aye, tis true. You're not touching him, but you're holding him by the oldest Druid trick in the book."

"And what is that?"

"Ocular Sinister, the *evil eye*, you dolt! You know very well what you're doing."

3

Brittany kept her left eye on the little man. "That's the second time you've called me a dolt. You're calling me a dull or stupid person and that's not very nice. I understand the meaning of a lot of words, so you need to be careful what you call me."

"Ha, ha, ha," laughed the voice as if he were having a rollicking good time. "Dolt, dolt, dolt," he taunted.

"By the way." She moved her elbow to become more comfortable on the grass, her eye steady on the little man. "You called me by my name the first time you spoke to me. Who are you and what are you doing on my grandfather's property?"

"My name is Shamus. I am an Elfin, as is the little man you have trapped in your vision. I am the Elfin Guardian and I've lived here for more than two hundred years. I should be asking, what *you* are doing on my property?"

"My grandfather bought this land from the county five years ago, cleared a few trees and built his house. There is no one on this land but myself and my grandparents. So, where do you live and how do you know my name?"

"I live in a very nice city, right under that great oak tree there. I know you are Jacob and Carol Ellis's granddaughter. I heard them say your name before you arrived yesterday and again since you have been here. I'll call you by your name unless you'd prefer me to call you Darlin', like your grandmother does."

"Let's leave my Monya out of this." Brittany scratched the side of her head with her right hand. "This conversation is giving me a headache. You won't have to hit me with your shillelagh."

Shamus laughed again. His voice softening, even though he remained concealed from view. "You know, Shimmy isn't feeling any too good either. You've had him standing on one foot for a long time. That Ocular Sinister is a very dirty trick you know. It freezes Elfins dead in their tracks."

"I'm sorry, I don't know that word. What's an Elfin?"

"You are a dolt," Shamus laughed. "An Elfin is what you would call *a little people*. The word is from our ancient language and it means elf-like. We are like elves, but we're smarter and our magic

4

is for good. Because our magic is good, it is superior to the magic of any elf."

Brittany scratched her head. "I thought the *little people* were called leprechauns. Are you saying you are not leprechauns?"

"Oh yes, we are not," said the Elfin Guardian. "Leprechauns are found in Ireland. We are indeed related to the leprechauns, but we are Elfins. We have some of the strengths and weaknesses of the leprechauns. I guess you could say we are descended from them as you are descended from the peoples of Europe, England and Ireland. "

"Are you going to show yourself, Shamus?"

"I don't want to. I propose that you release Shimmy. Go back to your nap, forget all about us and we'll have no further trouble."

"I don't want trouble and I don't want to make trouble. I want to *make* friends with you people. You've lived here for two hundred years and nobody even knows you exist."

Shamus's voice became deeper. "It's no wonder you didn't know. You are such a dolt. I told you only a few seconds ago that we are Elfins. We are *not* people."

"Okay, okay. I'm sorry. I want to be friends with you *Elfins*. You couldn't have a nicer dolt for a friend."

Shamus roared with laughter. "We don't need any *people* for friends. We've avoided you dolts for all this time and we aren't going to start making friends now."

"I'm beginning to think you don't have anything to say about it. As long as Shimmy is under my gaze, in this *Ocular Sinister,* he's my prisoner. Is that right?"

"That's right. For a dolt, you're pretty smart."

"Tell me," Brittany said. "Is it impossible for you to lie? My Potsy told me it is impossible for leprechauns to lie to a direct question. Is that true for Elfins too?"

There was a long pause in the conversation. "Your Potsy? That would be Bud Ellis. He has told you true. Another trick of those nasty Druids of yesteryear. May the curses of all time be on their mangy souls."

5

"Okay, Shamus. If you'll give me a couple promises, I'll set Shimmy free."

"It will depend on *what* the promises are. We don't have any 'pots of gold' or any of that nonsense."

"I don't want any gold. First, I want your promise you'll be my friends and number two, that you'll come any time I call you."

Silence and hesitation made the air heavy. Brittany strained to listen.

"Very well," said Shamus. "Now open both of your eyes and free Shimmy. The old boy is getting very tired."

Brittany blinked and opened both eyes. There was a slight rustling in the leaves and another little man appeared. He was dressed in black with a round-top bowler hat which had a shiny green ribbon for a hat band. A small four leafed clover stuck out of his hat band and he was carrying a long walking stick.

"I'll appear to you when you call me as long as you're alone. You'll be able to see me and any other Elfins with both eyes open. When you want me, you must say, *Shamus Mactavish O'Riley, please step forward*. Do you understand that?"

Brittany mouthed the words, *Shamus Mactavish O'Riley, please step forward*. She blinked again to make sure both eyes were open. "It's amazing. I can see both of you and you're moving around."

Shimmy realized he was free and made a dash for the giant oak tree.

"Hold right there young fella," Shamus said, pointing his walking stick at Shimmy. "Come over here."

After approaching, Shimmy stepped sideways standing as close as he could to Shamus and removed his hat.

Shamus's right hand shot out, snatching Shimmy's flop hat. He struck Shimmy several times about the head and shoulders with it. "You dolt! Why didn't you go invisible?"

The little man shrugged his shoulders as the Guardian handed him his hat back. "Now stand up straight and meet our new friend. Brittany, this is Shimmy. He is a decorator for the High Council and it is his job to gather leaves and other materials for construction and decorating in the city."

Shimmy, hat in hand, eyes peering upward from a half-bowed head, spoke in a soft voice. "Ga - Glad to meet you, Brittany."

"Nice to meet you too, Shimmy."

"Brittany, are we going over to Torgilson's store or not?" a voice called from the house.

"That's my grandpa, Potsy. I have to go now."

Brittany began to rise to her knees and stopped. "It sure has been fun meeting you guys. I'll see you tomorrow. Have a great day."

"Wait!" Shamus said. "Don't forget. You are being entrusted with one of the greatest secrets in this world."

Brittany stopped in mid-stride and looked back very solemnly, her head almost touching her chest. "I understand trust and I'll guard your secret with my life. No one will hear of you from me unless you say it is all right."

She skipped up the stairs, waving a final good-bye to her new friends as she entered the house.

Potsy met her in the hall near the door. "I'm ready to go any time you are."

"Right now is good for me."

"Good. My van is parked over by the shop. Let's get going."

Chapter 2

Torgilson's Store

Raising a cloud of dust, the gravel of the country parking lot spit and scattered from beneath the tires as the old van skittered to a stop and the engine was shut off.

Brittany jerked the handle, pushing the door open and sliding to the ground in one motion. "Is this the place, Potsy?"

"Torgilson's General Store," said Brittany's grandfather as he opened his door.

Brittany's eyes widened as they explored the old white wood structure. At least a hundred feet across the front with a porch running its full length. She stared at the old wooden chairs lined up willy-nilly against the peeling paint of the clapboard front.

"I'm afraid this is as close as you get to a modern store without driving into the city," Potsy said, as he began to ascend the steps.

Brittany quickened her pace to catch her grandfather's arm as he began to cross the porch.

Two elderly men sat next to the door, playing chess on the top of a small wooden barrel.

This is what I imagined a country store might look like, Brittany thought.

"Bud, I see you have a helper with you today," said the man in a straw hat and bib overalls.

"Oh, yes," Potsy said. "Brittany, this is Doc Watson and Mr. Younger. Doc is a retired professor of science and history from State University and Mr. Younger is a retired newspaper publisher. Maybe not totally retired. He writes an article once in a while -- when he wants to get the locals upset."

Potsy was, for the most part, the perfect southern gentleman. "Fellas, this is my granddaughter, Brittany. The scholar I've told you about. I picked her up at the airport yesterday and she's been learning about farm life this morning. She's come to spend the summer with us at Whispering Oaks."

"Most delighted to meet you young lady," Doc Watson said as he stood and removed his straw hat. "Your grandfather told me you'll be in the eleventh grade when school starts. Is that right? A little ahead of your age group aren't you?"

Brittany glanced up at her Potsy. "Yes, sir. Just one grade."

Potsy shrugged his shoulders. "He's an educator. He asks those kinds of questions."

"That's great." Doc Watson smiled. "Keep up the good work and keep an eye on that grandpa of yours, he's always into some kind of mischief."

"We hope you enjoy your stay in our village," Mr. Younger said as he rose and removed an unlit corncob pipe from his mouth.

"I'm sure I will, and thanks," Brittany said, with a slight bow and followed her grandfather through the wide double doors into the store.

As she took in the sights, she was fascinated by the size of the store. The ceiling was twenty feet over head with an old fashioned ceiling fan about every ten feet across the expanse. She smiled in delight as she discovered the area was covered by two foot square tiles of tin that had been pressed with antique flower designs. Upon taking a closer look, she could see the tiles surrounding the chimney pipe of the old pot bellied stove near the front door were tarnished by decades of heat and soot.

Potsy reached back, caught Brittany under the arm and directed her to the check-out counter near the entrance. "Brittany, this is Mrs. Torgilson. Mrs. Torgilson, this is my granddaughter, Brittany. She's here for the summer, so you'll probably be seeing a lot of her. If she comes in and picks up anything, you can put it on our bill."

"What a lovely child," Mrs. Torgilson said, looking right into Brittany's eyes. "How old are you girl?"

"I'm fourteen, ma'am, but I'll be fifteen before the summer's over."

Mrs. Torgilson reached across the counter and took the ends of Brittany's flowing blond hair between her fingers. "Your hair is beautiful. Do you bleach or color it?"

Brittany felt the blood rush to her face. "No ma'am, it's all natural. My mom claims I was kissed on the head by an angel when I was a baby."

Brittany placed her hand on her grandfather's arm. "We came in for lunch didn't we?" As she looked around, her gaze fell on the soda fountain that ran down a side wall of the store. Standing behind the counter talking to a customer was a young fellow about her age. He wore a white apron. He had dark hair and a big smile.

Potsy turned toward the soda fountain. "Come on. You have to meet Jinx."

Brittany sat on a stool next to her grandfather at the long red counter.

"Hello Mr. Ellis. What can I get for you folks today?" The youngster gave a furtive glance at the girl sitting at his soda fountain.

"Jinx, this is my granddaughter, Brittany. She's here to spend the summer with us. I told her she'd love your cooking. I'll have a burger deluxe. What would you like Brittany?"

She looked down, avoiding eye contact with the young man. "I'll have the same as you, Potsy."

Potsy looked at Jinx and smiled. "Don't worry, she'll warm up to you."

Jinx prepared the meals and placed the orders in front of his patrons as other customers came in and sat at the counter. Jinx im-

11

mediately directed his attention to them.

Brittany ate her hamburger with vigor and was almost out of her shy mood when Potsy put a ten dollar bill on the counter and slid from his stool. "I'll meet you at the front check-out when you're done."

Not able to keep sight of her grandfather, Brittany finished her sandwich and walked to the area of the front checkout.

Potsy returned from the back of the store, carrying a gallon of milk, a pound of butter and a loaf of bread.

After Mrs. Torgilson rang up the sale, Potsy signed the slip while she bagged the groceries. Sliding the gallon of milk across the counter to Brittany and handing the bag to Potsy, she said, "Did you tell her about our lion?"

"I thought I'd show her on the way out," Potsy said, nudging his granddaughter ahead of him toward the open doorway.

Potsy set the groceries in the van and slammed the door shut startling Brittany who was about to climb in. "Come on," he said, leading her about twenty feet down the road to the right. He pointed to an open area about fifty feet square along the side of the store. One side and the back of the open area had a twelve foot tall wooden fence. In the corner on the right stood a giant oak tree about eight feet in diameter. The foliage on the tree was so heavy and green that its shadow made the entire area appear as dark as night.

Bricks, painted white, created a line that ran across the entire front of the area. Large signs said "**Stay behind the white line** and **Beware of lion**."

Brittany squinted and stared hard, trying to get her eyes to penetrate the darkness. "Am I supposed to be seeing something, Potsy?"

"Just keep looking and tell me what you see. Start looking right in front of you and look all the way back to the darkest spot you can see."

Brittany strained all the harder, trying to pick up sight of anything. Next to her, just across the line of white bricks, was a deeply grooved semicircle radiating from the darkness to within six feet in front of her.

"This is very interesting, Potsy." She stepped forward to measure the depth of the semicircle with her toe. "What makes this strange track in the ground?"

Her ears were greeted by a roar from the deepest shadows. She stepped backward with a start, her grandfather jerked her still further as a male African lion charged.

Turning to flee, only her grandfather's firm grip kept her in place as the giant lion's charge was countered. As he reached the end of his chain. He made a sudden stop, followed by his legs flipping from under him until his rear was some six feet beyond the ruts he had trod.

Brittany, visibly shaken, buried her face in her grandfather's shoulder.

"Don't worry. He can't hurt you. Look, he doesn't have any claws."

The lion padded up and down at the full extension of his chain, growling a strange, high pitched noise that sounded very much like a cow bellowing from the bottom of a well.

"Yes, but he has teeth!" Brittany exclaimed.

Only when she had calmed down could she see that the lion wore a heavy leather collar with a steel ring on it. The ring was attached to a heavy duty logging chain.

"That animal belongs in a zoo. It must weigh hundreds of pounds and it could easily kill a person with just the swat of a giant paw."

"You're right, but that animal has been here for over six years. This lion has never hurt anyone, and besides, the Sheriff is Torgilson's cousin and wouldn't do anything unless it did hurt someone. Torgilson uses this animal to bring in tourists off the highway and boost sales in his store. You just remember to stay clear of this lion's compound when you come over here."

"Don't you worry about me. I love animals, but I sure don't plan to become any lion's lunch."

The ride to Whispering Oaks was less than five minutes, most of it on Potsy's private dirt road which turned off the blacktop a half block from Torgilson's store.

Brittany spent the afternoon watching her grandfather cut out a cabinet in his woodshop. She helped with spot sanding and applying stain to projects that were almost finished.

At five in the evening Potsy shut down his power tools, turned off the lights and pointed to the door. "Let's go down to the chicken coop and close the gate for the night. We can gather any new eggs while we're there. We'll see if the calves need feed and check the water in the trough."

"We gave the calves fresh food and water this morning. Do you think they've eaten all we gave them already?" Brittany asked as they walked out and got into Potsy's old green pickup truck.

"I wouldn't be a bit surprised; those critters seem to have a never ending appetite."

Arriving at the cow pens, Potsy tossed a portion of a bale of hay over the fence and went into the feed and grain shed to get a small pail of chicken feed.

Brittany watched as her grandfather threw a handful of chicken feed into the main area of the enclosure. Chickens rushed from all areas of the barnyard to get inside and eat the tasty morsels. Potsy closed the large chicken wire gate and turned the latch closed.

"Why do you lock them in at night?" Brittany asked.

"We don't want them to start roosting in the trees. If they do that, before long they start laying their eggs out in the brush. We'd loose those eggs and if they start nesting on the ground, they become easy pickings for predators. Chickens are kinda' strange when they nest. If they're sitting on their nest, you have to physically knock them off to get at their eggs. Because of that behavior, predators can catch them easily if they nest anywhere but on their nesting boxes here in the coop."

He closed the feed shed and turned the latch. "Let's go to the house and see what Monya has in mind for dinner."

Monya met them at the door as they approached the house from the parking area. "Brittany, darlin', how was your day? Did

14

you have any adventures?"

"Oh yeah." Brittany held Monya's hand as they entered the house. "We went to Torgilson's and I saw that giant lion. He's beautiful, but as far as I'm concerned, he's very dangerous."

Monya pointed down the hall. "Don't worry. He's just a tourist attraction. Potsy, go wash up and come to supper."

Potsy disappeared down the hall while Monya and Brittany went into the kitchen.

"And now young lady, is there anything you want to do while you're here this summer? Anything, that is, besides hunt, fish and swim?"

"Nope. All I can think about is going down to the river with Potsy and bringing home some big old catfish." She raised her arm and flicked her wrist forward as if casting a fishing rod. "I guess you can say I was born with a bad case of fishing fever. I can't wait to feel that old rod vibrate."

The next morning was filled with work around the farm. Brittany spent most of the morning in the barnyard feeding the calves and chickens. She fed the horses and even cleaned out the stable area. She finished mowing the two acres in front of the house and down to the pond that she had started the day before. As she drove into the shop to park the mower, Potsy was working on the table saw, cutting out some new cabinet fronts. He stopped when he saw his granddaughter.

"Potsy, I have a question for you," Brittany said as she shut the tractor off. "Why is this place called Whispering Oaks?"

Potsy turned his tools off and went to stand closer to Brittany. "Well, I'll tell you. Some folks around here think this place is haunted. They say that if you sit under the oak trees after the sun goes down, you can hear them whisper to each other."

"That's interesting, but I'm afraid I'll have to *hear* it to believe

15

it," she said as she slid from the seat of the tiny tractor. "Do you have any gum, Potsy?"

"I don't. I guess you'll have to go over to Torgilson's and buy some. You can drive my van down the road and across the pond dam. You'll find a parking space for it just before you get to the blacktop. Park the van and walk from there and you won't be breaking any laws." He held out his keys and dropped them into Brittany's extended hand.

"What do I do if I run into that lion?"

"I'm told that if you bite him on the nose, he'll leave you alone. I've never tried it, but that sounds pretty logical to me."

Brittany giggled as she left the barn.

She parked the van at the end of the dam road near the black-top and walked the last half block to Torgilson's store.

Arriving at Torgilson's store, Brittany could see what Potsy meant by 'attracting traffic off the highway.' There were lots of cars with out-of-state plates in the parking lot.

One family in particular caught her eye, a young couple with a toddler at the corner of the compound. It was almost the exact spot where she had stood when the lion charged the day before.

Maybe I should warn them to step back a bit. Before the thought could form into action, she heard the roar. At the sight of the charging lion, the young couple turned and fled, the baby crying in surprise.

"Whew! They're safe," she said aloud to herself as she turned back toward the store.

She looked down at the front of her old blue shirt to make sure she was presentable. The flap on her left pocket was open and the pocket looked as if it was bulging a little.

I never use these shirt pockets, she thought as she buttoned the flap. *I wonder if I could talk Monya into sewing them shut. Then I wouldn't have to be buttoning them all the time.*

"Hello, Brittany." Mrs. Torgilson greeted her from behind the counter next to the door.

"Hi. I thought I'd come over and pick up a pack of gum. I haven't had a chance to look around your store yet. Maybe I'll just browse for a few minutes."

Mrs. Torgilson, a woman with a jolly nature, spread her arms and smiled. "Make yourself to home, girl."

Brittany turned and started down the aisle. On her right, was the old fashioned soda fountain where she had lunch the day before. She stopped to take in the atmosphere. The floor in the fountain area was covered with black and white linoleum tiles, a red Formica bar trimmed with shining aluminum rails and twelve round padded stools ran the length of the bar. Ice cream coolers with tall plastic sneeze guards stood directly behind the counter, separated by an aisle to a grill against the back wall with a large hood above it. A small sign above the grill read, "Today's Special: Toasted PB&J with Ice Cold Soda, $1^{00}."

Brittany couldn't help herself. She slid onto a bar stool and looked across the counter at the young man on duty. Tall, thin, well muscled, with dark hair, he appeared to be a year or so older than herself. The soda jerk was drying his hands on a small towel as he smiled and approached her.

"How may I help you, miss?"

"I was just wondering about your special," Brittany said, pointing above the grill. "What is 'toasted' PB&J? Don't you mean, peanut butter and jelly on toast?"

The youngster's face lit up, his blue eyes sparkled and his smile got bigger. "Oh no. What we have is much more special than that. May I make you one?"

"If I don't like it, I guess I can take it home and give it to the squirrels."

He took a pencil from behind his ear and scratched Brittany's order on a small pad, turned and began to prepare the sandwich at the grill.

Brittany couldn't help but put her feet on the shiny rail in front of her and twist from side to side.

The fountain clerk said, "Go ahead. Everybody does it."

Brittany was caught off guard by the handsome face. "Does what?"

"Spins on the bar stools," the young man said, making a spinning motion in the air with his index finger pointed down.

Brittany pulled on the edge of the counter, the force of just a finger sending her spinning round and round. On the third spin she stopped herself. "Wow. I can see why everyone does it. It's a blast."

By this time the fountain clerk was setting her order in front of her; a small plate with a grilled sandwich and a glass of soda over crushed ice. The bread was thick, grilled with butter and the jam inside had chunks of strawberry in it. She took a bite.

"You're right," she said, her mouth still containing the first bite. "This is great."

The youngster stuck out both hands in front of him, palms up. "There ya go. Now you'll believe me when I tell you somethin's good." He reached his right hand toward Brittany. "Hello again. It's Brittany, right?"

Brittany felt her face flush as she took his hand. "Yes. We met yesterday."

"Correction. We were introduced yesterday. We did not *meet*. I was busy yesterday. I had to talk to my grandmother to find out who you are."

"Grandmother?" Brittany said.

"Guilty. I'm a Torgilson too."

Brittany rolled her eyes. "Of course you are. Potsy told me a little about you. I knew that. It just slipped my mind."

For the moment, Brittany was the only customer at the soda fountain. The two youngsters chatted for several minutes, until a little old lady came in and ordered a 'special'.

Brittany looked at her ticket, $1.14. She put a dollar fifty on the bar next to the tab and slipped from her stool. Jinx was busy, so she could only wave as she turned into the notions aisle.

"What a store. They have everything here," she said in a whispered tone as she looked at the large assortment of yarn, thread, notions and buttons.

After spending an hour browsing through the store, she found her way to the candy department, picked up a pack of gum, and headed for the front check-out.

"Will this be everything?" Mrs. Torgilson asked. "I saw you back there talking to Jinx. I knew you two would hit it off. What do you think of him?"

"Oh, Mrs. Torgilson, your grandson is awesome and he makes a great sandwich. I'll have to come and see him tomorrow if my grandparents don't have too much for me to do."

Mrs. Torgilson started to ring up the sale. "Did you want to pay for all this now, or did you want me to put it on your grandfather's bill?"

"Oh, I'll pay for it. I can afford my own gum."

"Great. That'll be two dollars and fifty-four cents. Did you want a bag for your gum? I see you have your ribbon in your pocket already."

"In my pocket?" Brittany felt the front pockets of her denim trousers. She knew her face was turning red. *I don't have any ribbon in my pocket,* she thought as she glanced down. Her shirt pocket was open *again.* The flap was not only open, but the button was *missing.* A small flat-pack of glossy green ribbon stuck out. The price ticket visible, two dollars.

Brittany dug two dollar bills and some change from her back trouser pocket, "I'm sorry, Mrs Torgilson. I didn't realize I had picked up the ribbon."

"The curse of Whispering Oaks," Mrs. Torgilson said, handing Brittany her receipt.

"What?"

"That's what your grand-dad calls it. He comes in every once in a while and winds up taking out something small that he can't remember picking up. He always pays for it, that's not the problem. The way the curse works, according to him, is -- he never gets home with the item he paid for."

A frown crossed Brittany's face and her eyes narrowed. "Well, this ribbon is going to get home, and I'm going to give it to my Monya."

Brittany waved off the bag that Mrs. Torgilson was holding, picked up her gum and her receipt and headed for the door.

Walking down the steps, Brittany watched the family that had been near the lion when she entered the store. The lion was walking up and down at the end of his chain, his head held high and his tail almost straight up in the air.

"That is a beautiful animal," she said in a soft voice. "I wish it were in a wild animal park somewhere and the Torgilson's had a bronze statue."

As she entered the street and headed toward the crossroad that lead to Whispering Oaks, she heard a rustling in the gravel behind her. She turned around.

Jinx appeared, jogging up to her.

"Hey! What's the big hurry?" Jinx said.

Brittany stopped and looked at him. "I thought you were working."

"I was, but my sister, Marie, came on duty at three, so I'm free to go. Marie and I come up here to visit our grandparents every spring from Atlanta. We both work at the soda fountain all summer. That's how we build up our college fund. I love it, she hates it. What can I say?"

Brittany turned to continue as Jinx came along side. "So tell me, what's your real name?"

Running the toe of his low-cut tennis shoe in a half-circle on the dirt, Jinx lowered his head and fidgeted. "My real name is Marion, but I don't run around telling everybody I meet."

"That's a cute name. So where'd you get the handle of Jinx?"

"That's hard to explain. I think your grandpa had something to do with it. Two years ago he came into the store. My grandmother

20

introduced us and told me about the curse of the Whispering Oaks. I made some foolish offhand remark about your grandpa being a little old shoplifter. I didn't mean it and I didn't think he was close enough to hear me, but I started having little mishaps right away and I've had them ever since. The strange thing is, I only have mishaps here at the store. When I go home to Atlanta, I play basketball, run track and do all sorts of stuff. I never have a problem. My grandmother said she thought your grandpa put a jinx on me, and folks hereabouts have called me Jinx ever since."

Brittany ducked her head, about to laugh and searched for another subject. "Don't you drive? How come you're walking?"

"Sure I drive. I got my license last fall, but like I said, I run track and play basketball. If you're going to do that, you need good wind. I walk or run pretty much anywhere I need to go in the village."

The couple walked along together until they came to the road that lead to Whispering Oaks. "Well, this is where I go south," Brittany said.

"I know, this is where I turn north. Maybe you can come by the store tomorrow or the next day and we can chat."

"Maybe you can come on out to Whispering Oaks and visit me," Brittany said, showing a toothy smile and gesturing toward the road.

"I don't know. I'd hate to see my jinx get any worse, if you know what I mean."

"You said your mishaps only happen at the store. You could come to Whispering Oaks and take a swim. We have a great swimming pond."

"Well," Jinx said, shoving his hands deep into his pockets. "If you promise you won't let your grandpa put another hex on me, I get off at two on Saturday. I could walk down as soon as I get off."

"Don't forget, you can come over before Saturday if you want to, and I promise, Potsy won't do anything to you."

"Great!" Jinx waved as he jogged away. "If I can get over before Saturday, I'll call first."

"Please do," Brittany said. She turned and crossed the street onto Whispering Oaks property, where the van was parked. She waved at Jinx who was turning now and then to get a final look at her.

Brittany pulled the van to a stop next to the house, hopped out, slammed the door behind her and bounded up the stairs.

"Monya. Look. I brought you some ribb . . .," her voice trailed off as her hand touched the pocket flap of her shirt. The flap was closed and the package of green ribbon was *gone*.

Chapter 3

Questions

Brittany sat on the edge of her bed and stared at the wall, thinking of the strange and unexpected events of today and yesterday. Yesterday she had met Shamus and today she bought a package of ribbon she didn't even know she was carrying.

She mouthed the sentence, "Shamus Mactavish O'Riley please step forward," over and over again. She didn't want to forget the words.

She felt like she was about to burst. She wanted to tell someone about the missing ribbon and about meeting Shamus, but she knew she had given her solemn promise. She felt that somehow, these two things were connected.

Questions raced through her mind like bolts of lightening. *Are Elfins real? Will Shamus come if I call him and will he truly be my friend? Are there other magical beings around here?* She wasn't sure what to believe. One question she wanted answered was: 'Did her encounter with the Elfins really happen?'

Brittany laid back on her bed. "I need to know," she said aloud. She sat up and took a deep breath. "Shamus Mactavish O'Riley please step . . ."

'*Knock, knock, knock.*' Someone was at her door.

"Just a minute," she said, opening the door to greet her grand-father.

"I was wondering if you were all right," he said. "I thought I heard you talking to someone."

"Oh, I'm fine. I was just talking to myself. I do that a lot, you know."

Potsy laughed. "I know you used to when you were little, but I thought you outgrew it. But then again, I do the same thing."

Brittany's complexion flushed, she smiled and changed the subject. "Monya's dinner was great, wasn't it? I love her home-cooked Southern style chicken."

"Me too," said Potsy, leaning down to kiss Brittany's cheek. "I'm going to see what's on TV. Then, after the news, I'm off to bed. I get pretty tired these days."

"Okay. Good night." A rush of curiosity came over her as she watched her grandfather turn toward the hall. "No, wait, Potsy. Would you please come in for a minute. I've only been here for a couple of days and I have some questions."

He stepped to the large chair by the window and took a seat. "Sure darlin', I'll be happy to answer any questions I can."

"The curse of Whispering Oaks, what is it? Mrs. Torgilson told me about it. Is there more to it than things appearing and disappearing? How long have you known about it? Does the curse affect the whole community or just the property?"

Potsy pulled at strands of white hair sticking from under his ball cap, just above his right ear. "Well, I can tell you some things, but don't let Monya hear you talking about the curse or anything like it. She'll be taking you over for special sessions with the Reverend, Pastor Kelly. Monya is a sweet, gentle woman, but she doesn't take kindly to discussions of fairies, leprechauns or tales of the supernatural.

"Five years ago, when I bought this land and started to build my house, I was going to clear off those two giant oak trees that grow just outside the front door. I didn't want them blocking our view of the pond. Strange things started happening right away.

24

Whispering Oaks - The Curse

Chain saw blades would break as soon as I cranked up. Brand new blades, straight out of the package, would have chunks missing out of them. One morning, my new chain saw was frozen up and wouldn't start. The strangest thing of all was when I went to put the saw back in its case, there was a stack of silver dollars in the case. It didn't take me long to decide to move the location of the house back twenty feet.

"I have the account over at Torgilson's because I keep buying things that I don't even know I have in my possession. That account has been open from the moment we moved onto this place. It's never anything major. String, ribbon, small swatches of cloth, fishing line and the like. Small things disappear from my workshop too. But, when something is gone, it is replaced by something else. I've got the neatest bunch of small fishing hooks that were left where I used to keep my tack hammer. They are unusual in that they look like lead headed jigs, but I think whoever cast them used gold instead of lead for the heads. These hooks are really magnetic to fish. When I fish with them, I put on a rubber rooster tail jig and I always catch blue gill and white bass, every cast.

"Yes. There are some strange happenings around here, but if you keep an open mind, none of it will surprise you. As far as affecting the community, that is the strangest thing. It doesn't happen all the time, but it does happen. Every once in a while you'll see people bring an elderly person down to the edge of the road on this side of the pond. I've also seen them bring a crippled child in a wheelchair. They set them out there in the evening, just as the twilight is turning to darkness. I've gone out the next morning and there isn't a sign of them. They're gone."

Brittany was really curious now. "You're telling me that you saw this and you didn't go out there and ask them what they were doing on your place?"

Potsy rubbed his beard. "At first I had the urge to run out there and find out what was going on. I started out the door, but suddenly felt it was more important to go to bed and get a good night's rest. In the case of the cripple child, I knew the people and asked them about it a few days later at church. They simply said the Old Indian Medicine Man, Waycon, told them to bring the child to Whispering Oaks. "

"I attended the child's funeral three days later. Pastor Kelly officiated. A doctor from Kansas City signed the death certificate."

Brittany frowned. "And this Waycon, have you ever met him?"

"As a matter of fact, we hadn't been here long when Doc Watson introduced me to him over in front of Torgilson's store. The old Indian bowed his head as he shook my hand saying that he knew me. He said I was the keeper of the keys. To this day, I have no idea what that meant.

"That's enough for now," Potsy said, rising from his chair. "It's getting very late and I have to get an early start in the morning. I'm going to the livestock auction to see if I can buy a calf or two."

Brittany hugged her grandfather and kissed him on the cheek as he turned from her door. "Tell Monya, I love her."

"I'll do that," Potsy said, fading down the hallway.

Brittany sighed and closed the door. She went to her dresser, took out her pajamas and headed for her bathroom to change. When she reentered her room she was still thinking about Shamus and Shimmy, and all the questions she had for the Elfins.

Walking to the window near the foot of her bed, she opened it, pressed her hands against the screen and breathed deep. The night air was sweet, smelling of honeysuckle and her grandmother's prize roses. She switched off the light, and as her eyes adjusted to the darkness, she looked out at the scenery bathed in the bright glow of a summer full moon. "This is such a beautiful place," she said.

Her gaze wandered through the yard, down across the pond and up to the forest and it's dark shadows. Tree toads croaked and fireflies were everywhere, lighting up the night. She looked above the trees and into the starry sky.

Thoughts of Jinx flashed into her mind. She didn't know why, it was probably because his eyes twinkled like the stars up there.

Whispering Oaks - The Curse

Perhaps his bubbly personality or his shiny black hair had excited her. *Maybe I'll call him Marion. Sir Marion, knight of King Author's court or maybe Marion, the Swamp Fox, hero of the American Revolution from South Carolina.*

Her thoughts raced back to the Elfins. *Should I call Shamus?* She sat down on her bed. *Not now. Maybe tomorrow. I'll take a walk down by the pond and I can call him then.*

Thoughts tumbled as she leaned back and stared up at the ceiling of her room. As she relaxed, she heard a whispering sound just outside her window. She concentrated and listened hard.

"She knows . . ." was the first words she could make out. Then she heard another word clearly, "Danger . . ."

Brittany's adrenaline pumped and the hair on the back of her neck stood up. She rose and tip-toed to the window, peered out and listened. The voices stopped. All she could see was the giant oak trees, their leaves clicking softly in the breeze.

"Huh?" Brittany said aloud. "Maybe the oaks really do whisper, but why would they say 'danger'?" *I hope that no one I love is in danger,* she thought as she closed the window and pulled the blue polka-dot curtains closed.

Moving to the small stereo she had brought from home, she turned on the radio. *Ugh! Nothing but static.* She turned it off and retrieved her MP3 player off of her dresser, placed the tiny earbud headphones into her ears and turned on some relaxing music as she lay back on her bed.

"Good mornin' darlin'," Monya said as she knocked and opened the bedroom door at the same time.

Brittany opened her eyes and realized that she had fallen asleep listening to her music. She turned off the MP3 player, pulled the earbuds from her ears and sat up.

"Good morning, Monya."

"Don't you think it's time you were getting up?"

Brittany could tell by the intensity of the sun on the window curtain that it was well after dawn. "What time is it?"

"9:35."

"Am I too late for breakfast?"

"How about waffles, eggs, sausage and hash browned potatoes?"

"Yum! Gimme a sec and I'll be right there."

"Okay, honey," Monya said, pulling the door closed.

Turning her MP3 player back on, the screen read 'low battery.' *Darn! Now I'll have to plug it in after breakfast. Falling asleep with it on is NOT smart. I'll have to be more careful in the future.*

Throwing on her housecoat, she slipped into the bathroom, washed up, put in her contacts and went to breakfast.

"Didn't that storm wake you last night?" Monya asked.

"What storm? I didn't hear a thing," Brittany said as she filled her plate and poured a large glass of juice.

"Oh, yes. Last night was one of those powerful thunder bumper storms. There wasn't a lot of rain. The rain that did fall was coming down sideways. The thunder and lightning was something else. The wind blew a great deal too, whipping, whining and screaming through the trees. It was enough to make a body seek shelter. Are you sure you didn't hear it, dear? There was one lightning strike very close, probably within a mile of this place, over toward town."

Brittany looked up from her breakfast and smiled sheepishly. "I fell asleep with my head phones on last night, I guess that's why I didn't hear anything. Don't worry, Monya. I plan **not** to make that mistake again."

"Good," she said, looking over her shoulder from the sink. "Your grandfather left for the stock yards. He said he'd be home around noon."

"Do you need any help with the dishes, or any other chores?"

"No, darlin'. Get your shower and get ready to help your grandfather with those calves when he gets home. I'm writing on

28

a new chapter for my book and I think I have it ready to go in my mind, all I have to do now is put it on the page."

It was close to noon as Brittany walked beside the pond and watched the road for the approach of her grandfather's old green pickup truck. She picked a large red rose from one of her grandmother's bushes, walked onto the small pier and sat down.

"Shamus Mactavish O'Riley, please step forward," she said in a soft voice.

Poof! There was a sound imitating a short, sharp puff of breath as if blowing out a candle. A small flash of light and a wisp of smoke accompanied by the smell of peppermint. There stood Shamus, a white napkin stuffed into the front of his black shirt, no hat on his head, and a very large sandwich clutched between his hands.

He looked as if he were about to take a bite, but stopped and exclaimed. "Don't you know it isn't polite to call people during their lunch? This had better be important! What do you want?"

"I'm sorry! I'm sorry!" Brittany blurted. "Could you please come back after lunch? I need to talk to you."

Poof! Shamus was gone. A wisp of vapor trailed away into the air. With his leaving, Brittany *again* noticed the faint scent of peppermint!

"Now that's interesting; was that smell created by his coming or his going?" Brittany asked the flower she was holding. "I'll have to pay more attention when he comes back."

As she looked across the pond, she saw her grandfather's truck coming down the road. She jumped up and ran to meet it.

The truck rolled to a stop and Potsy called to her from an open window. "Girl, hop in and we'll take these critters down to the cow pens."

Brittany got in and sat back watching a big bird as the truck jogged easily along. A large black hawk swept down close to the back of the truck as if inspecting the live cargo. It let out a loud screech and turned away, as if in fright.

When they reached the cow pens, Brittany was first to jump out and go to the back of the truck. "Potsy, how old are these calves? Do they need to be fed milk or can we start them on hay and grain right away?"

The truck was backed up to the cattle ramp to make it easy for the calves to get out. Potsy dropped the tailgate and opened the back door. "Come on girls, get out of there. This is your new home. To answer your questions," he turned to Brittany, "they can start eating hay and grain right away."

The little black and white calves came right out and then, from behind them, came a small pink piglet. It grunted and squealed as it followed the calves.

There was the sudden odor of peppermint in the air. Brittany turned her head to see Shamus. He sat on top of a nearby fence post. He was already talking to her. "This is totally unacceptable. We can *not* have a pig on this property. You have to tell your grandfather to get rid of that pig at once!"

"Potsy," she said. "You remember the story you told me about the chain saw?"

"Yes, I do. That was a strange one wasn't it?"

"I have a feeling, that if we don't get rid of this pig, we're going to have some things happen along that same line."

Shamus sat on the edge of the post, giving Brittany a glare-stare and a very mean, eyes-half-closed, frown.

"Potsy, I feel very strongly about this," Brittany said.

Potsy sniffed the air, took a deep breath and answered. "Okay."

Without another word, he picked up a stick and ushered the piglet back into the truck. "The Jensens, up the road a piece, raise hogs. I'll take this little guy up there and drop him off." He closed the back door of the stock rack, closed the tailgate and walked around the truck. He reached for the handle on the driver's door.

"Would you like to come along? We can stop at Torgilson's and have a sandwich on the way home."

"I'd love to," Brittany said, jumping into the passenger seat. She leaned forward and raised her right hand. She moved her little finger, giving Shamus a 'pinky wave' as the truck pulled away.

After they had left the farm road and moved onto the old highway, Brittany turned to her grandfather. "Potsy, do you know about the Elfins? The little people that live at Whispering Oaks? Have you ever seen them?"

"I've been aware of their presence -- in a way. I've never seen one, but I've *felt* their presence. I've never discussed them with anyone. Been afraid to. I mentioned something about them a few years ago to Monya, and she had me an appointment with Parson Kelly the next day. I wasn't going to talk to him about my suspicions or my hunches. He would have probably had me locked up in a nut house. I did speak to Parson Kelley's wife though. She was born in Ireland and believes in all kinds of leprechauns and stuff."

"You can talk to me about them all you want," Brittany said. "I've seen them, and I've talked to them. How was it, you knew exactly what I was talking about when I told you we couldn't keep the pig on the farm?"

Potsy smiled at his granddaughter. "Part of that was instinct, from having been exposed to these guys before and part of it was the smell of peppermint in the air. If you smell peppermint, lookout! Something bad, or at least unexpected, is about to happen. A couple of years ago, I told your grandmother I was going to the auction to buy a pig and when I went out to my truck, I had flat tires. Not one or two, but all four were flat. Thank goodness there were no holes in them, the air was just *gone*."

"That sounds pretty spooky to me."

"It sure was, and from that day until this, I've never mentioned raising pigs. I don't know what came over me this morning. I saw this little pig and had to buy him. It was like there was a strong force provoking me. I've never seen any pig that cute or that pink."

Potsy turned the truck off the highway and started down the

lane to the Jensen farm. "You say you've seen these little people, Brittany?"

"Yes, sir. But, please don't call them people. They're Elfins and they'll go out of their way to make sure you know that. It was by accident. I caught one by holding him in my gaze with my left eye while my right eye was closed. Shamus called it 'Ocular Sinister,' like it was something real bad."

"Ocular Sinister, that's an interesting term. It's simply Latin and means 'left eye,' but in legend, if you look at someone with your left eye only, you're giving them the *evil eye*. Who is this Shamus?"

Brittany took a deep breath. "Shamus is an Elfin Guardian. He's either the leader or one of the main guys in the Elfin world. He was watching over a little man named Shimmy that I caught with my left eye. Shamus was the one that popped up when we were at the cow pens and said we had to get rid of the pig. He's the one that always smells like peppermint."

"I see. Well, I can tell you this. Shamus has been a constant companion of mine since we got here five years ago. He's never done me any harm, but he has made me shake my head in astonishment on more than one occasion."

The truck idled to a stop in front of the barn at the Jensen farm and Potsy got out.

Brittany's nose was immediately assaulted by the strong odor in the air. *Yep. This is a pig farm. It looks clean and neat, all painted white, but there is no mistaking the smell in the air.*

A large man in gray overalls and a straw hat came out. He removed the glove from his right hand and extended it to Potsy. "Bud, good to see you. What brings you out this way?"

"Carl, I've brought you a piglet."

The huge fellow shook with laughter. "Bud, I'm in the business of sellin' hogs, not buyin' 'em!"

Potsy removed his ball cap and scratched his head. "I didn't mean that you should buy him. I just can't keep him over at Whispering Oaks. I thought he'd be happier over here with you."

Mr. Jensen leaned against the back of the truck and peered in at the piglet. "He is kinda cute isn't he? I don't think I've ever seen a piglet quite that pink before, and look at those eyes, they're a gray color I've never seen before. He seems to be watching and hearing every word we say. I'll tell you what, Bud. I'll take him off your hands and the next time I butcher, I'll wrap up some special cuts for you. This little guy won't be ready for market for another year anyway."

"That sounds more than fair to me," Potsy said. "You know, Carl, I was just mentioning to Brittany, my granddaughter, how pink he is." He opened the door, hopped behind the wheel of his truck and cranked the engine over.

The big man opened the tailgate, took the piglet under one arm, closed the tailgate and waved, signalling Potsy to pull away.

"Thank heavens for good neighbors," Potsy said as the old truck rolled onto the highway. "If you would have asked me if I planned to buy a pig, I would have said, no, but something came over me and I just had to have that little guy." Chasing the subject from his mind he turned to Brittany. "Let's head for Torgilson's and a big banana split. How does that sound to you?"

Brittany leaned back in her seat and put her feet on the dash. She crossed her legs at the ankles and relaxed. "That sounds great to me."

Chapter 4

Answers

Brittany sat on the edge of her seat, her safety belt already released as the truck rolled to a stop in front of Torgilson's General Store. "What's with all these people?" she asked, looking out the window.

"I don't know," Potsy said, opening his door. "Looks like that lion is still attracting lots of folks off the highway."

Brittany could hear the people talking as they walked past the truck. ". . . last month when I was through here they had a real lion."

Another man said, "One thing for sure, I won't be afraid to bring my kids down here to see the lion anymore."

"Let's go see, Potsy." Brittany closed her door. She wove her way through the crowd until she stood at the edge of the lion's compound. *Wow! Now what is that?* she thought.

There on the edge of the compound stood a great bronze, life-size statue of the lion that had been pacing up and down only the day before. She leaned forward to read the brass plaque stuck in the ground next to the statue. "This lion's work here is finished. He has gone to the safety and security of a wild animal park in California. We hope you will enjoy this life-size statue in his place." After the last word on the plaque, there was an emblem. It was the impression of a four-leaf-clover.

Brittany followed her grandfather into the store and back to the soda fountain.

Jinx was behind the counter and smiled as they sat down. "Hi folks, it's good to see you. What'll you have? Have you seen Grandpa's lion yet?"

Assuming they both wanted sodas, he dipped ice with two fluted fountain glasses and ran them to the brim with soda. As he set them on the counter in front of his customers, he continued. "You know, when that big lightning storm came through last night, Grandpa heard one strike that was particularly loud. He thought it hit the store so he came down here to have a look at the damage. He didn't come home until three in the morning, and when he got home, Grandma said he was stone drunk, walking into things and dragging a bottle of hooch with him. I'm afraid he's still home in bed."

Jinx appeared agitated. "I'm sorry, I don't mean to babble, but yesterday afternoon when I left the store, the lion was out there." He pulled the pencil from behind his ear, "What can I get you folks?"

"I'm hungry," Brittany said. "I'd like a burger and a small order of fries."

Jinx turned his attention to Potsy. "And you sir, what can I get for you?"

"I think I'll have the same."

"Two deluxe burgers coming right up." Jinx pushed the pencil through his dark wavy hair until it lodged behind his ear, flipped his little notebook closed and headed back to the grill.

Brittany turned to her grandfather. "I don't think we have to wonder what happened to that lion," she said in a whisper. "That four-leafed-clover on the sign looks like the one I told you about that Shamus wears in the band of his hat. It's turned at the same angle and everything."

Potsy placed his hand over Brittany's and whispered back to her. "Let's not discuss it any further. This is not the place. We don't want to send the whole village into a panic. There are enough superstitious people around here already."

Jinx set their plates in front of them just as three more people perched at the end of the bar. "I'm sorry I won't get a chance to talk to you folks. It looks like I'm getting busy."

When they finished their sandwiches, Potsy placed a ten dollar bill on the bar. "Hey. I thought we were coming in here for banana splits," said Potsy.

As they got into the truck he said, "You know, people used to take one look at that lion and leave, but now that it's a statue, they hang around and have a good time. The atmosphere is like a fair or a carnival."

Brittany clicked her seat belt. "Maybe, since the statue doesn't scare them, they want to make friends with it or something. I just hope Mr. Torgilson doesn't blame Whispering Oaks for his new statue."

When they reached the house, Potsy went inside to talk to Monya. Brittany took a walk down by the pond. She found her favorite stump, sat down and said, "Shamus Mactavish O'Riley please step forward."

There was a *poof*, a wisp of mist and the smell of peppermint.

"And, what is it you're a needin', girly?" Shamus asked, his left hand on his hip, his walking stick planted next to his right foot and his right arm extended its full length.

"Shamus, are you my friend?"

"Ya know I am, Lassie. I don't give my word to be passin' the time of day."

"Good. I have some questions for you. Did you have anything to do with that storm last night?"

"I did not."

Brittany scratched at her chin. "That's strange, because, from what I hear, that storm had a lot of Elfin earmarks about it."

"Earmarks, is it? Let's not be makin' fun of Elfin ears."

"Oh, I'm sorry, Shamus. Earmarks doesn't refer to anyone's ears. It means that it looks like the storm was caused by Elfin magic."

Shamus shook his head and pointed his index finger at Brittany. "Did you or did you not say, '*I wish it were in an animal park somewhere and the Torgilson's had a bronze statue.*'?"

Brittany jerked upright and blinked. "I guess I did."

"All I can tell you, is, you'd best watch what you say when you're carrying a Wish Fairy in your pocket."

Brittany fingered the new button on the left breast pocket of her shirt. "Oh my gosh! Wish Fairy? How did I get a wish fairy in my pocket?"

"When you went over to get yourself a pack of gum, I sent a young Wish Fairy, Millie, with you to pick me up some ribbon. She's barely a hundred years old and doesn't really know what she's doing just yet. She took a liking to you, and when you made that wish; well, you know. Do you want me to bring the lion back?"

"Oh, no! As a matter of fact, I'd like to personally thank Millie, if that's possible."

No sooner had Brittany finished speaking when a very pretty Elfin girl appeared next to Shamus. She had red hair, large blue eyes, a cute little outfit with a green flared skirt and white apron front. "Glad to meet you, Brittany, I'm Millie," she said as she curtseyed.

Brittany lowered her head in recognition. "Happy to meet you, Millie, I'll be very careful about my wishes in the future. It's like my Monya says, 'If wishes were horses, then beggars would ride.'"

The tiny girl in green opened her eyes wide, looked at Brittany and laughed out loud. "Are you asking for a horse? You'll have to rephrase that wish if you are."

"Oh no!" Brittany said. "I just want to thank you for the wish you already granted me and I promise not to wish for anything in the future -- unless I really need it."

Millie turned to Shamus. "She is a child of the Outer World, is she not?"

"Yes, she is, but, she is also our friend and you can trust her not to lead you into danger."

38

With that, the wish fairy vanished.

"Shamus, I have a few more questions for you if you don't mind."

"Okay, but keep them short."

"I've told my grandpa about you. Is that all right?"

"I don't think there's any harm in that."

"Would you allow my Potsy to see you?"

"Yes. But only you and he must know we're here."

"He wouldn't tell anyone about you."

"I'm sure you're right, I've known your grandpa for several years, stubborn, but intelligent."

"If Elfins live in the Inner World, why do you come to the Outer World? Is there something you need here?"

"We have been coming to the Outer World for hundreds of years. We primarily come to capture sunlight. It's very complicated, but we can only capture it in a couple of ways each season. For instance, the drops of dew as the sun first rises. Those drops capture the first sunbeams and are magic. We take them back with us. There are many things that exist in the Outer World that we can use, but we never steal. Each time we take something, we replace it with something of value."

"Why do people bring their elderly and crippled children to Whispering Oaks?"

"For many years, we've been taking in the sick and elderly from the human population and bringing them into our world. As a medium, we use an old Indian Medicine Man named Waycon. Most of the people in the village regard him as crazy, so we do not feel threatened. When people move to our world, the elderly become young and the cripple become healthy."

"Do you keep them forever?"

"We keep them for as long as they wish to stay. None have ever wanted to return to your world. If they elect to go back, they must return as they came to us. Elderly will be old and cripples will be lame. While they are with us, they are youthful, healthy and happy, and none want to return to the way they were."

"Don't they miss their families? Won't their families worry about them?"

"Yes. They do at first, but we allow them to visit their family members in dreams to reassure them that they're all right."

"What about all the loose ends the disappearance of a person causes? I mean, don't the police ask questions?"

Shamus smiled at Brittany. "I didn't plan to tell you all the secrets of our world right away, but . . ." He hesitated for a moment. "There is a certain Doctor O'Keif in Kansas City that comes down here when we have need of him. He signs the death certificate of the person that has disappeared. The grieving family buys a coffin from the undertaker, brings it home and puts in just the right number of sand bags to ensure the proper weight. They seal the coffin and call Pastor Kelly. A funeral is held and the casket is buried in the cemetery. Doctor O'Keif returns to Kansas City and that's it."

"I thought you said you didn't have any *people* friends. This Doctor O'Keif sounds like a friend to me."

"Doctor O'Keif is a friend of the population of an Elfin city near Kansas City. He travels all over taking care of death certificates. Although he is well known in the human world, he is a secret in the Elfin world and what he does for us is a secret in the human world."

Brittany scratched at the side of her head and changed the subject. "Why won't you let pigs live on Whispering Oaks?"

"Hogs root up the ground and destroy our gardens and sometimes tear up the entrances to our cities. Once, a hundred years ago, a great feral boar tore up the edge of the city and killed an Elfin. We regard life very highly, and since that time we forbid them coming onto the property."

Shamus leaned against his staff, both hands near the top. "The piglet that your grandfather brought onto the farm this morning could have been a real pig or it might have been an evil agent of our eternal enemy, the Nenuphar. In either case, it could have presented danger to the Elfins of our city."

"I noticed Millie was wearing green. Do most Elfins dress in

40

green?"

"Green is the uniform for those who are venturing out and about in summer. Once Elfins get to a certain maturity or develop their powers sufficiently, they can venture out in their favorite color. You may recall that Shimmy was wearing overalls and an old flop hat the day you met. The venturing colors are normally green in the spring and summer, brown in the fall and winter. If it snows, the color for that period is white."

"Why do you wear black?"

"Black is the color of the guardians. I am the senior guardian and I report directly to the High Council, the ruling body of our world."

"Does the High Council know about me and my grandpa?"

"The High Council is aware of everything in the Outer World.

"Can a person, who is not sick, go into your world and return?"

"I would say yes, I think Dr. O'keif does it in Kansas City, but it has never been tried in our city. People who come into our world want to stay and make a home with us."

Brittany and Shamus sat at the edge of the pond and talked for long hours, until Monya's voice came to Brittany's ear. "It's time for dinner. Come in and wash up."

"I'm sorry," Brittany said, "I lost track of time. I have to go in now."

Shamus fingered the watch chain hanging on his vest and fished a gold watch from his pocket. "Yes. It is getting late and I, too, must be going."

As Brittany rose, she turned to her new friend. "Shamus, is it all right if I call you tomorrow?"

Shamus leaned back on his heavy cane. "It will be fine if you call, but please, make sure it is after the noon hour."

Brittany turned and went into the house to wash up for dinner. Her grandfather was coming down the hall from the bathroom. "Potsy, can we talk after dinner?"

Potsy slowed as he passed her. "How about meeting me out in

41

the wood shop? I have a cabinet to finish for Mrs. O'Karon."

"Great," Brittany said, standing on tip-toes to kiss her grandfather on his cheek.

The phone rang and Monya answered it as Potsy and Brittany entered the kitchen. "Ellis residence. Yes. One moment, Carl."

Monya turned to Potsy. "It's Carl Jensen, honey," she said as she handed him the cordless phone.

"Hello, Carl, what can I do for you?" Potsy listened for a moment. "Gone? No trace, no signs? No, I didn't have a change of heart. I'm sorry to hear that. No. You don't have to do that. You don't owe me a thing. Thanks for calling. Have a great evening."

Potsy set the phone in its cradle and sat down at the table. Brittany watched as his expression appeared to become confused.

"That piglet we took to the Jensen farm this morning. It's disappeared out of a locked wire cage. Carl said the lock was still on the pen and there was no sign of tampering."

After dinner, Brittany and Potsy went to the woodshop, where he wiped down a cabinet that sat on his workbench and began to apply stain with a sponge as Brittany talked to him.

She told him of the conversation with Shamus and about meeting Millie.

"That sure explains a lot about what's been going on around here and it explains the curse of Whispering Oaks. You know, I went to the funeral of that little crippled boy, Billy Martin. There sure were a lot of tears shed for an empty coffin. But, at the same time, his mother seemed quite calm throughout it all."

"Would you like to meet Shamus, Potsy?"

"I certainly would. He sounds like a very interesting person -- er, Elfin."

"I think you'll just love him to death. He is so cool. He knows lots of stuff and has such great magical power, but he doesn't act conceited or like a bully."

"I'm sure he's as wonderful as you say, but if you don't mind, I'll form my own opinion."

Potsy dropped his staining sponge into a can and turned the

lid down tight. He set the container on the shelf and started for the door. "It's time for bed young lady. I know it's been a very exciting day, but there is another day tomorrow." He flipped off the light and pulled the door shut as Brittany exited ahead of him.

Brittany walked ahead of her grandfather, down the path toward the house, listening to the sound of crickets and breathing in the sweet smell of honeysuckle. Lightning bugs darted in and out of the rose bushes along the way. A bright moon was rising and silver light cast long tree shadows here and there as they went up the steps onto the porch.

Brittany held the screen door as her grandfather entered the house. She leaned against the open door watching the fireflies blink on and off as they played in the flower beds.

"Yep! This is a beautiful place," she said as she stepped inside and the door closed behind her.

Chapter 5

Millie

The morning sun had just crept over the tree tops of the forest and started to slide down the roofline of the house as Brittany tossed and turned. She was aware of a sound that had not come to her before. It was the big red rooster in the barnyard. He was greeting the day with his song of Cock-a-doodle-do.

Brittany's eyes twitched at first and then sprang open. "Oh my gosh! Shut up you stupid bird. If I have to hear that racket, maybe I'll sleep with my music player every night," she said aloud.

The quiet night had passed and now it was a bustling day on the farm. She sniffed the air for the sweet odor of honeysuckle, but the smell of fresh bread and sausage, along with the aroma of brewing coffee excited her taste buds. She threw back the blankets and vaulted from her bed. She hummed a happy tune as she showered and dressed.

The moment she arrived in the kitchen, she was greeted by a smile. "Good morning, darlin'," Monya said. She set a glass of fresh milk at Brittany's place. "How many eggs and sausages?"

Brittany slid her chair sideways and dropped into it. "I'll take one egg, two sausage links and one toast if it's not too much bother."

"You know better than that, darlin'," Monya said as she turned from the stove, a prepared plate in her hand. "We just finished breakfast. Potsy's on his way over to pick up the mail at the Post Office and then to O'Brien's Feed Store to pick up a load of hay and a couple bags of feed. Our little calves sure go through a lot. I think our grain is feeding more than those calves."

"Don't we feed grain to the chickens, horses and ducks, too?"

"Not really," Monya said, tipping her head sideways and closing one eye as if the powerful calculator in her head were working extra hard. "I think the primary feed for those animals is cracked corn, which is a grain, but it's a good deal less expensive than oats, wheat and barley. I'll bet it's those pesky white rabbits. There's a ton of them around here anymore."

Brittany set her glass down and pushed back from the table. "I think I'll go down to the pond if you don't need me."

Monya stood across the table from Brittany. "One thing I think you should do, is run into my office for five minutes and send your mom an email. You know, let her know that you're all right."

Brittany smiled. "Would you consider dropping her a note for me. I really wanted to walk down by the pond right now."

"I know you love that pond, but I think you should give your family a little consideration, and there's no time like the present."

"Okay," said Brittany raising her right hand. "I guess I just got in a hurry and wasn't thinking." She left the kitchen and went to her grandmother's office where she sat down in front of Potsy's computer. It was on a desk on the opposite wall from Monya's. He only used it for email and converting digital pictures into movies to email to family and friends across the nation.

A few clicks and her email screen came up. She inserted her mother's email address and started writing.

Hi Mom,

Monya insisted that I write you a note, so here I am.

I'm sorry I haven't written but I have been busy.

I'm safe and having lots of fun. lol.

Love, Brittany

She pressed the send button on the screen and it flashed 'Message successfully sent.'

Monya entered the office with a big smile. "Is that machine working all right?"

"Oh, sure," said Brittany. "I'm going to slip out and go down by the pond now if you don't mind."

Monya turned in her chair as Brittany was leaving. "I'll try to write another chapter on my new novel. If something comes up, I'll give you a holler."

Brittany pushed out through the kitchen door and walked down to the pond. She sat on her favorite stump and said, "Shamus Mactavish O'Riley, please step forward."

There was the familiar *poof*, a wisp of mist and the smell of peppermint.

"I thought I asked you not to call me until after the noon hour -- what is it that you're a needin' girly?" Shamus stod his left hand on his hip, his walking stick held high in his extended right hand. "You know, I have work of my own to do. I can't be spendin' all o' my time chatting."

"I just wanted someone to talk to," Brittany said.

"Someone to talk to is it? I'm not a television you can turn on any time you want. I have big responsibilities. You can't be callin' me every time you turn around. It's just not right."

"I thought you were my friend," Brittany said, covering her face with her right hand as if to cry.

"Oh, come now," Shamus said, his voice softening. "I don't want to hurt your feelings, but you must understand how busy I am."

Brittany wiped her eyes with the edge of her sleeve. "I'm sorry, I just don't have a lot of friends around here, and you're the only one I can talk to."

"Okay. Okay. I'll make you a deal. I'll call Millie out here and you can talk to her. How does that sound?"

"That's great. Are you sure it's not a bother?"

"It is no bother for me, and Millie loves to chat and flit around and do girly things. There is one thing I must tell you though. It's kind of secret." He turned his head from side to side as if scanning the area for a listening ear. "You must never allow her to eat sugar or candy that has sugar in it. I know how you humans love sugar."

"Oh my, is she allergic?"

"You might say that. Have you ever seen an adult human when they're drunk?"

"Yes, I saw Potsy when he was really plastered once. The things he did and said were hilarious."

"The reaction of an Elfin to sugar is much the same. The first sign is slurred speech and hiccups, then the giggles and shortly thereafter, they will become disoriented and after that they involuntarily take flight. This is very serious, so please, don't allow her to eat or drink anything that is made with sugar."

"You have my word. I won't."

"Good." Shamus leaned against his walking stick and spoke. "Millie Mactavish, please step forward."

Appearing in the same manner as Shamus, the little maiden bowed at the waist. "Yes, Master Shamus, how may I serve you?"

"You will be Brittany's companion for as long as she likes. Be good and mind your manners."

"Yes, Shamus," she said, bowing low and sweeping her right hand out from her face in some sort of salute.

Shamus tipped his hat and was gone.

"Shamus is very busy you know," Millie said.

"I imagine he must be," Brittany said, looking up the hillside toward the house. Her eyes caught sight of several white rabbits. "Oh, my gosh! Look at all the rabbits. Where did they come from?"

Millie was now standing on a small branch just above Brittany's shoulder. She broke into laughter. "Those aren't rabbits, those are my brothers and sisters. They've come to look at you. We don't get a chance to observe humans in the Outer World very often. We usually have to hide when they are about."

"Okay, there are fifteen or twenty rabbits out there and I don't see an Elfin among them."

Millie's laughter had her bent over, both hands on her stomach. She was laughing so hard she lost her balance and started to fall from where she stood. Like a gymnast, she reached back and grabbed the branch with her right hand as she fell. She pulled up hard, rotated her body and was standing upright on the branch, still smiling.

"I don't mean to laugh, but I guess you're not aware that Elfins are shape shifters."

Brittany blinked and turned to look at her little friend. "So, I give. Tell me about shape shifters."

"A shape shifter is a being with the power to turn into any warm blooded animal or bird they like. The problem is, we Elfins can be only one color for the body, a solid color. We can do the eyes too, but the body remains a solid color. That's why we prefer white rabbits. If you look really hard at the animal we have shifted to, you can see we don't *really* look like that animal. Oh, we are close enough to fool most people, but sometimes we make choices that are not good. Whoever heard of a pink bunny or a blue squirrel? White rabbits and white pigeons are the easiest."

Brittany watched as the rabbits hopped back toward the great oak tree near the house and disappeared. "Did they know we were talking about them?"

"One of the advantages of being a rabbit is that you can hear every word for a quarter of a mile."

"That's pretty impressive, but they must know we don't mean them any harm."

"Yes, but they have to get back to their work."

"Don't you have work you have to get back to?"

"I do, but for now, being your companion is my full time job. I can be your companion for an hour, a week or longer. Shamus said it was my full time job. I'm happy to do it."

"I thought Elfins didn't have any human friends."

"You're my friend," said Millie stepping to a branch closer to Brittany. "This city hasn't had friends in the Outer World for many years. Legend says we were befriended by some Indians that lived in this area about two hundred years ago. Since then, no one has been interested in the land or in its small inhabitants. Oh yes. Doctor O'Keif comes down from Kansas City. We sometimes see him, but he seldom comes to Whispering Oaks."

"Shamus told me you've been here a couple hundred years."

"The truth is, we came here a little more than four hundred years ago. Shamus sometimes pays no heed to the passage of time."

"How is it you are only a hundred years old and you know what Shamus knows?"

"We share all knowledge. It is passed on from one Elfin to the High Council and from them to all the members of our community, unless it is banned or held knowledge."

"Okay, so what is banned and what is held knowledge?"

"All knowledge goes through the High Council. If it is to be shared by all, it is passed down. If not, it is banned and only the Council will have access to it, but they may pass it to the guardians if it has to do with the security of the population. Held knowledge is what you Out-Worlders call personal or secret. It is usually kept by the High Council."

"Thanks for all the info," Brittany said. "You say you can shape shift. Can you shift into a girl like me? I mean, you are a girl, can you get bigger?"

"The Druid law which governs Elfins, forbids us from becoming like humans unless we are asked to become a specific someone by the human in authority."

"Who is this *human in authority*?"

"You are the human in authority right now."

"How about if you shape shift into a girl and we can sit and talk without me having to look up in a tree or down on the ground? I can imagine how stupid I'd look if someone came along and saw me talking to a tree."

"And, just which girl would you like me to shift to?"

Brittany became excited. *This is great! I get to design my own friend. The friend I've always dreamed of. This could be a lot of fun.*

Whispering Oaks - The Curse

"How about if you just stay yourself and pop up to my height, weight and age? Can you do that?"

Millie stretched her arms out and began to turn in a circle. The circle became smaller and smaller. A bright light glowed in the center of the tiny spiral. Dust and leaves rolled across the ground and the nearby roses shuddered. *Poof*, there was a soft noise, a flash of light and there stood Millie, her arms spread wide.

"How do I look?" Millie asked, glancing down at her clothes. She was wearing the exact same outfit as Brittany. Her eyes were still blue, her red hair dangled in long flowing pigtails with ribbons at the bottom.

Brittany stood in startled amazement, her mouth half open. "Wow! You look great," she said, reaching out to touch Millie's arm. "You feel real and look real to me."

"I can assure you, I am anatomically correct in every detail."

"I do have one question. What is that on your left wrist?" Brittany pointed to an ornately designed band encrusted with jewels that Millie wore.

"That's my *sparkler*. I see you are wearing one too."

Brittany looked down at her right wrist. "No, I don't have a *sparkler*, it's called a wrist watch."

Millie took Brittany's right hand in both of hers, studied her watch, scrunched up her face, closed her eyes and 'snap,' the jewel encrusted band around Millie's wrist appeared to be an ordinary wrist watch, the same model as Brittany's.

"There!" Millie said. "I have made both of our sparkler's *exactly* the same."

Brittany had Millie turn around several times so she could look her over. "Yep, you look like any ordinary girl."

"Why do you wear your watch on your right arm?" Millie asked.

"I'm left handed. I use my left hand for most things and I wouldn't want to bump my watch and break it, or lose it while throwing a ball or something like that."

"That's interesting. I use both of my hands equally well, but as you might guess, I've had plenty of time to practice. If you don't mind, I'll continue to wear mine on my left wrist."

Brittany and Millie walked down the dock on the pond and sat with feet dangling over the water. They sat for several hours and chatted. Brittany was as happy as she could be and so was Millie. Brittany felt she had truly found a friend.

"Millie, do you eat and drink like us humans do?"

"I do indeed! Why do you ask?"

"I was just thinking that it's past the lunch hour. We could go in the house and grab a snack."

"Do you have salad? I love salad. Is Outer World salad the same as ours?"

"How about some nice crisp lettuce, carrots, cucumbers and fresh tomatoes sprinkled with shredded cheese and covered with dressing?"

"That sounds wonderful."

"You wait right here and I'll run in the house and make us each a salad," Brittany said, springing to her feet.

"Will your grandmother mind?"

"Oh, no. She's a novelist. She doesn't do lunch. She does breakfast and dinner, but in between, she locks herself in her office and writes all day. Potsy and I fend for ourselves." Brittany continued up the path to the house.

In a few minutes, she was back with two small salads in paper bowls. She sat back down on the dock next to her new friend.

"Oops," Brittany said. "I have to go back in the house and get us each a fork, I forgot silverware."

Millie placed her right hand over the *sparkler* on her left wrist, then pointed to Brittany's shirt pocket with her right index finger. "Will those in your pocket do?"

Brittany glanced down at the front of her shirt. Two fancy silver forks stuck out of her pocket. "Whoa! I'll say they'll do," she said, passing one to Millie. "You know, plastic works just as well when you're eating from a paper bowl."

"I'm sorry, I thought I heard you say silverware."

"Yes. Yes, you're right. Millie, please don't do any more magic unless you tell me first, Okay?"

"Okay. I was just trying to help."

Brittany blushed and rolled her eyes. "Just let me know before you help any more."

Chapter 6

Cousins

Splashing her bare feet in the water of her grandfather's pond, Brittany turned to Millie. "It would be so neat if this water were clear, so we could see the bottom when we swim."

"Would you like it clear?" Millie asked.

"Like it? I'd love it."

Millie placed her right hand on her *sparkler* and then stuck the first finger of her right hand into the water. She turned her finger making a swirling motion. The murky green color began to recede. There was a swirl in the water that stretched out from where Millie sat and soon the entire pond was clear and clean.

"Holy cow! How did you ever do that? I can see all the fish. Woops! They can see us too. They're dashing under the dock and into the shade of the willows to hide."

"I just used my *sparkler*. You can use yours. It's not broken."

"I'm sorry, girl; it's like I told you. Mine is a wrist watch. Just a plain old watch and it doesn't do anything but tell me the time."

Looking up, Brittany saw her grandfather's old green pickup truck coming down the road. As he crossed the dam at the end of the pond, Brittany waved for him to come over.

Pulling his truck into the parking area in front of the shop, Pot-

55

sy got out. He held two or three pieces of mail in his hand. One envelope had been opened. He walked down to the dock where the girls sat dabbling their feet in the water. "Brittany, I see you've found a friend. I also see there is something strange going on." He motioned toward the clear water of the pond.

"Potsy, this is Millie. Millie, this is my grandpa, Potsy."

"Happy to meet you, Millie," Potsy said as he took her smooth pink hand into his. "I feel like I know you already. Are you from around here?"

Brittany watched her grandfather's face. For a split second, it went expressionless -- his eyes had an empty stare. "Yipes! A little static electric shock there," said Potsy, pulling his hand back.

"Yes," Millie said. Her large blue eyes lit up her smiling face.

Motioning for her grandfather to take a seat, Brittany patted a spot on the dock between the two girls. "Potsy, there is something I need to talk to you about. It's really important. I need your help and advice."

"Okay," Potsy said. "I'm sure that whatever it is, we can work it out." He took a seat, cross legged on the dock between to the girls.

"Potsy, Millie is Elfin. She is my friend and I want to make it so she can come and go around here without too many questions."

Brittany told him about the things that had happened in the past few hours.

"If I tell Monya she's from town, she'll want to know where she lives in the village and who her folks are. She knows everyone from church. If I tell the people in town she lives out here, someone might see Monya in town and ask about her. What can we do?"

Potsy pushed Millie's red hair back revealing her pointed left ear. "Yes. She's an Elf-type all right. Those ears are a dead give away. Sounds like you have quite the problem," Potsy said, pulling off his ball cap and running his hand through his thinning white hair. "The first thing we have to do is put this pond back the way it was. A clear pond without a filtration system in this part of the country will invite lots of questions."

Millie looked at Brittany, who was shaking her head as if to

56

say, yes, and rolling her eyes like a child caught with her hand in a cookie jar. Millie tipped her head slightly and clapped her hands. A thunderous pop rose up and the pond was as it was.

Potsy sat silent for a moment, then his face lit up. "I've got it. I would not normally try to deceive your grandmother, but we'll have to arrange for one of your cousins from out of town to pay us a visit." He looked at Millie. "Can you look like a person just by seeing a picture?"

"Yes sir, I sure can."

"Okay, you're going to be Brittany's cousin from California who's been going to school in England." Potsy pulled the envelope with a frayed edge open and pulled out a picture of his brother's granddaughter. "Here. Can you duplicate this face?" He extended a wallet size school picture to Millie.

Millie held the picture very close to her face, studying every dimension. Handing the picture back to Potsy, she extended her arms and moved off the dock onto the level ground. She started to spin round and round until she was almost a blur and then with a soft *poof*, she stopped. Her hair was no longer in pigtails, but was long and curly. She was now a honey-blond with occasional streaks of brown in her hair.

"Oh my gosh! It's Josie!" Brittany exclaimed.

"Yes it is," Potsy said. "Didn't you know? I just picked her up at the airport. It's a surprise visit."

"Potsy, this is the greatest thing ever, but can we convince Monya?"

"I think we can. You'll notice I don't have the hay on the truck that I went to get. The feed store was awfully busy and one of the clerks had called in sick, so I drove into the city to pick up a part for my table saw."

Potsy turned to Millie. "From now on, your name is Josie. You grew up in northern California, where you live with your parents, but you've been going to school in England for the past year. You've been living with your mother's parents during the school year. You are the eldest granddaughter of my brother Sam. You have a brother and a sister. You are visiting here while your parents are on a two month business trip to the Orient. They had to leave before you got home from school, so they took the younger children and you came here for a visit."

The Elfin girl blushed. "I know all of that. I did a mind-match with you when we met. I know all about my new self. The fact is, your grandniece did not come home. She stayed in England for the summer."

"Monya is awful smart. I think she'll know her own grand-niece," Brittany said.

"Well, I'll tell you what honey, there's no time like the present to find out," Potsy said as he started walking toward the house with the girls close behind.

The heavy screen door clicked shut behind them as they entered. "Monya, where are you? I've brought you a surprise. We're in the living room, where are you?"

"I'm in my office." Monya's voice rang from down the hall. "I'll be right there, dear."

"Don't be too long. This surprise won't keep," Brittany said.

"I was nearly done. I said I'd be right . . ." Monya's voice trailed off as she entered the room from the hall and saw Josie. She rushed to her and gave her a big hug and a kiss on the cheek. Tears welled up in her eyes and her glasses clouded for a moment. A blank look came to her eyes for just a second.

"Where did you . . .? How . . .? I'm flabbergasted." Monya turned to Potsy. "I thought you've been acting a little strange the last couple of days. Keeping a secret, huh?"

She released Josie from her embrace. "There is a twin bed and a set of bunk beds in Brittany's room. You can be in with her or use the guest bedroom. You choose."

Josie shrugged her shoulders. "I'll go in with Brittany, if that's okay."

"Great! That's settled. Potsy, put Josie's luggage in Brittany's room."

Stepping back Potsy said, "One more piece of news. Her luggage has been lost. You know those international flights."

"Well, I'll be," Monya said.

"I've already called her parents to let them know she arrived safely," Potsy said.

"I've got more than enough clothes that we can share," Brittany said as she took her *new* cousin by the hand. "Come on, Josie. I'll show you where you'll be sleeping."

As the girls left the room, Monya hugged Potsy and gave him a kiss. "You sneaky old man, you. You really know how to surprise me."

"I *am* going to the feed store now." Potsy cupped his hands to raise his voice and faced down the hall toward Brittany's room. "I'm leaving for the feed store. Would you girls like to go with me?"

As the jovial threesome cleared the porch, descended the steps and started up the path toward the workshop and Potsy's old truck, a large black squirrel sat on a branch and made clicking sounds in their direction. Josie looked up at the squirrel, smiled and waved. The squirrel immediately turned and disappeared around the tree.

As they walked down the path, Potsy turned to Josie. "Do you think this change will be all right with Shamus?"

"It is fine," she said as she hooked her arm under Potsy's, "and he said I should go, learn and enjoy myself."

Arriving at O'Brien's Feed store, Potsy backed up to the loading dock. A full complement of personnel was on hand and his truck was loaded in no time.

"Say, how would you girls like to stop at Torgilson's on the way home and grab something to eat?"

"That sounds great," Brittany said, nudging Josie. "I could eat a horse, how about you?"

"I don't think so," Josie said. "That sounds like an awful lot."

Potsy laughed.

Brittany put a hand to her face as she turned to Josie. "I could eat a horse is just another way of saying, I am very hungry."

"Okay," Josie said, "I'll help you eat your horse."

"Great." Brittany rolled her eyes. "Now, I'm going to have to watch how I say things."

As the truck entered Torgilson's parking lot, Brittany pointed outside. "Wow. I think the statue draws more traffic than the lion ever did."

"Can we go see?" Josie asked.

The truck rolled to a stop and Potsy pushed his door open. "Sure. Let's have a look."

A large crowd of people was gathered around the statue of the great lion. One small boy sat on it while his father took a picture.

Josie stood still, her head moving up and down just a little as if in deep thought. "I haven't been here since the night. . ."

Potsy frowned and took Josie's hand. "Come on girls; let's go get that sandwich I promised you." He started for the store, the girls close behind.

As Potsy was about to take the first step on the porch of the store, he noticed a gray car parked near the step. The license plate read, State Government 104. Without hesitation, he cleared the steps and entered the store.

As Brittany entered, she could see the number of patrons was far larger than usual. They found their way back to the soda fountain and slid onto their favorite stools.

Jinx turned away from the grill. He appeared very tired at first glance. The sight of friendly faces seemed to revitalize him. A big grin crossed his face and his eyes sparkled as he walked to the new arrivals.

"Hi, ya'all! It sure is good to see a familiar face in here today." He wiped the counter in front of Brittany. "What can I get you?"

She answered for the whole group. "We'd each like a burger and small fries with a soda to drink."

"And... a horse," interjected Josie.

Jinx's eyes widened as his head spun toward Josie.

"She's just making a joke," Brittany said, half leaning over the counter. "This is my cousin, Josie, from California."

"How do you do?" Jinx said. He scrawled their order on a check and walked back toward the grill. He placed three burger patties on the grill, poured precut fries into a basket and set them into the hot oil to cook, then returned.

"It seems you folks only come in here when there's something interesting going on. The last time was the lion thing and this time it's *that* guy." Jinx moved his eyes to the right and gestured with his head slightly. At the end of the bar sat Mr. Torgilson with a small, slender man dressed in a black business suit.

"Who is *that* guy?" Brittany asked.

"He's some big shot from State University. He's here to study supernatural and unusual activity in the area. I guess the Curse of Whispering Oaks has reached out and caught the attention of a lot of people. Maybe he thinks we have aliens." With that, Jinx walked down the counter to welcome two new arrivals. In a few minutes he was back with three burgers and sodas.

"Thanks, ya'all. I'd like to talk more, but I'm getting a little busy here." He laid their check on the counter and went back to tend the items cooking on the grill.

Putting mustard and ketchup on her burger, Brittany took a bite and smiled. "Wow. That Jinx sure makes a mean hamburger."

Josie raised the top of her bun and looked at Brittany. "Mean?"

"I'm sorry. What I meant to say is, this hamburger sure is good."

"Oh," Josie said as she smiled and took a bite.

Josie sat between Brittany and Potsy and ate slowly compared to the other two.

"If you don't want to eat all of that, you don't have to," Brittany said.

"It is good, but I am pretty full." Josie pushed her half-eaten burger aside and took a sip from her soda. "My! This is good. What is it? I've never tasted anything like it before." Her statement was soon followed with a hiccup.

Brittany looked into her eyes. They looked larger than normal and the pupils were dilated.

"Th..is isth re..ally goood, hic," Josie said as she reached for her soda. Her hand wavered as if unsure of the exact location of the glass.

Brittany grabbed the glass and moved it out of her reach. "Potsy, we must get her out of here, NOW!" she whispered.

Potsy tossed a ten dollar bill on the bar, tucked one of Josie's arms under his and he and Brittany hustled her out of the store between them. Her feet were off the ground, trailing behind them as they dashed down the stairs into the parking lot.

Brittany opened the door of the truck and hopped in. Potsy braced himself and lifted the girl up. She was unexpectedly light. He almost threw her into the roof of the cab. Brittany pushed her down in the middle seat and buckled the belt. "She's about to take involuntary flight," Brittany said. She dropped into the seat next to the door and buckled her belt as the door slammed shut.

Potsy turned to go to the driver's side. He was met by Mr. Torgilson and *that* guy. "Bud, this is Mr. Emongaton, that's pronounced E - mo - na -ton. He's here from the university. He studies unusual happenings, UFOs and that sort of thing. He heard about my lion and came right down."

"That's nice." Potsy extended his right hand by reflex, but withdrew it as the men stepped closer. "Glad to meet you Mr. Emongaton. I've got to go now."

"Is someone ill?" Mr. Emongaton asked. "We saw you bring those girls out of the store. Is one of them sick?"

"Oh no, Brittany and Josie, my granddaughter and my grandniece, they're just clowning around. Josie just arrived from California and they're pretty excited. They haven't seen each other for quite a long time."

The people outside the truck could not see the occupants through the darkly tinted windows. If they could, they would have seen Josie making faces at them.

Potsy rounded the front of the truck and sprang inside. "Whew. That was a close one."

"I'm sorry," Brittany said, "I didn't realize there was sugar in those sodas we drank. It really gave Josie a buzz. She's starting to calm down now."

Whispering Oaks - The Curse

"I think the best thing to do is try her on a little taste of various soft drinks until we find out exactly which brands, if any, she can tolerate," Potsy said as he drove out of the parking lot.

"That was a strange sensation," Josie said. "I don't think I have ever experienced anything like that before."

"You have an allergy to sugar. If anything you eat or drink has sugar in it, you can expect this same reaction again," Brittany said.

"In my world, I never have heard of such a thing."

"Shamus has heard of it. He's the one that warned me not to let you have sugar."

"I'm glad he did. I would hate to embarrass you and give myself away. There would be all kinds of people from the Outer World chasing me."

"Don't you worry. Settle back and relax. We'll be home soon and we can go in the house and take a nap if you like."

Josie's eyelids sagged heavily and her head tilted slightly. "Just keep that guy away from me," she mumbled. "He's a mean . . ." She fell asleep without finishing her sentence.

Brittany sat up straight, her eyes squinting as she studied Josie. "Potsy, I think this sugar stupor thing that Elfins have is a cycle. Big pupils, hiccups, slurred speech, loss of balance, involuntary flight and lastly, sleep. Josie looks exhausted and she's out like a light."

"I'm sure you're right," Potsy said. "But I noticed that she did make one very critical observation about Mr. Emongaton. That's a pretty heavy duty judgement to make when you've only seen him from a distance and you haven't even talked to him."

"Yes, Potsy, but it's my impression that these Elfins have very well developed instincts and intuitions."

Potsy drove the truck across the pond dam and turned toward the cow pens and the feed storage shed. "I suppose you're right. I've lived with them for five years and didn't know it."

When the truck was backed into the feed shed, Potsy and Brittany got out and unloaded the hay bales and grain sacks. As they got back into the truck, Josie woke up.

"Oh my, how long have I been asleep?"

"About twenty minutes. How you feelin'?" Brittany asked.

"I feel great, like it's the start of a new day."

The evening passed quietly after a very special dinner Monya prepared to celebrate the arrival of her granddaughter and grand-niece. The family retired to their rooms and went to bed.

"I think it's working out fine," Brittany said to Josie. She went to her bathroom, removed her contacts, brushed her teeth and changed into her nighty. She slid between the sheets of her bed. "You know somethin', Josie? I enjoy having you with me as much as I enjoy having my real cousin, Josie, with me."

Josie went into the bathroom, brushed her teeth and put on her night clothes. When she returned to the room, she turned back the blankets on her bed, slipped between the sheets and answered Brittany's comment.

"I'm very happy being your cousin."

Brittany flipped off the lamp. "Good night, cousin."

Potsy usually woke up with a clear head, but this morning was a little different.

"Potsy! Potsy!" It was Monya, standing over him, shaking him awake.

He sat up to find himself nose to nose with his wife. He blinked trying to become fully alert. "Wha... What is it? Is there a fire?"

"No. But there might be if you don't tell me who the girl is that's sleeping in . . ." There was a slight hesitation. "I mean, *over* the bed in Brittany's room." She took Potsy's hand and pulled him from the bed. He followed, Monya pulling him all the way. Brittany's door was slightly ajar. Monya pulled Potsy to the door and pushed him up next to the door jamb, almost into the room.

Potsy looked in. Brittany was half curled on her left side with her blankets pulled in disarray and crumpled around her body. Potsy raised his eyebrows as if to say "So?" He began to turn away from the door.

Monya grabbed the hair on his chin between her thumb and first finger and moved his head to redirect his vision. His head turned involuntarily toward Josie's side of the room.

There she was, floating four to six inches over the top of her bottom sheet, a sheet neatly covering her body.

Potsy's eyes opened wide in surprise. He turned his head toward Monya, shrugged his shoulders and smiled a broad smile. He shut the door softly and ushered Monya down the hall to the kitchen.

Monya sat in her place at the kitchen table, her arms folded, a look of absolute disgust on her face. Potsy knew that look. She was ticked.

He slid down into a chair next to his wife. "Honey. I was going to explain what's going on around here as soon as you got used to Josie."

"I don't think you realize this is a modern world. I spend most of the day at my computer and I get emails from Josie and her mother regularly. I got an email from her mother this morning, saying she was going shopping in Tokyo today. I was going to get the girls up for breakfast and tell them about that email. You really had me fooled. Her parents are in the Orient, but Josie is in England with her maternal grandparents. Now, who's *that* girl?"

Potsy rubbed his face with both hands. "You've got to promise you'll sit right there and not move while I explain what's going on."

"Oh! Is this going to be one of your long stories? If it is, I'll make some coffee and we can call it our morning chat."

She went to the sink and started preparing the coffee pot for the morning's brew. The gurgling pot began to fill almost instantly. Monya poured two mugs full of the delicious dark liquid and set one in front of Potsy. She sat down in her place at the table, opened a packet of sugar substitute and poured it into her cup along with a dash of cream which she stirred vigorously.

"Well," she said, "I'm waiting."

Potsy took a sip of his coffee and started. He told her about everything that had happened since Brittany arrived. He was careful not to leave out anything. He recounted the experience with the pink pig and the meeting with Mr. Emongaton. A meeting that he suspected was much more than chance.

Monya sat with her eyes closed most of the time, opening them only when she took a sip of her coffee. "Are you expecting me to believe this yarn? I think you've really outdone yourself this time, Bud Ellis."

"I promise, Carol, it's true. Every word is true."

The grandparents did not realize they had been sitting at the table for two hours. The girls were up. They had showered, dressed and come down the hall, but hearing Potsy explaining, they stayed in the shadows until he was done. They now walked into the kitchen.

"It's true Monya, I promise," Brittany said, sitting down beside her grandma and taking her hand.

"It is, indeed," Josie said. "There is one very important thing. May I have your permission to continue as your grandniece? Without your permission, I must revert back to being myself."

Monya looked at the pretty, blond-haired girl standing behind Brittany and smiled. "Yes, you may continue to be my grandniece, as a matter of fact, I insist that you do. The people in the village are already nosey enough. Being my grandniece will keep them from getting too deep into our business."

Chapter 7

Some Research

*I*t had been a couple of days since the excitement at Torgilson's store. Potsy planted corn while the girls played around the barn, hauling fertilizer out to the field with the small tractor.

After they had fed, cared for the animals and gathered eggs as part of their daily routine, they went to the pond and swam.

This morning was a little different; when the girls finished their chores and went up to the workshop, they found several boxes stacked almost in the doorway.

"Potsy, what did you order?" Brittany asked.

"Oh, you gals are here," Potsy said, coming from behind a divider wall, wiping his hands on a red rag. "The delivery truck from Capital City just left. You can unpack those boxes and put the contents on the large workbench and those empty shelves there."

"Yahoo! This is like Christmas," Brittany shrieked, as she ripped the tape and pulled the flap open on the first box. Josie stood on the opposite side of the box, brushing packing peanuts aside and withdrawing a large bottle of soda pop.

All of the boxes were filled with soft drinks, juice, cookies, candies, and other confectionery delights as well as baked goods of all kinds. But, only one package of each item.

"Wow, Potsy. Are we going to have a party?" Brittany asked.

Potsy looked around the shop as if to make sure no one was near. "As a matter of fact, no. When you get everything unpacked, you should find a dozen tablespoons in that yellow box there. We're going to take a tablespoon full of each soda and cut up each and every confection so Josie can taste test it. I want to make sure we don't have anymore experiences like the one we had at Torgilson's."

"What a great idea," Josie said. "But, won't this take an awful long time?"

"It might take a while. We'll have to write down the name of every item we test; if we make a mistake, we don't want to make it twice," Potsy said.

"I'll go in the house and get my notebook and record the names of all of these items," Brittany said as she emptied the last box and set it aside.

"No. Wait," Potsy said. "I have a complete packing list for all of this merchandise. We can use it and put a check beside each item as we test it. If it tests bad, we'll put a circle around it. It's here on this clipboard." He handed the board to Brittany.

The girls unfolded and flattened the boxes they had emptied. Potsy picked them up and started for the door. "You have the plan; I'm going over to the hardware store, but I'll be right back. See how many of these products you can get through before I return. I talked to Jinx and he said only the most expensive soda pop is sweetened with sugar, so, hopefully you won't find too many bad items. Just in case though, read the labels on everything before you sample it."

Potsy started to leave the shop, as he reached the door he said, "Keep this door closed and locked while I'm gone, and don't let anyone in." He turned the latch and pulled the door closed behind him.

Brittany unfolded the packing list, picked up a pen and started with the first item. She opened a small bottle of soda pop, poured a tablespoon full. Josie took the spoon and gulped down its contents. "Wow! That is as good as the soda at Torgilson's soda fountain."

Whispering Oaks - The Curse

"The label says it's sweetened with an artificial sweetener," Brittany said.

"I could drink more of that."

"Maybe you could, but we better stick to the plan. You don't want to fill up on something and not be able to go on with the test. From the looks of that shelf, we still have another hundred items to test."

Josie placed her hands together in front of her face as if to pray; then keeping the heels of her hands touching, she spread her fingertips and placed them at her temples, her thumbs under her chin.

"Is there something wrong?" Brittany asked. "Do we need to stop?"

"Oh, no," Josie said. She dropped her hands to her sides as she walked to the door, flipped the lock and twisted the knob. "I just thought we might be able to use some help with all this testing." She pulled the door open wide and three small white rabbits and two black squirrels scurried in. As she was about to shut the door, a large black hawk flew through the opening and landed on the desk in front of Brittany.

Josie cocked her head sideways as she looked at the hawk. "Don't you have sky patrol today?"

There were six small *poofs* and the smell of peppermint spread throughout the workshop. A guardian, dressed much like Shamus, stood on the table top in front of Brittany and five other Elfins were on the floor in front of the desk.

"No," replied the Elfin Guardian in front of Brittany. "Virgil has sky patrol today. I was just up visiting with him when I heard your call."

"You will all have to be about our size, and look like Outer World children," Josie said.

The Elfin on the desk leaped to the floor and all of them began to spin like tops. There was a soft *POOF* and six teenagers stood around the desk.

"How may we be of service?" asked the dark haired boy who had been the hawk.

"Brittany, this is Phillip," Josie said, pointing toward the young man. She started down the line of boys and girls. "This is Wyatt, Gunnar, Angus, Alice and Savannah. I've asked you all here to help with testing these confections to make sure they are not harmful to Elfins."

"Wait a sec," Brittany said, "it might be a good idea to have several test subjects, but I'm not too sure Potsy would approve."

"Oh, sure he would. Besides, this way, we can get done sooner and go down to the pond for a swim," Josie said.

"Okay. Since you've gone to all this trouble, let's get on with it," Brittany said as she opened the next bottle of pop and poured a spoon full and handed it to Phillip. Each Elfin picked up a spoon and held it out so Brittany could pour something into it.

Brittany took her time, reading ingredients, carefully measuring soda and cutting cookies to ensure uniform size and recording the name of who was testing the product.

As she wrote down Phillip's name next to *Chocolate Chip Cookie* on the packing slip, she noticed he was chewing the cookie very slowly, then "Hic..." She looked at his eyes. They were dilated. He stepped back a little and tilted his head slightly.

"This cookie isth really goood," Phillip slurred as his feet came off the floor and he began to drift upward like a carnival balloon.

"Grab him!" Brittany barked pointing across the desk at the airborne youngster.

Wyatt and Josie were closest to Phillip, but he was away and over their heads out of reach by the time they got to where he stood.

Brittany reached the package and read the ingredients section again. There was no mention of sugar anywhere.

"Thith stuff ith really great! You guys need to try it," Phillip said as his head bounced like an errant balloon against the rafters of the shop twenty feet overhead.

Wyatt had picked a loose chocolate chip cookie from the desk and broken it into pieces. When Brittany looked up from reading the package she saw all the Elfins but Josie had a small piece in their mouth chewing it. Brittany poured three small paper cups full of milk and handed them to Wyatt, Angus and Gunnar. "Here, drink this!" she commanded.

All three Elfins tipped up the milk and washed down the cookie. Alice was caught up by involuntary flight and Savannah simply stood still, chewing, a look of anticipation on her face.

Savannah, Angus, Wyatt and Gunnar did not lift off. They stood, looking upward at Alice and Phillip with sober faces.

"It's the milk!" Josie shouted. "The milk reverses the effect of sugar."

"Crazy," Brittany said. "But why didn't Savannah go up?"

Savannah pressed close to the desk. "I know. I didn't go up because there weren't any of those little brown chunks in the piece of cookie I had. It was just cookie."

"That must be it, the chocolate chips in those cookies have sugar in them and that isn't listed on the ingredients section. It just says chocolate chips," Brittany said, looking up. "Hey, can you guys come down here and get a glass of milk?"

Both of the flying Elfins turned as if they were about to descend, but they stayed pressed against the rafters.

"I guess they'll have to wait for the sugar to wear off a little so they can come down," Josie said. "Was I in that condition when I drank sugar soda at Torgilson's?"

"Actually." Brittany laughed. "I think you were a little worse."

As their friends hung suspended above their heads, the rest of the group finished the testing.

"That's great," Brittany said as she wadded up wrappers and threw them in the trash can. "Now, let's go to work cleaning up the samples and placing them in the cabinet on the far side of the shop next to Potsy's small refrigerator."

All of the treats had found their way into the refrigerator or onto the shelves of the cabinet except the chocolate chip cookies, two candy bars and a package of chocolate covered raisins. These were in the large trash barrel near the desk with crumpled newspapers on top of them.

There was a metallic squeak and the workshop door opened. *POOF*, the Elfin teenagers changed to squirrels and small white rabbits, all of which scurried under benches and the table saw, out of sight.

"Hi girls," Potsy said as he closed the door and set a small bag on the table saw. "How is our project coming?"

"We're done, except for cleaning up," Brittany said.

A knock came on the door and it opened almost at the same time. There stood Mr. Emongaton. The girls gasped with surprise as the stranger entered the room. "I'm sorry to barge in on you like this," he said. "This is your place of business isn't it? Mr. Torgilson said you do wood work and I'm in need of a small box. It needs to be made of black walnut." He pulled several folded pieces of paper from the inside pocket of his suit jacket. "I have a drawing and the specifications for it right here." He laid the papers on the edge of Potsy's desk. "Do you think you can make this for me?"

Both girls backed to the other side of Potsy and peered down at the drawing. Brittany folded the packing list and stuffed it into the back pocket of her jeans.

"This looks like a box trap to me," Potsy said.

"Yes. That's exactly what it is," Mr. Emongaton said. "I believe there are creatures on or near your property that I am looking for and this is the only way to catch them. Can you make up a box like this or not?"

Brittany looked at the man -- a strange looking character, small, thin and almost skeleton-like. He had a very narrow face, a sharp pointed nose and chin, squinty bright gray eyes set deep in a bright pink complexion. A pair of small round powder blue colored spectacles hung low on his nose.

"Yes. Yes, I can make a box like this for you. It might be a little while though. I have other projects I must complete first," Potsy said, picking up the paper.

At that moment, the people standing around the desk heard rustling in the rafters above their heads. Everyone looked up.

Oh my gosh! Thought Brittany. *My friends will be exposed. We'll all be caught.*

"Brittany," Potsy said, "I see you have some of your friends in here again."

Two white pigeons cooed as they perched calmly on the rafters some twenty feet above.

"My granddaughters love all the animals of the forest," Potsy said to the man in black. "I'm surprised there aren't deer and ducks in here, too."

Mr. Emongaton's attention turned to Potsy. "It's not ducks or deer that I'm concerned with. What I'm after is much smaller. Just make sure you build the box exactly as it is specified. No nails or screws, no metal at all. Can you do it?"

Potsy placed his hand on the back of the smaller man's coat and pointed him toward the door. "Oh, I'm sure I can. Don't you worry about a thing. I'll have your box ready for you by next week. I'll call Torgilson at his store as soon as I get it ready. You'll be around there somewhere, won't you?"

"Yes. I'll be at Torgilson's." The man in black edged through the half-open door, looking up at the two pigeons in the rafters as he stepped outside. "Those birds look happy."

Potsy glanced up at the pigeons. Both had their heads buried under a wing and they appeared to be fast asleep. "Yep. They'll be here until Brittany goes outside; she feeds them, so they follow her around like puppies." He stepped outside with Mr. Emongaton.

As Mr. Emongaton reached his car, he suddenly stopped, turned around and placed the long, skinny first finger of his right hand in the air as if he had just remembered something. "There is one more thing. With your permission, I'd like to place my box down by your pond, or perhaps over by your feed shed when you get it finished."

Potsy looked around. "I'm sorry, I can't allow you to place any kind of trap on my property. Just the thought of it would upset my wife and the girls. They're not tree huggers, but it's like I said in the cabinet shop. . ."

Mr. Emongaton chimed in, "I know, they love all the animals of the forest." He got into his car and stuck his elbow out through the open window. "I notice you said *animals* of the forest, not *creatures* of the forest." His eyes narrowed as he watched Potsy's face for a reaction.

A wide grin crossed Potsy's face. "Now you're sounding like my wife. You know, animals, creatures, critters, varmints. Those kids love 'em all and I wouldn't have it any other way. I like 'em myself."

v   Mr. Emongaton started his car and began to pull away.

"Don't forget," Potsy said, "I'll call you at Torgilson's as soon as I get your box finished."

As Potsy entered the shop he noticed the black squirrel that always sat on the lowest large branch of the giant oak. The squirrel barked a disdainful greeting and scurried around the trunk of the tree, out of sight.

Brittany looked up at her grandfather. "Potsy, that man had the eyes of a pig. As a matter of fact, between the eyes, he looked a great deal like the pig we took over to Jensen's Farm last week."

Potsy smiled. "You know, I think you're right."

"Isn't this private? How'd he get in here?" Josie asked.

"My cabinet shop is a business," said Potsy, raising both hands and looking around the shop. "It's open to the public. People can come in here, at least in the front section, without being invited."

Chapter 8

The Box

Three days had passed since the unexpected visit from Mr. Emongaton. Potsy had gone to his cabinet shop and turned out several projects, but he had not gotten around to starting Mr. Emongaton's box. There was something sinister about this man and Potsy was not at all sure he wanted to be involved with building anything for such a person.

He kept going to his desk, picking up the drawings, starting to read them, '*All wood must be black walnut, planed to one quarter inch thickness,*' and dropping them back onto the desk.

It was Saturday, not a day that Potsy would normally work in his shop, but he was there, cutting up a large piece of black walnut. He cut a twelve inch wide plank into four foot lengths and began to plane one down to the thickness of one quarter inch. The big machine whined as its sharp blades began to eat away at the rough surface. The wood came out of the planer, hard and shiny, as if it were already finished. He cut them into one foot long pieces and set them up on the work bench.

As he stood admiring the pieces of walnut, a soft knock came on the metal shop door and it opened. Brittany and Josie slipped through the door, towels over their shoulders. They were dressed in similar blue bathing suits.

"Hi, Potsy," Brittany said, giving her grandfather a hug. "We're on our way down to the pond for a swim. We thought we'd come by and see you on our way."

Brittany stood close to Potsy's work bench and touched the smooth surface of the black walnut boards that he would use to make Mr. Emongaton's special order box.

"Josie, look how beautiful this wood is," Brittany said.

Walking to the workbench, Josie began to run her fingertips up and down the shiny surface of a piece of black walnut. Her fingers had passed up and down the entire length of the wood three or four times before she spoke. "You are so right. It is beautiful. I don't think I have ever seen anything so lovely in my life." The words of her sentence seemed to come slower as she spoke.

Potsy and Brittany both looked at Josie's face. She had a far off look in her eyes and a smile that seemed to get wider as she rubbed. Her hand was now rubbing in small circles on the surface of the wood slab. A crackling charge in the air and blue static-like lightning bolts came out of her fingertips, which seemed to be stuck to the wood. Her eyes rolled back in her head and she began to fall forward. Brittany caught her and pulled her back to a nearby chair.

Potsy dropped the piece of wood he was measuring at the other end of the work bench and rushed to the girls. "What's going on? I don't understand!" He held Josie upright in the chair. "I think it's time to call Shamus."

"Shamus Mactavish O'Riley, please step forward!" Brittany said with a trembling voice.

Poof. There stood Shamus on the end of the work bench. "What is it you're a needin', girly? You know, it's not past the noon hour."

Brittany looked up, fear and excitement in her voice. "Shamus, something has happened to Josie. She's very weak. She's acting like she's very sick."

Shamus looked around the shop and smiled at Potsy. "Aye, tis good ta' finally meet ya' face to face, Bud Ellis."

76

Whispering Oaks - The Curse

Potsy tipped his head as he held Josie upright. "I'm sorry the circumstances couldn't be better, but something seems to be wrong with Josie."

Shamus walked over to a piece of the black walnut and kicked it. "If she touched this, I'm not surprised. This Druid poison has made her weak. No other wood, no other substance on this earth, nothing but black walnut will sap the life force out of an Elfin. If an Elfin touches the stuff, he'll be drained right down and become limp as a rag."

"Will it kill? What can be done? What can we do to help her?" Brittany asked. She rubbed and patted the hand of her friend who was now slumped down in the chair, her face toward the floor.

"Kill? No, it can't kill unless it penetrates the flesh. An arrow made of black walnut can kill. As for what you can do, you're doin' it. Just keep her away from the walnut, talk to her and pat her hands."

Brittany looked up at Shamus, standing on the end of the work bench, "Is this state uncomfortable to her? Is she hurting?" Tears welling up in Brittany's eyes.

Shamus began to laugh. "No. She isn't hurting. Being under the influence of black walnut is for an Elfin like being under the influence of alcohol is for a human. The wood fouls all the senses and drains the body of energy. The Elfin just goes to sleep. If they are in constant contact with the wood, they can sleep for months."

Potsy leaned down, patted her face and rubbed his fingers against the cheek of the limp girl. Almost instantly, Josie opened her eyes and raised her head.

She took Brittany's hand between both of hers and smiled up at Potsy. "Thank you both for believing in me and loving me." She stood, still holding Brittany's hand. "Weren't we on our way to the pond? I thought we were going swimming."

Brittany let out a giggle and headed for the door. Both girls laughed as they left the shop, closing the door behind them.

Potsy sat down in the chair where Josie had been. "I'm sorry my family and I got mixed up in your world. If there was something I could do to remedy this mess, I'd do it in a hurry."

"I can assure you that it is not your fault. If there is blame to be had, it is mine alone," Shamus said. "It was I who sent a young, inexperienced, Wish Fairy with Brittany when she went to Torgilson's to shop. Josie liked Brittany very much and wanted to please her, so when Brittany wished the lion to be exchanged for a statue, Josie granted the wish. It would not have happened if I would have sent a guardian or a messenger Elfin as I normally do."

"I guess, after the lion disappeared, Mr. Torgilson called the university and asked for help. There's a Mr. Emongaton that has just arrived. He's got his nose into everything and he has asked me to build him a box trap."

"Humph," Shamus said. He dug a small pipe out of his pocket and lit it. He pointed the mouthpiece at Potsy, smoke rising slowly. "You can rest assured that your friend, Mr. Torgilson, did not call this *Emongaton*. Mr. Emongaton is not what he appears to be. The black squirrels that you see in the oak trees, those are guardians. They have reported that Mr. Emongaton is, indeed, a Nenuphar wizard. His only purpose here is to capture as many Elfins as he can and carry them back to his world with him."

"And how do you know this?"

"First off, Nenuphars consider themselves the smartest creatures on earth. They are very conceited. For example, Mr. Emongaton's name. What if you spelled it backward?"

Potsy picked up a stick and traced Emongaton backward in the sawdust on the floor. The tracing spelled out *Not A Gnome*.

"Oh my gosh!" Potsy exclaimed. "Is it true? Is he a gnome or what?"

"Not only are Nenuphars conceited, but they are also liars," Shamus said. "This particular one is not only a gnome, but a powerful being of the Nenuphar clan. He may even be a Wizard. Their only hold over humans is the fact that they can make them very sad. They can read your mind by shaking your hand or by holding onto an object that you are holding onto with your bare hands. They have to touch bare skin with theirs to make contact. Whatever

78

you do, never shake hands with Mr. Emongaton unless you have on gloves that would protect you from an electrical shock."

"Electrical shock?" Potsy said. "I got a static electricity shock from Josie the first time I met her."

"Yes," said Shamus. "I'm sorry that happened. I've scolded her about that. It's a reflex. If an Elfin meets an Out Worlder, we automatically go for a mind match. The static electricity, as you call it, is an indication that you have experienced a mind match."

Potsy leaned back on his stool. "That makes sense. I don't think I'll be in a hurry to shake hands or give him a warm welcome."

Shamus pointed his crooked pipe at the drawings on Potsy's desk. "My Guardians tell me that you are building something, a trap for the Nenuphar. Do you have a *contract* with Mr. Emongaton to build this Elfin prison? Did you promise him anything?"

"I don't think so. I told him I'd have it done by next week. If that's a promise, then I did make one."

"Nothing else. You're sure?"

Potsy rubbed his bearded chin. "I'm pretty sure."

"Did he ask you or tell you to construct it exactly as the plans said?"

"I told him that I *could*, I didn't say I *would*."

"Good." Shamus took a drag from his pipe and blew out a large smoke ring. "You see, when the project is done, it will be a box-trap. A gold coin or other irresistible item will be placed on the release trigger and when an Elfin goes in to pick it up, the door will be released and the unsuspecting Elfin will be trapped."

"But I thought you guys could just 'pop' from place to place. I've heard that you can be on the ground one second and high in a tree the next."

"That's true, but when the prison cell is made of black walnut, there's no escape. . ." He hesitated and took a slow, thoughtful drag from his pipe. "Unless there is a gold portal for the Elfin to escape through."

The tiny man pointed his index finger to an open space on the workbench next to Potsy. "You must build a portal into the prison cell, so that no Elfin can be held."

Potsy heard a sharp 'pop', like a cap gun going off. There on the workbench lay a solid gold piece about the size of a quarter. He picked it up. It felt heavier than a quarter, but it was very thin.

"Brittany told me you didn't have any pots of gold."

Shamus laughed. "The fact is," taking another drag from his pipe, "we don't keep our gold in pots, therefore, we don't have *pots of gold*, and that, my friend, is the truth."

"I'm not interested in your gold, pots or no pots. Just tell me how I'm supposed to put this portal into the box-trap without Mr. Emongaton finding out that it's there."

Shamus pointed the mouthpiece of his pipe at Potsy again. "I've given you the portal. You are the craftsman. You figure out how to place it so that it won't be seen."

Potsy pointed to the drawing on his desk. "How about if I put it right here? It'll be in the top and toward the back in the dark, a hard spot to see."

"Yes. Excellent. Would you please call me when you finish the box?"

"I sure will," Potsy said. He turned the drawing on the desk so he could read it clearly. He put his finger on the page. "Right about here."

Poof. Shamus was gone.

Potsy whistled as he cut the mortises, tenons and joints to fit the pieces of the box-trap together. But before he assembled it, he cut a round spot with his drill press on the inside, top portion of the box. Using wood glue, he placed the gold piece into the round slot and covered it with a paper-thin black walnut slug of the same size and glued the rest of the box-trap together. The sliding door worked smoothly and fell with the slightest jar of the trigger.

"There. It's done," Potsy said aloud. He set it on a high shelf for the glue to dry. "I'll have Brittany call Shamus tomorrow to have a look at it and see if the portal works." He switched off the light and closed the door. "I'd better get over to the house and give Monya the lowdown on this Mr. Emongaton."

Whispering Oaks - The Curse

I wonder, he thought as he walked up the stone path toward the house, *should I tell her I have finally met Shamus or would that be too much for her to believe right now?*

Chapter 9

Dilemma

After breakfast, the entire family gathered in the woodshop. Potsy pulled the box-trap from the shelf and placed it on the work bench.

"There it is," he said. "What do you think of it?"

"That's a very pretty trap," Monya said. "It's as lovely as a brand new jewelry box and there's no varnish on it. It shines without it. Have you called Mr. Emongaton, yet?"

"No, I haven't. I'm going to have Shamus take a look at it first. I want to make sure the escape portal is working properly."

Brittany spoke the words. "Shamus Mactavish O'Riley, please step forward."

Poof! There on the work bench stood Shamus. "Hi there, I've been waiting for your call."

His little round face suddenly contorted with anger and his right hand shot out as he pointed. "What is this woman doing here?" His voice, almost deafening, crackled and thundered throughout the large metal building.

Josie leaned down toward the work bench and spoke softly. "Shamus, this is Monya, grandmother to Brittany and wife to Potsy." Her voice was smooth, just above a whisper.

"I know who she is," Shamus said in a normal tone. His chin jutted out as he gritted his teeth, and his body physically shook as he struggled to control his rage. His voice rose with every word he spoke, getting louder and louder. "It's fine if one or maybe two Out Worlders know we are here, but you tell more than that and pretty soon they believe in us and if they believe in us, they start to look for us and when they can't find us, they *hunt* us! Mrs. Ellis, there," he pointed a finger at Monya, "was our best friend in the Out World because she had the strongest *disbelief* in this entire human community. Even that Irish preacher, Pastor Kelly, that she holds in such high esteem, has been heard to say that he believes we are real."

Shamus's voice calmed as he went on. "Pastor Kelly is friends with the old Indian Medicine Man, Waycon. People in town take their crippled children and elderly to him. The Medicine Man believes in us and brings those people to us to care for. He has never seen us, but he comes to the edge of Whispering Oaks and offers prayers and chants for our continued benevolence. We grant his humble wishes because he believes so mightily."

"It's my fault," Potsy said. "I told Monya so she would not fear things that she does not understand."

"I promise I'll never tell anyone about you or any other Elfin," Monya said, her eyes wide at what she was seeing.

Shamus was calm now. "I understand, but I'm not sure the Council will. You've created quite the dilemma for them." Shamus walked up to the trap and struck the corner with his shillelagh. "Could we get on with the reason you called me here?"

Potsy pointed. "I want you to inspect the trap and see if the escape portal is installed properly." He turned the open door of the box toward the Elfin Guardian.

Shamus entered the box without hesitation and pushed the trigger. The heavy door slipped forward and crashed down with a bang, locking him inside.

Poof! There stood Shamus on the far end of the work bench. "That portal works wonderfully," he said. "The hard part is that black walnut makes us very weak and tired. I almost collapsed, just walking to the trigger."

Monya leaned forward. "Potsy told me about the black walnut putting Josie to sleep. Is there anything that can be done to combat the effect?"

"We use black walnut to build our confinement centers in the Inner World, you know. It's where we keep Elfins that choose to disobey the rules."

"Do tell," Potsy said. "And how do your workmen who build the confinement centers handle the raw materials without being put to sleep?"

"Our workmen and our Guardians wear special clothing and take a special protective bath to make sure they are not affected by the power of the black walnut. We have a special blue water pool for this. The bath also protects against anyone being able to make a mind match. Nenuphars and Elfins can obtain a mind match by touching any bare skin you know. We can also do it if we touch an object you are touching at the same moment we touch it."

Potsy frowned as though he were puzzled. "You said wearing gloves that would withstand an electrical shock would protect against a mind match."

"Yes it will. A dip in the blue spring is better."

Monya couldn't believe her eyes. "Have you had the protective bath recently? How long is it good for?"

"No. I have not had it recently. It's good for about a month, but I will have it before I come to the Outer World again and I'll make sure all of our Elfin population working in the Outer World have it. You can never tell when one of Mr. Emongaton's Nenuphar henchmen will be lurking about."

Shamus leaned toward Potsy. "Please don't surrender this box to Mr. *Not A Gnome* until we've talked again. Excuse me, I'm being called by the Council." *Poof*, he was gone.

A light rain fell as the family left the wood shop and started up the path toward the house. The path was constructed of cobblestones which were slick in the rain. Monya's light shoes had smooth soles and she hadn't taken three steps from the shop when her feet went out from under her.

"Oh!" Monya yelled as she came down hard on her right hip.

Potsy was at her side. "Are you alright, honey?" He started to help her up, but she grimaced, moaned and motioned for him to put her down.

"No," she said. "I think I broke my hip. You'll have to call an ambulance."

Brittany and Josie were now at Monya's side.

"Maybe I can help," Josie said. She placed her right hand on her *sparkler*, bowed her head a little and put her right hand on Monya's hip. There was a flurry of blue static electricity flashing around her hand and a soft pop, like the noise of a cork gun. Monya's head, drenched in rain, jerked upward.

"Yahoo!" she shouted, waving her arms. "Get me up! The pain's gone! It's a miracle! Thank you, Josie."

Potsy helped her to her feet and the family went into the house.

Monya went to the linen closet, picked up towels and handed them out as she reentered the kitchen. "This is turning out to be a lovely day, isn't it?" she asked of no one in particular.

"Thanks to Josie, it's a great day." Brittany said.

"I'll say," Potsy said.

Monya opened the fridge and brought out a large head of lettuce. "You all sit back and relax and I'll whip up some lunch."

In moments everyone had a bowl of salad in front of them.

Shamus transported himself to the great gold circle in the main hall as he had a myriad of times before. A four inch wide solid gold line made a circle in the white marble floor marking the area from which Elfins could leave and return to their city. If an Elfin was summoned from outside, by magic, he could leave from anywhere he happened to be, and he was authorized to return to the place of his origin. For normal business, anyone going out or coming in would leave and arrive through the gold circle in the main hall. As a result, it was a very busy place. Much like an airport on a holiday.

The main hall was a gigantic room, the size of a large gymnasium. The walls were beautiful and ornate, white with lots of gold decoration, much like the interior of a great church.

Shamus walked down the hall to a set of large doors made of heavy wood. The Guardians, two of which, stood on either side of the great door, opened it for him and he was allowed to enter the chamber of the High Council.

At the far end of the large room, five thrones sat against the wall. The one in the center was tallest and set up the highest. The other four descended on either side in sort of a half circle, so each chair could be seen by the occupants of all the other chairs.

Shamus appeared before the Council. "You called me, Grand Master Enis?" He bowed at the waist, tipping his bowler hat.

"Shamus, you understand that we can't have too many people in the Outer World knowing of our existence. Particularly since we know there are Nenuphars in the area. Their wizard is in the Outer World for one purpose only -- to capture as many of us as he can. He will try to get a foothold into our city and capture our world. If he is successful, the Nenuphars will have enough magic to power their city for hundreds of years. "

"Yes, Grand Master Enis, I know, but these are honorable humans and they will not give away any secrets. I feel they will help us without rewards for themselves."

Grand Master Enis shifter in his chair. "Do you believe we should try to protect the humans?"

"I do. The human, Potsy, has already been working to our benefit. He has built a trap for the Nenuphar Wizard that has an escape portal. The Nenuphar will bait this trap with a gold coin. They know that we cannot resist gold in *any* form. An Elfin will eventually go into that trap, even though you have issued an edict telling all Elfins to stay clear of it."

"So, what do you propose?"

Shamus pushed his hat back on his head. "If we help them, we will be helping ourselves. We should bring them here for a bath in the blue spring. If we don't and they come into contact with a Nenuphar, he will make a mind match and we will be compromised."

There was a gasp from all five Councilmen as they leaned forward on their thrones.

"You can't do that," said Master Tock, the Councilman sitting second on the right of Master Enis. "They already know too much. I say we wash their minds clean and take our chances with the Nenuphar that is supposedly here."

Shamus took a step forward. "Master Tock, I can assure you that there is a Nenuphar Wizard in the human village. I have given my word to the Outer World girl, Brittany. I shall be at her call and be her friend forever."

"If her mind is washed clean, you do not give up your sacred vow. If she calls you, you will respond. You can carry on your friendship from the moment she calls you," said Master Tock.

"If her memory is washed, she will not know how to call me," said Shamus. "Doesn't that border on a violation of my trustworthiness?"

Master Enis rose, tapping his long gold staff on the floor as he stood. The rest of the Council also rose. "The Council shall retire and discuss this dilemma. We must either wash their memories clean or give them the most intimate secrets of our world and send them back to their world with that knowledge. That would create a great bond of trust on our part."

In a few moments the group of long haired, white robed elders regained the platform and sat on their thrones.

"Master Yojen has made the following suggestion," said Grand Master Enis. "We will bathe them in the blue spring and return them to their home. There has never been a human brought into our world and returned to theirs."

Whispering Oaks - The Curse

"Yes," said Shamus, stepping forward one step. "That is true, but we are being hunted by the Nenuphars and if they get into the city, all are doomed. I think, with human help, we can bring disgrace to the wizard that has been sent. Make him believe there aren't and never have been Elfins at Whispering Oaks. We must project the impression that humans can defeat Nenuphars without magic."

Master Yojen leaned forward. "What about Waycon, the old Indian Medicine Man that comes to the meadow to pray to us for help? I, myself, have spoken to him in his dreams. He knows we are real."

"None of the other humans in the village believe his stories," Shamus said. "When a human has a serious problem, they go to Parson Kelly. He will, as a last resort, send them to see Waycon. Doctor O'Keif comes from the city to ensure all the paperwork is done so no alarm is raised in the human world and Pastor Kelly performs a closed casket funeral."

Master Yojen raised his right hand. "We are not dealing with humans in his case. We must make sure the dark wizard cannot mind match with Waycon. If the Nenuphar wizard places hands on the Indian and makes a mind connection, he will know we are here."

"Perhaps we should bring the old Indian to the city and bathe him, too," Shamus said.

"The medicine man believes in magic," Master Yojen said. "Since he is only one being, we can take a goat skin of blue spring water and instruct him to wash his entire body with it. We can appear to him in a dream, and leave the goat skin bag nearby. Shamus, would you please send Phillip or another senior guardian to help carry out this task?"

"Aye, sir. I will."

Grand Master Enis leaned forward. "Why has this Medicine Man not been bathed in blue spring before?"

Master Yojen half-rose from his chair as if to argue a case. "Sire, the Indian has been around for eighty years and we have not been threatened by the Nenuphar before."

Grand Master Enis banged his long gold staff on the floor beside his throne. "Yes, fine. Shamus, bring your humans before us, we will examine their hearts to see if they will, indeed, help us."

Chapter 10

The Council

Potsy passed the salad dressing to Brittany as the door bell rang. "I'll get that, honey," he said as he slipped from his chair. He opened the door and saw no one there.

"Down here on the rail," Shamus said.

Potsy looked at the porch rail directly in front of him. "Why didn't you just pop up inside the house? We're having lunch. Monya made a lovely salad. You can join us."

"I didn't 'pop up,' as you call it, in your house, because Elfins cannot enter a private residence without being invited, and that's something you should tell your family; neither can Nenuphars. They should never be invited in. Once they've been invited in, they can cross the threshold any time they like."

Potsy stepped outside and extended his right hand, bowing slightly. "Please come into my house. Please be my guest for lunch."

Poof! Shamus stood before Potsy, almost his same height. He smiled, removed his bowler hat and entered the residence.

"Monya, look who's come to join us for lunch," Potsy said as he followed his guest into the kitchen.

"I'm delighted to see you," Monya said.

"Master Shamus," Josie said. "It's fun being our normal size in the Outer World, isn't it?"

Monya set a bowl of salad in front of Shamus. He answered as he placed his hat on an empty chair next to him. "Yes, I enjoy being this size, but then again, I just enjoy being." He leaned his walking stick against the same chair and picked up his fork.

The small group finished their lunch, chatting over the situation that had been created by the sudden appearance of the Nenuphar Wizard in the village.

When the meal was finished, Shamus pushed his salad bowl back a few inches and put his elbows on the table. "There is one thing we must do that is very important." He looked into the faces of everyone at the table. "You must all come to the Inner World to meet with the High Council."

"How long will that take?" Monya asked.

"It will only take a short time."

"What if someone comes by while we're gone?" Potsy asked.

"That's all been taken care of. With your permission, we'll have someone here to take each of your places while you're gone."

"Then you have it," said Monya.

There was a knock at the front door. Potsy went to answer it.

"Please come in," Brittany heard him say from the kitchen.

Everyone at the table watched the hall leading to the front door as Potsy walked back into the kitchen, but there appeared to be no one with him. As he took his seat at the table, he gestured, pointing toward the floor.

Looking down, Brittany recognized the four visitors immediately. "Monya, this is Phillip," she said, pointing toward the young Guardian dressed in black. She introduced the two girls behind Phillip. "This is Alice and Savannah, and this... I don't know this girl."

Josie laughed. "This is my sister, Ruby. How are you Ruby?"

The tiny girl smiled up from the floor. "I'm fine and I'm here to help."

Shamus stood by the table. "We must have your permission to

duplicate each of you."

Almost in unison, everyone at the table said, "You have it."

The newly arrived Elfins stepped back from the table and began to turn. The turns changed to a blur and *poof*. There in the kitchen next to the sink stood duplicates of Monya, Potsy, Brittany and Josie.

The Potsy figure came to the edge of the table and spoke. "We will be here to take care of the property, feed the stock and be seen while you're gone."

He stood close by as Shamus spoke in his deep voice. "Don't forget your orders. Don't eat or drink anything while we're gone."

Phillip, who had assumed the roll of Potsy, bowed slightly and said, "As you say, Master Shamus."

Shamus ushered the family out of the kitchen. "Okay, folks," Shamus said to the family. "Everyone hold hands." He stopped short of the door and banged his staff on the floor. A blue light, looking much like tiny lightning, radiated out from his walking stick.

Brittany took Monya's left hand in her right and Potsy's right in her left. Potsy took Shamus' hand and Monya took Josie's. Brittany felt a tingling in her fingertips. She looked over at Potsy. He was *gone* right before her eyes. The next second the entire group was gone. There was a blinding flash and she could feel a different floor under her feet.

Shamus' voice came to her ears. "You can open your eyes."

Brittany opened her eyes. The family was standing in the center of a large gold circle in a great white cathedral with high ceilings. Although it was the largest room Brittany had ever seen, it seemed warm and friendly.

There was a hustle bustle atmosphere as Elfins came and went in all directions. The arrival of the family seemed to go unnoticed by the throng of Elfins around them.

Wow! Grand Central Station, thought Brittany as she heard the voices of the quickly passing crowd. She still had her grandparents' hands in hers, but as she looked into their faces, she did not recognize them. Her Monya was long and lean with soft white skin, large blue eyes and long auburn hair. Her Potsy had no beard, his hair was full and blond with lots of curls and the pot belly that she had spent her entire life getting used to, was gone.

Potsy extended his arms and Monya ran into his embrace and kissed him. Brittany pressed between them. "Hold it, you two. Don't forget, we're here on business."

Brittany turned to Shamus. "Excuse me, but did we shrink when we came to the Inner World?"

"As a matter of fact, you did not," said Shamus. "If you look at your grandparents, they are probably taller than you remember them. People lose some of their height as they age."

"So, you're small in the Outer World and full size in the Inner World? Why is that?"

Shamus looked down at Brittany and smiled. "We find it much easier to remain invisible and move around in the Outer World if we remain small. And if we are discovered by a human, we are not intimidating. We can usually convince them that their imagination is working overtime and we leave unseen."

Brittany blushed and raised her eyebrows. "I know what you mean." She followed close behind Shamus as they walked down a long hall and came to a large wood double door. Guardians on either side of it stood to attention as Shamus approached. The Guardians opened the large doors, revealing another grand room.

In front of them was what appeared to be a throne, but instead of a chair for a king or queen, there were five. The one in the center was the largest, but the other four were nearly the same size with lower backs.

"Right this way," Shamus said. He led the way to a side door and opened it.

Brittany was surprised to see an open, airy, well appointed room. It was not quite as large as the throne room. Every few feet along the wall was a beautiful green house plant in a large white pot. In the center of the room, the main floor was sunk two feet below the level of the entrance area. There was a large round table made of wood in the center of the space with lots of chairs. The wood of the table shimmered and was very glossy.

At the table sat five white haired Elfins, dressed in white robes with blue trim. The figures all rose as the family entered.

The family walked down the three steps to the level of the floor where the table was. Brittany was surprised that this area was also spacious. A white shag carpet caressed her feet. She watched the five at the table.

The Elfin in the center spoke. "The Ellis family and Josie, please come and have a seat. We are happy you are here." The Elfin leader signaled them to sit as he continued, "Please be seated. My name is Enis, I am the Grand Master." He extended his left hand. "This is Brine and Pace, and on my right," he turned slightly, "is Yojen and Tock. I'm sure you are aware that we are the High Council for *this* city."

"For this city?" Potsy echoed. "Are you saying there are more cities like this one?"

"Oh yes, there are many cities like this in the world." Enis raised a finger. "There are also many cities that are occupied by the Nenuphar. They are our mortal enemies. They attempt to capture and enslave our people. The only magic they know is black.

"In the beginning, we befriended them. We helped them establish their civilization on this continent. But soon they discovered that if they used force, they could turn our people into slaves. They usurped our magic and used it to power their cities and extend the lives of their populations."

"What can we do to help?" Potsy asked.

"The first thing we'll ask you to do is go to the blue spring pool and bathe."

"Is this the pool Shamus told us about?" Brittany asked.

"Yes," said the Grand Master. "If a Nenuphar Wizard ever touches your bare skin, or touches anything you are holding, he can get into your mind and learn all you know about Elfins. The blue spring has the power to create a shield against such an invasion. We give you this, not only to protect you, but to protect all the Elfins you have ever had contact with."

"Holy cow," Potsy said. "I almost shook hands with that *Not A Gnome* guy when we were at Torgilson's store and again in my wood shop."

"If you had," Enis said. "He would know all you know. Please follow Shamus. We have determined he is right. You are, indeed, worthy humans."

"Come this way," Shamus said, leading the family up the stairs and into a hallway that led to a smaller room. "Potsy, you go through this door." He pointed to his left. "Girls, through that door. Remove all of your clothing, then go out the door in front of you. You will find a pool. Jump into the pool and sink to the bottom. Make sure your hair gets as wet as your feet. Return to this room. Allow all the moisture to dry and get dressed."

The girls stood in their room, each slowly taking off one garment at a time and hanging them on the hooks provided.

A loud "Yahoo!" and a splash was heard, just outside their door to the pool.

Brittany finished undressing and stood behind the door. "I'm not going through that door if Potsy is out there. I don't care how many of my diapers he changed."

"Don't worry," Josie said. "I've heard of this before. When you go through that door, no one can see you and you can see no one."

"You heard her," Monya said, pulling the door open wide and going out to the pool.

Brittany ran through the door and hit the water. Two more splashes followed her.

When she looked for the others, she could not see them. Thinking they had left, she dove deep, swam a while, then climbed the ladder and went back into the dressing room. A thick fog formed in the room that covered her to the neck. She found a bench and waited for the water to drip off her body. The door opened and there stood Josie. Brittany could only see her from the neck up.

Josie sat beside Brittany, wringing water from her long hair.

Now the door opened again and there stood Monya, her head floating above the fog bank.

"Hey. That's a nice pool," Monya said. "I swam the full length of it twice and I didn't see anyone."

"You didn't see anyone because the modesty shield is on," Josie said. "There could have been a hundred Elfins in the water with you, but you wouldn't know it."

"Yipes!" Brittany said. "Does that mean they saw me?"

"No, no. Like I said, the modesty shield is on. No one saw you and you saw no one."

As they dressed, the mist in the room ebbed and faded until, by the time they were clothed, it was gone. The soft moist air that had been in the room was now clear and dry.

Monya was fully dressed. "You know what, I wouldn't care who saw this beautiful body," she said, patting her flat tummy.

Potsy and Shamus stood waiting in the hall as the girls came out.

"Is everyone ready to go?" Shamus asked as they all came together on the golden circle in the cathedral room. "Hold hands."

There was a flash of light, and everyone stood in the living room of the Ellis home.

Potsy patted his stomach and scratched his beard. "Yep. We're back."

The Elfins that had replaced the family came forward from the kitchen, smiled, waved and *poof*, they were gone.

Monya turned to Potsy. "We have a lot to do to protect our friends. Let's get to it."

Shamus stepped near the door. "Potsy, you can give the trap to Mr. *Not A Gnome* any time you like. I think you'll be safe in his presence. Keep in mind that he is very dangerous. And *never* invite him into your home. Your shop is a business, open to the public, so he can enter there without an invitation." *Poof*, he was gone.

"I think I'll take that trap over to Torgilson's store and if Mr. Emongaton is there, I'll deliver it to him. If he's not, I'll give it to old man Torgilson."

Brittany took hold of the back of Potsy's shirt. "That's a great idea. Can Josie and I go along? We'd like to get a burger -- and a soda."

Josie smiled at Brittany. "Visit Jinx, don't you mean?"

Brittany shrugged her shoulders. "Okay, so I like his diet soda better than ours."

Chapter 11

Medicine Man

Mr. Emongaton sat in his car on the dirt road, high on the ridge, a pair of binoculars held to his eyes. He scanned the other side of the canyon below him.

Old man Torgilson said it was over here. I'll find it, he thought as his gaze passed over tall pine and oak trees on the heavily wooded and brush covered hillside across from him.

There! That must be it. His eyes focused on a small cabin made of earth and wood on the far canyon rim, just below a great stone outcropping. The grey color of the old wood and mud that chinked the logs caused the building to nearly disappear against the grey limestone canyon wall behind it.

 Looks like Torgilson was right. You can drive right to it on these dirt roads if you know where it's at.

He watched the scene for a moment. A large dark skinned man with long gray braids, wearing a red and white checkered shirt appeared at the doorway. The man walked to the wood pile, picked up several pieces and went back into the cabin.

Mr. Emongaton threw his car into gear and followed the road around the canyon rim until he came to a small fork in the road. He turned right and followed the road back until it came out under the limestone overhang and stopped in front of the cabin.

The tall Indian came out of the cabin and closed the door. He sat in a very old wooden chair that leaned against the front of his house.

Mr. Emongaton watched the man as he eyed him. He stepped from his car and walked up to stand before the old man. No expression crossed the Indian's face.

"I'm from the university. I study unusual and paranormal activities. My name is Emongaton. I understand your name is Waycon. I hope I have not come at a bad time." He extended his right hand in greeting.

The old Indian sat perfectly still, hands folded in his lap. He did not make eye contact. Mr. Emongaton could see the Indian's gaze took in all of his features, yet, he did not move to take his hand.

"If you are *not* from the village, what do you want here?" The Indian's voice was deep and his words slow but strong, punctuated by a right eyebrow that rose just a little when he finished speaking.

"I was told by the people in town -- er, in the village, you can explain the strange things that have happened around here."

"What has happened around here?"

"You know." Mr. Emongaton could hear his own voice indicating impatience. "You have to be aware of the lion at Torgilson's store. What happened to that lion?"

"I have not seen that lion for many days. It is cruel to keep any creature on a chain without his freedom." The old Indian leaned forward slightly. "Would you like to be chained so you could not do things that are of your nature?"

"I'm not here to discuss what makes animals happy, I just want to find out what you know about the disappearance of that animal."

"So, *that* animal is free?" The Indian's demeanor did not change, he remained still, his hands folded.

Mr. Emongaton's patience was wearing thin. "He's gone," he blurted. "There's a statue in his place. Where is he? Who did this? I

100

was told in the village that you know the answers to strange questions." He held a long slender finger in the air. "The people in town said you could tell me what is going on. Can you tell me what happened to that animal?"

"It seems, you know more about this lion than I do. I have prayed for years that the lion would be set free, but I never prayed for a statue. It is obvious to me that my prayers did not make this change."

Mr. Emongaton's voice suddenly became raspy and his eyes narrowed, a snarl crossed his mouth. "This is not the answer to a prayer. This is magic. Elfin magic." His tone lowered and almost growled. "Do you know of a city of Elfins in this area?"

Waycon did not move a muscle and his voice remained at the same level. "So tell me about the Elf-men. Do they have great medicine?"

"Elfins! Not Elf-men. They're little Elfins. They live in the forest. Do you know anything about them?"

"Sorry, I can't help you. I don't think I've ever seen one of these Elf men."

Mr. Emongaton jerked his car door open and jumped in. "I'm sure you know more than you're telling. I'll be back another day." He spun his car around in the dirt and headed back to town. A large cloud of dust followed his car as he raced up the road and out of sight over the far canyon rim.

The Indian watched the car speed down the dirt road and make a turn on the canyon rim. He could see a plume of dust following the car for a long time as it sped along the top of the far ridge.

A black squirrel came out from beside the cabin and jumped up on the small table next to the Indian. The Indian crushed a couple of pecan nuts between his hands and pulled the meat from one, handing it to the squirrel. "You know Chirpy, we will have to keep an eye on that man. I think he's nuts."

The sun was beginning to set as the Indian stood. "Tonight, we must go into the forest and thank the great spirit for giving the lion its freedom and ask that he protect us as long as this strange man is in the valley."

The Indian went into his cabin and came out wearing only a loincloth, arm bands and a special buffalo horn headdress. A small bag hung from a leather thong around his neck. He carried a rattle gourd with a single feather hanging from it and a long peace pipe.

Turning at the edge of his cabin, he followed a well-worn trail into the forest. In a few minutes he found his way through the trees to an open space surrounded by tall pines. Kneeling at a ring of stones, he started a fire, the flames opening into a small roaring blaze. He danced around the fire, chanting, shaking his gourd and holding his pipe high in the air, stopping to face different directions as he chanted and sang.

He knelt and removed a small burning branch from the fire and lit his pipe. He blew out a ring of smoke and set the pipe aside. Lying back on a pile of nearby leaves, a smoke induced trance soon brought him sleep.

The sun set behind the hills and darkness soon followed. The fire subsided, smoke swirling about his body. He dreamed of the great spirit.

Master Yojen came to him through the swirling smoke. Waycon's spirit rose from his sleeping body, sat on a nearby log and spoke with Master Yojen of the events of the day.

Master Yojen laid a large drinking skin, a strangely curved bow and a quiver of arrows next to Waycon's sleeping body. "The water in this flask is not for drinking. You must put it in a basin and wash your body from head to foot. Wash your hair and the bottoms of your feet. This water will protect you from the prying eyes of the black crow. Remember. The black crow is evil. The bow and arrows are your protection from the black panther if it comes to hunt you."

Whispering Oaks - The Curse

"Yes, Master Yojen. I will protect the secrets of the spirit realm." The medicine man lay down, returning to his body and Master Yojen disappeared.

The old Indian awoke from his sleep feeling refreshed, the skin of water, the bow and quiver of arrows next to him. Picking up the skin, he went to a large nearby rock with a deep rounded basin in the top. He took a cloth from the small pouch and began to wash from head to foot. Freeing his braids, he washed his long hair. Lastly, he sat on the edge of the basin and washed his feet. As he pulled his feet from the blue water, a vapor like steam began to rise as his body dried. The blue water remaining in the basin turned to vapor and blew away in the breeze.

After dressing, he picked up his pipe and gourd, slung the bow and quiver of arrows over his shoulder and returned to his house. He was now ready to deal with the man in black, the crows and the panther, should they come his way.

Chapter 12

Banshee

Mr. Emongaton sat in his darkened motel room eyeing the candle in the middle of the small table. The painted cinder block walls of the old building were rough with their many coats of paint. The sparsely furnished accommodation did not bother him in the least. He was here on a mission. He had to succeed if he were going to bring wealth and prosperity to his city.

He leaned forward, struck a stick match and held it over the candle's wick. The slightest touch of the match and the wick burst into flame. It was a *black* flame, appearing red, yellow and orange like a regular flame only in the middle portion. The outer edges and the center of the flame that licked the air two inches above the candle were black.

Sitting back in his chair, he studied the flame and placed his open hands near it. "By the power of the Druids of long ago, I command you, the Banshee of Death to appear!"

The flame became darker, the top of the candle fizzed and bubbled, a black cloud began to appear as it started to hiss like a Roman candle on the 4th of July.

The black cloud from the candle stretched along the ceiling and high into the room. It began to form the physical shape of a human in a long flowing black robe with a hood. The shape settled on the chair across from Mr. Emongaton as it gathered more form.

The candle regained its black flame and a feminine voice came from under the hood. "Why have you summoned me Nenuphar Wizard?"

The Nenuphar Wizard smiled, blew out the match that was about to burn his fingers and cast it into a nearby trash can. "I believe there are Elfins in this area. I know there are signs of Elfin magic, but I can not locate them. I believe the human population is helping them. I think they live at a place called Whispering Oaks on the other side of the village. I have observed from the air, but there seems to be nothing but wild forest there. It is private property and that stops me from flying low enough to see. I can drive onto the property in a car, but I can not go off the main road more than twenty feet. There is a business there, but I have been inside and saw nothing unusual. I think the entire place is protected by Elfin magic."

"What do you propose I do to gather the information you want?" asked the dark robed apparition.

The Wizard laughed with a squawking cackle. "You, my friend, are the strongest dark power on earth. Humans cannot resist you. You can walk through the walls of their homes. Go to them as they sleep and find out what is in their minds and hearts. If you will -- discover the secrets of Elfins."

The Banshee rose from the chair, stood next to the door. She pointed at the candle. "Remember, I am free on this earth only as long as that candle burns, guard it well." She turned and assumed the shape of a great black panther. "I shall return when I have gathered information for you Nenuphar Master."

"Very good," said the Wizard. "While you are gone, I shall go as close as I can to Whispering Oaks and place this trap that Mr. Ellis delivered to me today."

 The Banshee lowered her head slightly and sprung through the closed door to the darkness of the night outside.

Mr. Emongaton picked up the black candle, placed it into a

large metal and glass lantern and set it back onto the table. "There," he said. "If anyone should enter my room, they will not be able to bother the burning candle." Waving both hands over the candle he cast a spell, picked up the box trap and went out to his car. In a few minutes he had traveled the short distance to the edge of Whispering Oaks. He crept through the grass and wild berry bushes until he reached the fence. He found a spot where the grass was worn down. A rabbit path perhaps, set the trap and camouflaged it with grass.

The Banshee moved swiftly through the village, discovering the lay of the land and becoming familiar with all the surroundings. She moved quickly from one shadow to the next, almost invisible. An unexpected small stone wall appeared before her. She sprang over it in her stride.

"Eeeyoweee!" She let out an awful scream and vaulted backward to the other side. She lay down in the tall grass and panted, her tongue hanging out almost to the ground. She licked the aching pads of her front feet.

It seems I have found the holy sod of this village. A grave yard. If I had taken one more step, I could have been burned up and been sent back to the Under World. I thought I was dealing with Elfin magic, not both Elfin and Human.

She rose from the ground and began to walk with a slight limp. She came to a garden plot next to a house. The soft dirt of the strawberry patch was cool on her aching pads as they pressed deep into the soil. She crouched for a moment and sprang up assuming the shape of a woman wearing a black hooded cape as she walked toward the street.

She looked down at her hands. They were red, burned like she had touched the hot burner of a stove. She wanted to put them in cool water.

The curtain of the night began to draw back and streaks of gold began to appear on the eastern horizon. *I must return to the safety of the Nenuphar Master and the Black Candle while the sun shines upon the earth,* she thought.

"Hi there." A voice came from the other side of a small stone wall with a short iron fence above it. The Banshee was now in front of a residence next to the grave yard.

"How are you this morning? Look at that sunrise. Isn't this the start of a glorious day?" The cheery voice belonged to a plump, red-haired woman on the other side of the iron fence. Her right hand was protruding through the bars. "I'm Mrs. Kelly. Parson Kelly's wife, and that's his church there." She nodded her head toward the large white structure next to her house.

What an opportunity! thought the Banshee. *My first mind to read, and this one is being offered to me.*

The Banshee drew near the fence and started to reach for the woman's outstretched hand when she saw it. The woman had a cross on a gold chain around her neck. Banshee drew back with a start. She looked to the east, seeing the side of the church. She saw the shadow of the cross on top of the church was working its way down the sidewalk as the sun rose. In seconds that cross would be upon her and she would burn. She turned and crossed the street.

When she was out of the woman's sight, she fled as fast as a black wind can blow. She rushed into the Nenuphar Master's room and hid herself in the metal lantern on the table.

Within the hour, the Nenuphar Wizard returned. He had set his trap next to Whispering Oaks and was feeling good. "Banshee, are you here?" he asked as he closed the door.

"I am here." The Banshee's voice came from the lantern.

108

"Come out and talk to me. What have you found? Did you learn anything?"

"I'm not coming out as long as the sun is crossing the earth. Why didn't you tell me there are so many churches in this village? I counted five. Lots of Hallowed ground. That's what I found! I was almost burned up twice. I learned that there is a Bible in almost every house in this village, and if there isn't a Bible protecting the people, there are horseshoes full of magic hanging upside down nailed to door posts. I saw one house with several shamrocks painted on the door frame. I am powerful, but I must have war, violence, anger and derision to spread death and pestilence."

"Never fear, my dark friend," said the Wizard. "I have set my trap and in a couple of days we will have our first Elfin under our power. After that, it will be easy."

The Nenuphar Wizard sat down in his chair and closed his eyes. His day's work was done.

Brittany bounced up from the large recliner as the doorbell chimed. She dropped the TV remote. "I'll get that."

Josie turned from her spot on the couch and watched as Brittany opened the door.

"Hi, I'm Serena Kelly, Parson Kelly's wife," said the woman. A big smile covered her face as she pushed back the screen door and stepped into the house. "I need to see your grandpa. Would you call him for me, please?"

Josie rose from the couch and started for the kitchen. "I'll call him, if it's okay with you, Brittany."

"Go for it cuzzy. I'm sure Potsy will answer your call as promptly as he would mine." She looked at her cousin. "I think he's out in the south corn field on his tractor. I don't think he can hear that

109

dinner bell from that distance."

"It's worth a try. If he doesn't hear it, one of us can drive out on the four wheeler and get him."

Josie stepped through the kitchen door onto the side porch, picked up a heavy metal rod and began to stroke the inside of the triangle bell hanging on the porch. Releasing the rod, she placed the first finger of each hand on her temples and spoke softly.

Potsy sat in the cab of his big tractor, pulling a weed rake through the new corn field a quarter of a mile from the house. He heard an unusual tone in the cab, like a chiming bell. He immediately shut down the tractor and listened to see if the tone would be repeated. He heard Josie's voice. *"Potsy, you're needed at the house. Mrs. Kelly is here to see you."*

"Whew," he said. "That sounded just like Josie."

He stepped from the tractor, walked to his truck which he had driven to the field earlier, jumped in and headed for the house.

"Bud, it's good to see you," Mrs. Kelly said, rising from the couch as Potsy walked in. "May I speak to you privately?"

"Let's step into the kitchen," Potsy said. "Would you care for a cup of coffee?"

He poured two cups of coffee and sat down at the table across from Mrs. Kelly. "What can I do for you?"

"I'm here because of the legends that say Elfins live on Whispering Oaks. I haven't told my husband, but being Irish I believe these old stories. If they are true I'm afraid I have some bad news," she said, taking a sip of her coffee. "I was in the yard this morning, just as the sun was rising and I heard a Banshee scream."

"A Banshee? I thought the Banshee was an Irish myth."

"I can promise you that a Banshee is on the prowl in our community. I think I saw her. A woman wearing a long black hooded cloak. She was just outside our yard on the sidewalk. When she saw my cross, she ran away. Legend says that when you hear the cry of the Banshee, it won't be long before someone dies. I walked beside the wall alongside the graveyard and saw several large paw prints. It looked like a lion or some other big cat had walked there. It appeared the animal had started to cross the wall. There were two spots where the grass was scorched on the cemetery side. A Banshee cannot walk on hallowed ground."

"What does the Banshee want?" Potsy asked.

"I don't know," she said. "There is a good deal of gossip around town making reference to this Mr. Emongaton and the strange disappearance of the Torgilson's lion. No one really knows why that man is here, but he makes me nervous. And now this Banshee."

"What do you suggest?"

"Protect your home and family. Make sure everyone wears a cross. Hang crosses on your walls and in your windows. Those are the only things I know that the Banshee fears."

"When is this creature out and about?"

"She can come out anytime she wishes, but she prefers to roam from dusk until dawn."

"How is it you know so much about this mythical creature?"

"I was born and raised in Ireland and met my husband when he was a missionary there. Just growing up there is a lesson in understanding mythology."

"Thank you for letting me know. I'll see that we take the necessary precautions."

Mrs. Kelly slid her cup away and pushed her chair back. "I'm very grateful you listened to what I had to say."

Potsy stood and walked behind Mrs. Kelly as she went out the door. "A year ago, I would have had a hearty laugh, but today I believe every word you say."

He pushed the window curtain aside and watched as Mrs. Kelly's car disappeared through the trees and across the pond dam.

"Monya!" he called.

"Yes," she answered from her office.

"Would you please meet us in the kitchen?"

"Be right there."

Potsy continued without looking. "Come into the kitchen, girls. I have something to tell all of you."

"What's up Potsy?" Brittany asked as Monya arrived and sat at the table.

Potsy related what he had heard from Mrs. Kelly to the family. "For the moment, we don't know how serious this is. We'll keep our eyes and ears open for a while and if this starts looking like it's related to Mr. Emongaton, we'll call Shamus."

Monya turned to Brittany. "In the meantime, darlin', I'm not using the second computer in my office. It's about time you sent an email or two and let your family and friends know how you're doing."

Brittany rose and motioned to Josie. "Come on. I'll show you how to send an email. That way, when I get back to Utah, you can write to me. Right now I want to send an email to my friend Stephanie and let her know how much fun I'm having."

Josie's eyes grew larger as Brittany spoke.

Brittany recognized the questioning look. "No! Silly! I won't be telling her that all of my adventures have been with Elfins. I will, however, tell her about my new best friend."

Josie smiled. "Great. Let's go learn email."

Brittany dropped into the chair in front of the secondary computer in Monya's office and began to open her email program.

Josie spoke quietly. "Is your friend far away?"

Brittany looked up and smiled. "Yes, but she'll have this message in minutes."

Chapter 13

Terrors

Brittany and Josie came into the wood shop laughing and jostling each other. As the table saw came to rest, Brittany approached her grandfather.

"Potsy, may we borrow your van? We want to go over to Torgilson's and get something to drink. The calves are fed and we threw out a little extra chicken feed as we gathered the eggs. We folded the laundry and Monya says she doesn't need us for anything else."

Potsy reached in his pocket and retrieved his van keys. "Don't forget to park it on our property and walk the rest of the way. I don't want to have any unscheduled meetings with Chief of Police O'Neil or Sheriff Fitzpatrick."

Brittany took the keys and stood on tiptoes to kiss her grandfather's cheek. "Don't worry Potsy; we know the rules and we won't embarrass you." Brittany tossed the keys in the air over her head as she turned toward the door. Josie pulled the door open and bowed slightly as her friend passed.

The spirit of summer fun was in the girls as they mounted the stairs at Torgilson's store. This was a happy day for them. Brittany noticed a group of people around the lion statue as she moved through the door.

"What would you like to do after our sodas?" Brittany asked.

Josie turned to her as they entered the store and started down the aisle to the soda fountain. "I think I could go for a swim, how about you?"

They laughed as they slid onto their favorite stools and spun around a few times.

Although the laughter was ignored by other patrons at the counter, Jinx took quick notice and came over. "Okay! Enough of this happiness," he said as he wiped the counter in front of Brittany. "What can I get you ladies today?"

The girls calmed down to a snicker or two and Brittany spoke. "Jinx, old boy. What are you so sour about?"

"Isn't it obvious? I'm not having as much fun as you are." He raised his nose into the air slightly. "I know what you want. Two ice cold sodas coming up!"

"Make those *diet* sodas," said Josie.

Jinx stepped to the ice bin and scooped two glasses full of ice and held them under the spigot to fill them. He returned to the girls, setting the drinks down and flipping two straws on the counter.

"Say. How'd you girls like to go with me this afternoon? I get off in an hour and I was thinking of driving over to Hunter's Landing. They're having Berry Days over there. We could join in the festivities. They've got a great carnival going on and we could taste all the berry treats they make. They've got all kinds of ice cream, cakes, pies and the greatest raspberry milk shakes you ever tasted."

Brittany ran her fingers up and down the side of her glass and turned to Josie. "What do you think, cousin?"

"Sounds fun," said Josie, "but I'll have to be careful because of my sugar allergies."

Jinx leaned against the counter to make sure he was heard. "Don't you worry. I'll be right there every minute to make sure you don't get anything with sugar in it. There are lots of people with sugar allergies and the folks at Hunter's Landing use sugar substitutes to make sure everyone can enjoy themselves. All you do is say

114

'sugar free, please'."

Brittany leaned onto the counter, her face near Jinx. "There's just one little problem. We have to go home and ask our Potsy."

Jinx leaned back, slung his wiping rag onto the shelf behind the counter and got a very serious look on his face. "You tell your Potsy you will be with one of the most responsible people in town. He's cool. He'll say yes. Tell him I'll be by your house to pick you up at six o'clock. Hunter's Landing is on the other end of the county."

The girls sat quietly and finished their soft drinks. As Jinx passed them on his way to deliver a customer's food, the girls slid from their stools.

Brittany, pulled a wadded dollar bill from her pocket and laid it on the bar. "Pretty confident aren't you? We'll see you at six."

"Okay, okay." Potsy put his hand to his forehead. "It's your summer and I want you to enjoy it, but you know what Mrs. Kelly told me yesterday. If that Banshee takes a notion to come after you while you're off the place, there's nothing we can do to help."

"Potsy, I promise we'll be extra alert. We'll leave at six and we'll be home by eleven," said Brittany.

Leaning forward in his chair, he let his hand down the side of his face and twitched nervously at his beard with his thumb. "You wouldn't consider ten-thirty, would you?"

At six o'clock, Jinx drove into the yard in his grandfather's new Suburban®. The girls grabbed their hooded sweatshirts from the back of the couch and raced out the door.

115

Monya was on the porch to give the girls a hug. "You girls be careful and don't be late. You know, it doesn't hurt to be a few minutes early."

The front passenger door closed and the large vehicle pulled out of the yard and across the pond dam, turning right toward the highway.

The sign at the edge of the highway read "Big Timber 1 mile." Jinx pointed. "We can shave fifteen minutes off our time if we go through Big Timber State Park. The road is excellent, just a little curvy."

Brittany looked at Josie, sitting next to the door in the front seat. Josie nodded approval. "If the roads are good, let's go for it. Potsy told me, there isn't a prettier spot on earth than Big Timber State Park. I'd like to see it."

"Me too," said Josie.

"Oh, my gosh. Your Potsy is so right. The hilliest area in the state with lots of winding roads. There are deep canyons and crystal clear streams. The big attraction is the tall pine and oak trees. That's how it got its name. Its a preserve, you know."

Brittany patted Jinx's arm. "Okay, Mr. Tour Guide, give us the full tour."

They exited the freeway and turned onto the road marked 'Big Timber, Hunter's Landing.' Before long they were on a narrow two lane road with a double yellow line down the middle. The road ran up and down hills and turned back and forth as it snaked its way through the trees.

Brittany looked out through the windshield, her eyes taking in the giant oak trees standing close to the road towering skyward, creating a tunnel over the road now and then.

Josie was half leaning out the window, waving and giggling. "I've heard of this place, but I didn't know it was this close to Whispering Oaks!"

Brittany looked out and saw a black squirrel standing on a branch in a very erect manner. Her eyes moved to the open sky and there, making lazy circles, was a very large black hawk.

"Oh my gosh," said Brittany. "Are you telling me. . ."

Josie quickly turned to Brittany, placing a finger over Brittany's lips.

"Jinx, Jinx." Josie leaned across Brittany trying to get the driver's attention. "Jinx, I need to stop for a minute. Can you stop right here?"

The reluctant driver found a viewpoint turnout around the next bend and pulled the truck over. He slammed the transmission into park and turned toward Josie who had a strange look on her face.

Brittany quickly picked up the conversation. "Oh, she's got to go -- bad!"

Josie had already opened the door, dropped to the ground and started to walk to the far side of the nearest great white oak tree.

Brittany remained turned, looking at Jinx as she slid backward toward the door. "We'll just be a minute, maybe three."

"Wait!" Jinx said, reaching under his seat and bringing out a fresh roll of bathroom tissue with the wrapper still on it. "My grandfather says even the most rustic powder room should have paper."

Brittany hesitated for a second, then took the paper, looking back at Jinx with a big smile. "Your grandfather is right. He's so understanding." She closed the truck door and darted down the path she had seen Josie take.

As Brittany rounded the tree out of sight of the car, there was a flash and a soft poof. She came alongside Josie just in time to see a large black rabbit scurry into the underbrush.

Josie's voice sounded. "I told you! This is Brittany! She is my friend. I trust her with my life."

A deep voice came from under the foliage. "We can see that. It is very dangerous to make friends with humans. No one in this forest has had a human friend since Senator Thomas O'keif died, err...

went to the Inner World in 1966. Now, that man was a friend to all Elfins."

"I remember that name from my history class," said Brittany. "They called him the Great Conservationist." She placed her hand to her face. "Oh my gosh! Shamus talked about a doctor from Kansas City by that same last name."

Poof. A guardian suddenly appeared before the girls. He was much larger than any of the guardians from Whispering Oaks. His deep resonant voice continued. "Senator Tom did not really die. He and his wife live here with us at Big Timber. He drafted the legislation that made this place a state preserve, you know. And yes, Doctor O'keif from Kansas City is his son. He is at the age where it won't be long before he joins his parents and comes to live with us. His son, Doctor Raymond O'keif will then take his place."

Josie blushed slightly. "I'm sorry. Brittany, this is Blaise. Blaise is senior guardian of the Big Timber Elfin city. He does the job here that Shamus does in our city."

"I'm very honored to meet you," said Brittany, taking the Elfin's hand.

"What?" Blaise had a strange look on his face as he turned to Josie. It was a look of total confusion. "I could not make a mind match!"

Brittany laughed. "The water from the blue spring really works doesn't it?"

"We can only stay one more minute," said Josie. "Give me your hand and I'll tell you everything we know about what is going on at Whispering Oaks."

Blaise took Josie's hand as if to shake it, but held it still. Nothing was said. Brittany watched as a blue aura wrapped around their clasped hands, their eyes fixed on each other. When they released their grip, their hands fell limp at their sides and their chins dropped to their chests for just a moment. They blinked and returned to normal.

"Thank you for the information," Blaise said. "I'll double my patrols during the day and triple them at night. If your Council

118

needs anything, tell them to send a night hawk or an owl and we will be happy to give them all the help we can muster."

"I will. Thank you," Josie said. "We must go now. Our ride is waiting."

Josie started to move around the tree, looking back at Brittany. Brittany pulled the wrapper off the toilet paper and spooled off several turns. She handed the wad to Blaise. "Thanks, big guy," she said. She tucked the paper roll under her arm and dashed to catch up with Josie.

When they reached the truck, Brittany slid in first, pressing up beside Jinx. She handed him the roll of paper as Josie closed the door. "Tell your grandpa that this stuff sure came in handy."

"Happy to," Jinx said, taking the roll and sliding it into its place under his seat.

"Oh my gosh!" Brittany said. "These are the greatest milk shakes ever." She wiped the edges of her mouth with a napkin.

"I've eaten a whole bunch of blackberries before, Josie chimed in, "but I have never tasted anything this good."

"What did I tell you?" Jinx beamed from his seat across the table. "This festival has the flavor of every berry there is and the way they serve them, you never tasted anything better."

Brittany smiled at Jinx as she rose and dropped her empty cup in a nearby trash receptacle. "What do you say we take in a few of the rides and attractions before we try anymore eating?"

"We've done just about everything there is to do and the sun is going down." Jinx pointed toward the midway. "We'll have to leave soon to be able to make it home by ten."

"I think I told Monya we'd be home by eleven." Brittany shrugged her shoulders as she hooked Jinx's right arm with her left. Josie followed suit and hooked his other arm. "How about one more ride on the Ferris wheel?"

As the youngsters stood in line to purchase their tickets, Josie stepped off to the side. "I went with Brittany last time, Jinx. You go this time."

"Okay," he said, turning to Brittany. "Okay with you?"

"Sure."

As they were about to board the Ferris wheel, a breeze came up with intermittent strong blasts of wind. Jinx pointed to the west. Dark clouds blotted out the setting sun. "This weather is getting scary," he said.

Brittany shrugged. "Who knows? Maybe it'll go away as fast as it came up."

Comfortably seated with her escort, she leaned back and began to watch the carnival below them. Lights blinked on everywhere. "It's not sundown yet, but look at that sky, it's as black as midnight."

The Ferris wheel came to a stop with their chair at the very top. Jinx edged a little closer to his date. "Ever wonder what it would be like to be kissed on the top of a Ferris wheel?" he whispered.

"I guess there's always a first time," Brittany said. She leaned back against Jinx's arm and closed her eyes. *My first kiss! This is great! What an experience!* Brittany could feel Jinx getting closer.

Suddenly, there was a cold blast of air that startled them both. Brittany looked around at the sky as the chair rocked violently. Off to the right the face of a woman appeared close up in the clouds, heralded by loud cackling laughter. Brittany easily recognized the shape of a head, shoulders, arms and hands. The woman's long flowing hair disappeared into a menacing black cloud. Brittany watched, petrified by fear as the head turned toward the teenagers and let out a scream that chilled her from head to foot. The cackle of her laughter resounded like loud thunder.

Brittany clutched at the cross she wore around her neck and held it up like a shield in front of her.

Jinx reached to the other side of her, wrapped her in his arms and pulled her across his lap leaning over her to shield her with his

120

body.

Clouds gathered quickly after the apparition passed, lightning jumped from cloud to cloud as it began to rain.

The machine started to move and both youngsters let out a loud sigh of relief. Their moment on top of the ride had been a long one. When the Ferris wheel operator opened the safety bar, both youngsters jumped out. Brittany took hold of Josie's hand and the group made a dash for the parking lot.

As they piled into the truck, Josie spoke with wide eyes. "Did you see that? That, my friends, was the Banshee."

Jinx cranked the engine over and put the car into gear. "See it? Haw! We were almost part of it. I swear that thing was looking right at us."

Brittany held her hands to her face, still shaking. "Mrs. Kelly said that the Banshee can scare a person to death. I believe it."

A steady, but soft, rain fell on them as they returned to Whispering Oaks. It was quiet for most of the ride, but as they arrived home, they began to feel safe and a cheerful atmosphere returned.

"It's only 9:30," said Brittany. "Would you like to come inside and join us in a glass of ice tea or a cup of hot chocolate?"

Jinx lowered his head. "I'd better go on home. My grandma will be worried about me. She always gets worked up when I'm out after dark and it gets worse with the rain."

Brittany patted his arm. "No worries. We'll be by to see you at the store."

Jinx waved as the large vehicle pulled out of the driveway and across the pond dam road on its way into the village.

The next day, the *Weekly Gazette* was a little late coming out because there were so many happenings the previous day.

Potsy browsed the front page. All the stories seemed unrelated on the surface but as he read through them, he could see what they all had in common.

"Mrs. Kelly was right. The Banshee is loose in the village," he said. He looked around the table at the girls and Monya. "There's a story here about lightning striking a large pine tree next to the church. The resulting fire scorched the cross on top, but the rain put the fire out. There's a story about Frankie Stubbs, the town drunk, being found dead this morning in the alley behind the Fisherman's Inn bar. It says the coroner's first report indicates he might have been scared to death. There's another story here that took place outside of Hunter's Landing. An old goat herder reported to Sheriff Fitzpatrick that a lion, or a bear, attacked and killed sixteen of his sheep, but none of his goats were harmed."

Josie leaned against the table. "Potsy, that's because goats, especially horned goats, are a sign of good fortune, faithfulness and prosperity in the Under World."

Potsy poured another cup of coffee. "Brittany, I think it's time to call Shamus."

Chapter 14

Treed

Brittany sat at the table, her hands wrapped around a warm mug of hot breakfast chocolate. Monya and Josie sat beside her. They listened carefully as Potsy related to Shamus the information he had received from Mrs. Kelly and Sheriff Fitzpatrick. When he finished, he handed the newspaper to Shamus.

"What do you think we should do to prepare?" Potsy asked.

"It's obvious that *Mr. Not A Gnome* as he calls himself, is also a Nenuphar Master. A most powerful Wizard. This makes him much more dangerous than I had thought. The mere presence of the Banshee means there is a black candle somewhere in the village. We must find that candle and extinguish it with blue water." He reached into his vest pocket and brought out two small vials. Each one glowed with a blue color. He handed one to Potsy and one to Brittany. "You must find the black candle and put it out. If you are successful in doing that, it can't be relighted for thirty years."

"What is this *black candle* that you speak of?" Potsy asked.

Shamus raised his eyebrows. "A black candle is the Nenuphar Master's direct link with the Under World. He can use it to come and go between this world and his. He can also use it to convey any number of dark creatures from the Under World."

123

Potsy rubbed his chin. "Are you telling me that this guy could bring all of the resources of the Under World against us if he wanted?"

"Probably not at this time. He must be pretty powerful in his world or the Banshee would not be here to serve him. But, I'm sure he is restricted to a small force of soldiers until he can definitely prove to his leaders that there are Elfins here. So far, all he has seen is you, Josie and Brittany."

Potsy leaned forward. "I'll go into the village to find Doc Watson and see what he knows about Mr. Emongaton. State University is a small school and he should know something about him. That's *if* he's ever been there."

"While you do that," Shamus said, "the girls can go through the forest to the west and talk to Waycon. If this Nenuphar Master is half as smart as he should be, he'll be watching the Medicine Man and will attempt to read his mind at the first opportunity."

Monya left the room and returned in a few moments with a jewelry box. She opened the box and dumped it on the table. "I want each of you to wear a cross while you're off the property. Brittany, you already have one, but everyone else needs one."

There were at least a dozen crosses on the table; fine gold, silver, wood and even some that appeared to be made from two sizes of horseshoe nails with leather neck chains. Josie quickly picked up a silver cross and fastened the chain around her neck. Potsy chose a gold one.

Shamus picked up one made with horseshoe nails and passed it to Brittany. "Here, take this one with you. Give it to Waycon when you see him. After you tell him about the Banshee, ask him if he would like to return to Whispering Oaks where we can protect him."

Monya pointed to the cross in Brittany's hand. "That cross is made from silver. It's just shaped like nails to remind the wearer of the crucifixion."

Brittany shoved the cross into her shirt pocket and buttoned it. "Wow, it's bigger than all the rest and that thing is kind'a sharp."

Monya handed Brittany a small backpack. "Here, I don't want you girls getting hungry on the way. I've put in some sandwiches and a couple of diet drinks."

Brittany and Josie picked their way along the narrow forest game trail, heading south toward the river. The high forest canopy made walking cool, but occasional patches of blackberry and wild raspberry bushes caught on their clothing and slowed their travel.

"There must be another way to get to Waycon's house," Brittany said, carefully pulling a raspberry vine away from her trouser leg.

"There is," Josie said. "We could follow the road, but it would take us hours to walk that way."

"Look," Brittany said, "it's the boundary fence. Once we crawl through it, we'll be off Whispering Oaks."

Brittany took hold of the middle strand of barbed wire with her left hand and pulled up as she stepped down on the bottom strand creating a hole for Josie. Once Josie reached the other side, she held the wire so Brittany could crawl through.

As the girls looked back toward Whispering Oaks, a large black hawk drifted over the oak trees and gave a sharp screech.

"It's Phillip wishing us well," said Josie.

The girls waved, turned and started down the path. The forest had been harvested on this side of the fence a few years before so there were fewer trees. The sun was warm as they moved down hill toward Waycon's house. They soon came to the area that Waycon used as his ritual site. The uneasiness that Brittany had felt in the forest disappeared as the sun crept higher.

They entered the ritual site. It was in a grove of dense pine trees with large oaks scattered here and there. In the center was a fire pit, and on one side stood a natural basin atop a large rock formation. A cool breeze rustled the leaves of the oak trees and caused the scent of the pines to swirl through the air.

"This would be a lovely place for a picnic," Brittany said.

"Yes, it would," Josie said, pulling off the backpack and laying it on the top of a shoulder high flat rock. "This will serve us nicely as a table."

Placing the sandwiches and sodas on the smooth surface, the girls leaned against the rock and started to eat their lunch.

"Monya sure makes good sandwiches," Brittany said.

Turning her head from side to side, Josie exclaimed. "Look for a tree that you can climb, and get up into it quick!"

Without a thought, Brittany ran to the nearest pine tree with low hanging branches and jumped to get a grip on a limb. She swung herself up, pressing her feet against the trunk and settled on a heavy branch about five feet above the ground.

As Brittany looked around, she saw Josie standing on top of the large rock they were using as a table. There was a crashing noise, the breaking of brush and loud grunting.

A huge black feral hog burst from the thicket and stood next to the stone table, grunting and drooling as he looked around. He had all the characteristics of the wildest beast. His great jowls sagged as he opened and closed his huge mouth sniffing the air. He turned his head and looked directly up at Brittany. The beast was so large his back was almost even with the top of the rock where Josie stood.

"Hey fat pig!" Brittany called to the animal. "Would you like the rest of my peanut butter and jelly sandwich?"

The hog looked up at the branch and the taunting girl. He lowered his head and charged the pine tree. There was a loud crack and the tree shook violently. Brittany nearly fell from her perch. She flung her sandwich toward the pig and grasped the branch with both hands as the vibration caused the limb to buck like a bronco.

The great swine's nose twitched and he quickly found the half eaten sandwich. His jowls flopped and the noise he made as he chewed was like a wet string mop splashing up and down on a concrete floor.

126

Brittany looked down at the trunk of the tree where the great beast had struck. The wood was cracked, making a long splinter up the center of the tree.

I don't think this tree can take many more whacks like that, she thought.

Josie had been watching the hog closely. "I've heard of these animals, but I've never seen one. Here, hog, have my sandwich too," she said, tossing it near the pig's head.

The great pig slurped up the morsel and turned his attention to the girl on top of the rock holding a soda can. The beast reared up and placed his front feet on the stone table. His gaping mouth opened as he pressed against the stone and tried to force his snout closer to Josie. She stepped back a little and began to pour her soda into the beast's open mouth.

The hog kept his mouth wide and lapped at the soda with his tongue as it drizzled. When the flow of soda stopped, the beast rolled his eyes and took a couple of chomps at Josie. She tossed the can to the ground and the pig chased it like a dog playing fetch.

Josie placed the index fingers of both hands just behind her eye, next to her temples and lowered her head. The giant beast yelped like a piglet, squealed and ran, crashing through the brush and out of sight. Josie dropped her hands and raised her head, showing a big smile.

"Whoa! What happened to that hog?" Brittany asked.

"While I was pouring the soda into his mouth, I made a mind match. In his youth, he was frightened by a large wolf that broke down his pen and carried off one of his siblings. I simply told him the wolf was here and about to eat him."

"Is he likely to come back?" Brittany asked as she swung to the ground.

"I don't think so. I figure he'll be half way to Arkansas by the time he quits hearing the wolf panting in his ears."

Brittany went to the stone table and picked up her soda which had remained undisturbed during the pig's attack. "My soda is still half full. Would you like to share with me?"

"No thank you, I had plenty before I shared with the pig. Let's get on our way. We need to talk to Waycon and get back to Whispering Oaks."

"You're right. Let's get going."

The girls followed the path down and around until they came to Waycon's cabin. The old Indian was sitting outside his house, watching a large black crow making lazy circles in the sky.

"Waycon," Brittany said as she approached the Medicine Man. "My name is Brittany and this is Josie. We're from Whispering Oaks and we have a message for you."

The Indian rose and shook hands with each girl. "Come inside. We are being watched."

Brittany glanced up at the crow as the girls followed Waycon into his cabin. The black squirrel that had been sitting on the ground next to Waycon followed the group inside, found his way to a window sill and began to chirp.

"Quiet Chirpy," Waycon said. "These are friends. You keep an eye on that crow."

Chirpy squeaked once and turned to look out the window.

The girls conveyed their message about the Banshee and gave Waycon the heavy cross that looked like nails. He slipped the leather thong over his head and smiled. "You must leave now and get back to the safety of Whispering Oaks. The Black Jaguar is the ruler of the underworld and kills without cause. It is often in the company of crows."

"Do you want to come to Whispering Oaks with us?" Brittany asked. "You would be much safer there."

"I've lived too long to be afraid," Waycon said. He slung a quiver of arrows over his shoulder and picked up his bow. "I'll walk with you as far as the property line."

When the group reached the fence, Waycon held the barbed wire so the girls could crawl through. "You girls take care of yourselves, and stay alert at all times," he said, turning back down the trail toward his home.

The girls slipped down the path into the forest and found their way home. The last rays of a beautiful sunset were lighting up the sky as they reached the house. Monya was on the porch.

"Welcome home," She said. "I was about to send out a search party."

"We completed our mission," Brittany said as she bounced up next to her grandmother. "Is Potsy back yet?"

"As a matter of fact . . . ," Monya hesitated and raised her right hand to point a finger down the driveway. "There he comes now."

Potsy pulled his van up near the workshop, slammed the door and walked to the edge of the porch. "It's good to see everyone here," he said. "I made some interesting discoveries while I was out. The big one is the fact that nobody at State University ever heard of Mr. Emongaton." He brushed past the girls and started into the house. "Let's talk about this inside."

The family joined Potsy at the table. "As soon as dinner is over, I'll take Brittany and find out where this Nenuphar Master is and try to put out that black candle."

"What about me?" Josie asked. "Can I go with you?"

"No, not this time. I'd hate to tell Shamus I lost one of his Elfins to the Nenuphars."

Brittany turned to her grandfather. "Potsy, you should have seen Josie today. We got treed by a big old feral hog. She made a mind match with it and chased it away."

Potsy looked at Brittany with a scowl on his face. "If she were to make a mind match with a Nenuphar, she might be dead or injured. You and I, on the other hand, would not be affected. According to Shamus, we'd feel a little tired and depressed. All the Nenuphars want is your joy and happiness."

Josie nodded in agreement. "There is one more thing you need to remember. If a Nenuphar gets you into a *mind-match*, they can force you to do things. Things you would not otherwise do."

"Kinda like hypnotism?" Brittany asked.

"Yes and no," Josie said. "Nenuphars can make you do things *against* your will, they can leave orders in your mind that would make you do evil or they can take away information. Their primary reason for attacking humans is to drain their spirit from them. They steal all the positive energy from the human and the human becomes very melancholy. Sometimes to the point of self-destruction. If the protection of the blue water were to wear off and you're attacked with a mind-match, simply think of the Great Wall of China, as if you are on one side and the Nenuphar is on the other. In your mind, he can not climb over it. He must remove the entire wall, stone by stone. As soon as you set up that wall, run. Get away."

"Sounds like a great plan to me," Brittany said.

Monya was now at the table with several plates. "Here Brittany, wash your hands and set the table. The roast is ready and we can have dinner. Potsy, you and Josie can get washed up too."

Chapter 15

The Beast

Brittany pressed her back against the exterior wallboards of the old building, a foot away from her grandfather. She could feel her heart beating in her throat. It was nearly midnight. The moon was full and it made the surroundings very bright. Where there were shadows, they were dark and deep; the kind of blackness one did not expect on a moon-lit night. Two hundred feet away, the old neon sign of the Riverfront Motel stood in the shadow of a large tree. It buzzed and crackled as night bugs swarmed to it. Although it was on, it gave little light and Brittany could barely read its message, "Vacancy."

Brittany and Potsy watched the motel room where Mr. Emongaton's car was parked for over an hour. There were no lights on, but there was light that flickered like a candle burning near the window. They moved to the end of the building near Mr. Emongaton's room and waited. The wind came up, a light breeze blowing from the street, past their hiding place.

She struggled to put her long hair back under the edge of her dark blue ball cap. She and Potsy had dressed in dark clothing and smeared their faces with black grease paint to avoid being seen, but her long blond hair was not cooperating.

131

Mr. Emongaton stirred in his chair beside the table and opened his eyes. "Princess of the Under World, come out and join me for a cup of tea." He rose and placed two cups on the small table next to the candle lamp. He smiled as he waved his hand over the silver tea pot on the table. Picking up the pot, he began to pour a dark liquid into the cups.

A hiss sounded from the lantern as black smoke began to fill the room. Just as suddenly as it started, the smoke cleared and the figure of a woman wearing a black hooded cloak sat in the chair across from him. Steam rose from the cup in front of her as she sniffed the air.

"Licorice tea. My favorite. Did you have a good day Nenuphar Master?" she asked.

"I did. But I have been impatient for the night. I want you to go to the old Indian Medicine Man and make a mind-match with him. I want to know all he knows. I am sure he has an alliance with the Elfins."

"To make a mind-match with a human, I must take on the flesh of the beast. When I have gathered the information you want, I will take his life. When I am in the flesh of the beast, I cannot resist the urge to destroy. Last night I roamed the area. I had a great deal of fun. I took on the flesh of the beast and killed nearly a whole heard of sheep. I flew down between two buildings that smelled of liquor. There was an old man there, drinking from a bag. I screamed and flew close to his face. He fell over backward. I think he was dead."

"Do what you will, but first get my information."

The Banshee set her cup down and slid back from the table. "I shall return before the clock strikes the fourth hour of the new day," she said, stepping to the door.

Mr. Emongaton smiled and tipped his head. "Good hunting,

my friend. In your absence, I shall go to the edge of Whispering Oaks to retrieve my trap. I am sure I will have my first Elfin to-night."

With a hissing sound, a plume of smoke rose from where the Banshee stood, now a great jaguar, a black panther, stood next to the door. The outline of the great cat seemed to shiver as she walked through the door and out into the parking lot.

Being smaller and more agile, Brittany slid carefully past her grandfather, looking around the corner to Mr. Emongaton's door. As she peered around the corner, she saw the great panther come through the door into the parking lot. The huge cat sniffed the air as she turned her head from side to side, her mouth opening wide as if to catch as much of the breeze as she could. Brittany froze, afraid to move. The cat sprang over a car in the parking lot and out of sight through the shadows.

Brittany slumped back against her grandfather and pressed hard against the building. Fear spread goosebumps over her body. She wanted to melt into the wall. Her legs were weak and her heart raced. It was hard to breathe. She knew she must be shaking.

"Are you all right?" Potsy whispered.

Speech would not come. She nodded her head indicating she was okay. She regained her composure and slid back to the corner.

Mr. Emongaton was coming out of the motel room. He locked the door, went to his car and drove away.

Brittany turned and grabbed Potsy's arm. "I just saw the Banshee. I saw her come out of that room."

"That was Mr. Emongaton, honey. I saw him too."

"No. No. Just before he came out, she came out."

"I didn't hear the door," whispered Potsy.

"She was in the shape of a black panther. She didn't open the door. She came out, right through it and jumped over that car there."

Potsy edged around Brittany, whispering as he came up on the sidewalk at the front of the motel. "That would make you one of the few people in history who have seen her and haven't died." He patted his granddaughter's shoulder and encouraged her to come along.

They walked to the door and Potsy tried every trick he knew for picking the lock, but nothing seemed to work. Short of breaking the door down, there seemed to be no way they could get in. In frustration, he stood back from the door.

Brittany, who had been standing by patiently, stepped forward, put one hand on her wrist watch and took a hold of the knob with the other. She turned it, pushing slightly. They were in.

"How . . . ?" Potsy said.

Brittany held up her right wrist so her grandfather could see. "It's not a watch, it's a *sparkler*."

Potsy closed the door behind them. There on the table stood the lantern and in it, burning brightly, was the *black candle*.

Waycon watched in the cool night air outside his home. All was quiet as the panther approached. A dark shadow from the limestone cliffs shrouded the entire cabin. The panther jumped to the porch and flashed through the closed door.

In seconds the big cat reappeared on the porch. The panther sniffed the air and a woman's voice ushered forth. "Where are you, Indian?" The animal shuddered from head to tail like a wet dog shedding water. "I am taking on the *flesh of the beast* so I can eat your heart."

The swish of an arrow cut through the darkness and struck the cat in the ribs just below its heart.

Whispering Oaks - The Curse

"Yee. .. ow!" screamed the cat as it jumped sideways from the porch and rolled on the ground in front of the cabin. As quickly as it had fallen, it sprang up, its fangs glistening in the moonlight. Another arrow rattled through the big cat's ribs and it rolled and spun around. It now faced the direction from which the arrows had come. There in the moon's shadow stood the Medicine Man wearing his loincloth and ceremonial headdress. He had another arrow drawn as he watched the big cat. The panther lunged from sixteen feet away. As the cat attacked, the arrow burrowed deep into its chest.

The woman's voice came again as the panther landed on the Medicine Man. "You can't kill me with your mortal weapons, you foolish little man," she roared. "But I can kill you!"

The great cat pounced on the Indian, forcing him down into the dirt. His bow was knocked from his hand as he tumbled to the ground. He felt the claws of the great cat entering his body as he fell backward.

The Indian was almost immobilized as he was pinned under the huge animal, his left arm pressing up under the cat's chin and his right hand lying on his own chest. The cat became calm as she raised her head. "Now, you shall know the sting of death in the mortal realm," she growled. She made a lunge at the Indian's throat, her great fangs dripping saliva in the moon light.

"Yee . . . ow!" The panther screamed. "You have killed me!"

There was a loud *poof* as the panther seemed to explode into the air. A black cloud rose above the Indian and drifted away as smoke in the wind. There he lay, holding the cross that had been around his neck. He had plunged the long nail that was the base of the cross deep into the panther's throat and now it dripped with black blood.

Chirpy, the black squirrel, ran to his friend's side and chattered to his longtime companion.

"Chirpy, the Banshee is dead. The beast is no more, but I am afraid that I too shall die soon."

The squirrel ran around and around his friend as fast as he

could and *poof.* When he stopped he had assumed the figure of a very large man dressed like Waycon. He scooped his friend up in his arms and started to run through the forest toward Whispering Oaks.

"No my friend, you shall not die. You may be dead in the Outer World, but you have a long life ahead of you," said the huge figure. He held Waycon gently as he skipped over the fence that was the boundary of Whispering Oaks.

Potsy placed his left hand on the top of the candle lantern and reached for the small hook on the front that held the lantern shut. "Ow!" He pulled his hand away. "That thing is hot."

"Try to flip the latch up with your pocket knife," Brittany suggested.

Potsy pulled his knife, but to no avail. It was as if the latch was welded shut. "We can't pour blue water on the flame if we can't get the lantern open."

"Let's take it with us," Brittany said. "We can bust it open and pour water on it later."

Potsy hooked the bail of the lantern with his left hand and pulled up as if to leave. He was dragged back violently. The lantern could not be moved. It was stuck to the table and the table to the floor.

Brittany raised the first finger of her right hand to her lips to signal silence and spoke softly. "Potsy, I hear a car outside."

The intruders rushed into the closet and closed the sliding door, all but an inch shut. They tried to be calm and quiet as a key rattled in the old door lock.

Chapter 16

Trapped

Brittany stood behind her grandfather as he peered through the narrow opening in the door of the closet. She held onto his right arm just above the elbow. Her left hand rested on her own right wrist, on the *sparkler* Josie had given her.

The key in the old lock rattled slightly and the door opened. As Brittany had feared, Mr. Emongaton was in the room. He dropped his room key onto the table and withdrew a box from under his cloak. Brittany leaned closer, so she could see better. It was the box trap Potsy had built. As the wizard set the trap on the table, Brittany could hear a soft bumping and scratching noise from within the trap.

The Nenuphar Master sat down at the table and turned his head from side to side as if he had detected a noise in the room. He leaned over the box trap and listened to the soft thumping inside. He opened the end of the trap and reached inside with a gloved hand.

"I've got you now, you little Elfin bugger." He wrestled his hand around trying to get a grip on the creature inside. "Now, come out of there."

Brittany held her breath as she watched. *Oh my gosh! He's caught*

137

one of my little Elfin friends, she thought. *And what about us? We're trapped in a closet six feet from that nasty little monster.*

As the Nenuphar Master pulled the creature from the box, back end first, there was no mistaking the fluffy white tail of a rabbit from where Brittany stood. Her mind screamed. Her heart felt like lead in her chest. *Oh, no!*

"What?" Screeched Mr. Emongaton.

Brittany's hand shot to her face. She knew her mouth had not moved. *Has he detected us?*

"What is this?" He held the rabbit by the scruff of the neck to the window and pulled back the curtain so the moonlight flashed into the room for a moment. He threw the rabbit across the room and it bounced off an overstuffed chair and landed on the linoleum floor. It skittered through the darkness out of sight.

Mr. Emongaton pounded his fists on the table and groaned a painful sigh. "Now I have to go reset my trap. I need a better place to set this trap and I need to figure out a way to keep stupid cotton-tail bunnies out of it." He picked up his key and trap and dashed out the door.

As the door opened the frightened little bunny made a run for it, but it was closed too quickly and the rabbit sat silent on the floor next to it.

Hearing the car leave, Brittany squeezed her grandfather's arm and whispered. "Can we get out of here now?"

Potsy slid the closet door open and put it back exactly as he had found it as they exited. "Yes. Let's get out of here."

Brittany's attention was fixed on the black candle on the table. The light of the wick suddenly burst into a very bright flame lighting up the entire room. It flickered for a second and became very dull, as if it were about to go out.

"That was strange," said Brittany. "What do you suppose that flash means? Do you think someone is trying to come from the Under World"

"Maybe. Either that or someone was leaving from this world to the Under World," Potsy said. "Shamus said it was their medium for coming or going."

Potsy opened the motel room door for Brittany to pass, the cottontail rabbit dashed between her feet on its way outside and hopped away as fast as it could.

Brittany jumped into her grandfather's truck and pulled the door shut quietly. She buckled her seat belt and turned to Potsy. "I don't want to be in that predicament again. I was sure we were going to be caught by that mean old wizard."

"What makes you think that wizard is mean?" Potsy asked.

"Let's see, sworn eternal enemy of the Elfins. I saw him throw that poor little rabbit. Do you think that might give me a clue?"

"Okay," Potsy said. "I guess we can assume that he is mean."

"Speaking of that poor little rabbit," said Brittany. "Do you think Mr. Emongaton will notice he's not there when he gets back to his room?"

"I think Mr. *Not A Gnome*'s mind is definitely somewhere else. I'll tell you one thing, he sure has a temper and gets frustrated pretty easily."

Potsy drove onto the road across the pond dam and turned left, parking in front of the workshop. He was laughing as he got out of the truck. "It's good to have a little comedy relief after that frightening experience." As he came around the front of the truck, he almost ran into Brittany. She was frozen where she stood. Her right hand extended, pointing toward the grain shed.

"I think we have company on the place," Brittany whispered.

Potsy pulled her down behind the front of the truck. "Maybe he hasn't seen us."

"Maybe not, but he might have noticed that this truck wasn't here when he drove onto the place and he might have seen our headlights."

The bright summer moon had gone behind a heavy dark cloud and the entire area was totally black. Potsy and Brittany heard the engine of the car start down by the cow pens. The headlights came on and the car quietly followed the road up across the dam and off the property.

"Do you think he saw us?" Brittany asked.

Potsy looked high over head at the dark yard lamp on the pole next to the workshop. "I don't think so, but I'm sure he would have if I had got that light repaired yesterday like I planned."

As they walked onto the porch, they heard the call of a great horned owl in a neighboring tree. As the cloud hiding the moon crept by, they could make out the silhouette of the large bird.

The motion sensors on the porch detected their presence and lights came on. In the light, the eyes of the great owl reflected blue.

"That has got to be an Elfin sentry," Brittany said. She opened the screen door and stepped into the house.

"Good night." Potsy said as he waved to the sentry and ducked through the door behind his granddaughter.

Chapter 17

Acting

Brittany and Josie sat at the end of Potsy's workbench, watching as he rolled out a large surveyor's map of Whispering Oaks. Shamus, who had just arrived, sat on a tall stool looking down at the map.

"Why do you have a survey map, Potsy?" Brittany asked.

Shamus ran a finger along the boundaries of the property. "These have been the outer markers of this property for hundreds of years. The High Council will be putting a protective dome over the entire property for whatever period of time they feel is necessary to protect us from the Nenuphars. Kind of like putting a sheet over a bed. The barrier will only reach two hundred feet in the air. If a Nenuphar flies over it, they will be looking down on the camouflage blanket. They will only see the natural forests, rivers and streams that the Council wants them to see."

"It's been rather exciting around here for the past few days," said Potsy. "I wish we could figure out a way to convince Mr. Emongaton to go away."

"Yes, a lot of excitement," Shamus said. "But you don't know the half of it. I'm afraid our chance for getting rid of Emongaton disappeared with that lion."

"Would anyone care for a cup of coffee, tea or a soda?" Brittany asked as she walked to the small stove next to the refrigerator. "I have a couple pots on over here. Just say what you'd like."

Shamus raised a hand. "I'd love a cup of tea."

"A diet soda for me," said Josie.

"And I'll have a cup of coffee if you're serving," Potsy said.

"Great," Brittany said, making two trips to the table carrying drinks.

Shamus stirred his tea once, removed the tea bag and took a sip. "You don't feel that you were successful with your mission last night, but it may make you happy to know that the Banshee has been sent back into the Under World. Waycon killed her with the silver cross he wore around his neck. Unfortunately, Waycon was also killed by the panther."

"Oh no!" Brittany exclaimed, covering her face. A gusher of tears rising in her eyes.

Shamus reached out his hand and patted Brittany on the shoulder. "Don't cry child. He was killed in the Outer World, but Samuel was with him. He was barely alive when he was brought to our world. He is now alive and stronger than ever, but he can never walk in the Outer World again."

Brittany calmed herself and dried her eyes on the sleeve of her shirt. "Samuel? Was that the black squirrel we saw at Waycon's house?"

"Yes, Samuel has been his constant companion for all these years, disguised as a squirrel, Waycon has called him Chirpy."

Potsy looked hard at Shamus. "If the Banshee is sent back to the Under World, does that mean she can come back? The black candle is still burning."

"Yes, she can come back. But, not for thirty years. The black candle still burns because you could not get to it. Mr. *Not a Gnome* had placed a spell on the lantern and therefore you could not open it."

"How is it that Mr. Emongaton can come onto our property without our permission?" Brittany asked.

Whispering Oaks - The Curse

"The road and your grandfather's cabinet shop are 'public areas'," Shamus said. "He can leave his car and walk twenty feet in any direction in a 'public area', without the permission of the property owner."

"That explains how he was able to walk right into this shop without being invited," Brittany said.

"Yes," Potsy said. "And last night we saw him setting his trap down by the cow pens."

"The Council is fully aware of the trap's exact location and all Elfins have been warned to stay clear," Shamus said.

"How about if I bundle up the trap and take it back to him?" Potsy asked. "I told him he couldn't place a trap on my property."

"You can't do that, Potsy," Josie said. "If he were to find out you are on to him, he would suspect you of having ties to the Elfin world. It would put you in danger."

"I guess you're right," said Potsy. "But we need to do something."

Shamus sat quietly and then raised his tea cup. "Potsy. Have you had problem with foxes or skunks in your hen house lately?"

"I never have. Why?"

"I think you should check your fence around the chicken coop and be alert. You never can tell when a fox or a skunk might come along."

"I'll do that. My chickens are pretty important to me."

"In the meantime, with your permission, I'll take this map back to the Council so we can start setting up a perimeter to guard Whispering Oaks," said Shamus.

"Great," Potsy said, rolling up the map and handing it to Shamus.

Shamus stepped from the stool and *poof*, he was gone.

"Well," said Brittany. "Potsy, if you don't need us, Josie and I are going down to the pond. Jinx is coming over to swim with us this afternoon."

"You girls go and have a good time. I've got plenty of work to do this afternoon. I'll see you later."

143

The girls left the workshop and went into the house as Potsy took a shovel and stepped aboard his ATV. He rode down to the cow pens where he set to work, making sure all the animals had plenty of food.

After feeding the calves, he got a pail of chicken feed and entered that area of the chicken coop. The gate was open and many of the chickens were out in the field chasing grasshoppers and other bugs. As he threw out the chicken feed by the handfuls, the chickens came from the yard and the coop, scratching and picking up the food in their beaks.

After feeding, he grabbed his shovel and started walking around the outside fence inspecting it and looking for any possible holes. Soon he spotted a metal spike holding down a section of chicken wire. He kicked the spike popping it out of the earth. He dug a little trench under the fence and threw fresh dirt back onto the spot.

"At sundown, I'll be back to close your gate so you hens better be inside as usual," he said, stepping up on his four wheeler.

Brittany and Josie swam and played in the pond. They ran and jumped off the small dock, crashing into the water, trying to see who could make the largest plume of water. As they took a break, they saw Jinx and another boy walking down the pond road. They each carried a rolled up towel.

"Hey. You guys look like you're ready to swim," Brittany said.

Jinx sat down on the dock next to Brittany. He pointed his thumb over his shoulder at the boy about to sit down behind him. "This is Mr. Emongaton's nephew, Bob. He's come down from Capital City to spend a little time with his uncle, so I invited him to come with me since he doesn't know anyone around here. I hope that's okay."

Jinx pointed to each of the girls. "Bob, this is Brittany and that," he extended his first finger, "is Josie. They're Bud Ellis's grand-daughters I was telling you about."

Bob leaned forward to extend his hand to Brittany. Josie's eyes grew large as she watched. *No! No! Don't take his hand! He's looking for a mind match,* screamed Josie in her mind to Brittany. Both girls sprang backward into the pond making a large splash. They both laughed as they splashed and paddled into deeper water.

"Glad to meet you, Bob," Brittany said as she rose shoulders high out of the water and made a big splash toward the boys. "Are you guys here to swim or sit around chatting all day?"

Josie came to the surface at the far end of the pond after swimming over a hundred feet under water. A large beach ball floated near where she had surfaced. She rose up under it and flung it at Jinx who blocked it with his forearm.

Jinx immediately pulled off his shirt and trousers, exposing his swim trunks and jumped into the pond making a splash. "Yeah!" he screamed. "This water is perfect. Come on Bob, jump in."

The young man about the same size as Jinx, looked a little frail as he sat on the pier, his towel under him. "I'm sorry. I'm not feeling so good all of a sudden. If you don't mind, I'll sit this one out."

Jinx swam back to the pier. "Are you sure you don't want to join us? Are you going to be all right? Do you need an antacid or an aspirin or somethin'?"

Bob scooted back from the edge of the pier, away from the water. "Oh no. I'll be fine in no time. I'm sure of it."

"You just sit and relax," Jinx said as he climbed up on the pier then sprang into the water.

Josie swam to the pier and spoke to Bob. "Come on, fella, jump in here and get wet."

"I'm not feeling like swimming right now. Maybe later," said Bob, pushing his powder blue sunglasses up on his nose.

"Okay, just don't say you weren't invited," she said, flailing the water as she swam away. Water splashed up on the pier and Bob withdrew a little more.

Potsy rolled up on his four wheeler as Josie jumped into the

145

pond. "Would you kids like to go to Torgilson's for a burger?"

The three swimmers hurried to the pier and started drying off in response to the invitation.

"I'm so hungry, I could eat a horse," Brittany said as she slipped on her jeans over her swimsuit and finished dressing.

"And I'll help you eat it," Josie said. She laughed as she dried her hair.

"If it's all the same to you," Jinx said. A smile crossing his face. "I'll have beef."

Potsy ushered his charges to the soda fountain and sat down next to Bob. Jinx's sister, Marie, was working behind the counter and came up to serve them. "What can I get you?"

Potsy leaned forward. "As for me and the girls, we'll have burger deluxes and diet sodas." He turned to Bob. "What will you have? And how about you, Jinx?"

"I'll have whatever you're having," Bob said.

"I'll have a burger D," said Jinx. "But, instead of french fries, I'd like onion rings."

Marie wrote the orders on her pad and looked up at her brother. "You always have to be different, don't you?" She spun on her heel and went to the grill.

As his sister turned away, Jinx scrunched up his nose, arched his neck and stuck his tongue out at her back.

"Now, is that nice?" Brittany asked.

"If only you knew. That girl has been picking on me since I was born. She started out stealing my baby bottles and she still isn't happy letting me live my own life. I love her, but she sure makes things hard sometimes."

As the group was finishing their meals, Marie came back down the counter and stood in front of Bob. "So, did you enjoy your swim?"

Whispering Oaks - The Curse

"Fun was had by all," Bob said.

Potsy took a last sip from his straw, set the glass on the counter and put a twenty dollar bill on the bar to cover the check. "Girls, it's time we were leaving. I have to get back before sundown and close up the chicken coop. We don't want to be having varmints in our coop again."

The sun was sinking low in the west as Bob entered the motel room. The Nenuphar Wizard sat in a large chair next to the window reading from a book, a very thick book with a leather binding.

"Sia Robearus, soldier of the realm, where have you been?" Mr. Emongaton asked.

"Please call me Bob. I'm here posing as your nephew. I don't want to be discovered anymore than you do."

"Why did his Great Majesty send such an insolent soldier?" The wizard demanded.

"If you had done your job, I wouldn't have been sent," the young man said, a sneer crossing his face. "Your failures got the Banshee sent back. You said I could befriend this Jinx person and I would learn the secrets of Whispering Oaks."

Mr. Emongaton sat up. "I said you *may* be able to discover secrets. I did not say you *would* discover secrets."

Robearus dropped into a chair next to the table. "I made a mind match with that young man and I got nothing. His mind is a jumble of lost thoughts. The only useful thing I was able to find is that he has a passion for that golden haired granddaughter of Bud Ellis. He daydreams too much. It was difficult to separate fact from fiction."

"What happened when you made mind matches with the rest?"

"Nothing. I didn't get the chance. They do not honor formal introductions. They greeted me from far away, with smiles and waves. They were in a pond at Whispering Oaks."

147

Mr. Emongaton straightened up sharply. "How did you avoid the water?"

"I simply feigned illness for a moment and they accepted it. They are as gullible as you said they would be." Robearus sat at the table and fingered the edge of the lantern holding the black candle. "Uncle. Yes, Uncle, that's what I shall call you, Nenuphar Master. Why don't we just call in an army and destroy this entire population of humans? They mean nothing to us."

"You need to pay attention, my young friend. Did you not just remind me that the Banshee has been destroyed by this very population that you want to attack?"

"But," Robearus raised a finger for emphasis, "we could easily destroy the entire population and make it look as if some natural disaster had struck this entire area. Once their human protectors are gone, we can find the Elfin population and take them back with us. To hear you tell it, there is enough magic here to supply us for a hundred years."

The Nenuphar wizard pointed to one of the two beds in the room. "Lie down and rest. I will call you when it's time to go out. We must be patient."

Potsy went to sleep with his bedroom window open. His twelve gauge pump shotgun rested in the corner by the door. He had told Shamus that he would be ready for any sort of ruckus in his hen house.

A clatter, with screeching and clucking from the hen house drew him from his slumber. Jumping from his bed, he grabbed his shotgun and headed out the door. Leaping onto the ATV parked next to the porch, he rode toward the hen house. Monya and the girls were in the van and traveling, just moments behind.

Potsy raced down the hill to the cow pens and found Mr. Emongaton's car parked in the middle of the road near the chicken coop. Potsy ignored the car, drove around it, jumped from the four wheeler and opened the chicken coop door. The flashlight taped to the barrel of the shotgun came on and 'BOOM', the shotgun went off.

"Take that you dirty fox!" Potsy screamed.

Frightened chickens fluttered around the coop making all sorts of noise.

Potsy exited the chicken coop closing the door behind him. As he came out of the small building, there in front of his car stood Mr. Emongaton and his nephew. Both men's eyes were wide with a look of total surprise. Mr. Emongaton had the box trap under his arm.

Monya stopped the van. The girls, in their night shirts, hopped out through the sliding door. "Did you get that skunk, dear?" she asked as she closed the driver's door.

"No. It was a fox and he was too quick for me." Potsy's eyes fell on Mr. Emongaton. "What are you doing on my property?" he growled.

"I . . . I was. . ." Mr. Emongaton stammered.

"I told you. You can't place a trap on my property. I think you would have set that trap and not said a thing if that pesky fox hadn't come along and ruined your plan," said Potsy. "Monya. Move the van. Mr. Emongaton is leaving."

Mr. Emongaton and his nephew drove out of sight.

There was a *POOF* and Shamus stood next to Potsy. "Now, that was the best job of acting I've seen in years."

Chapter 18

Taya

As Brittany and Josie finished breakfast with Monya, the telephone rang. Monya rose and answered. "Ellis residence. Yes, honey. She sure is, would you like to speak to her?" She carried the cordless phone to the table and handed it to Brittany. "It's your mother, darlin'."

"Hi, mom," Brittany said. A big smile on her face. "Oh, you bet. It's about a hundred times more exciting here than I expected it to be." She tossed her head from side to side, a grin from ear to ear. "No. You can tell my friends I'll get on the internet and update them as soon as I get time. Tell them this is a working farm. There's stock to feed, grass to mow and lots to do." Her grin dropped from her face. "Well, I'm learning to work and to enjoy it. Monya and Potsy are great teachers and I'm making some fantastic friends here." She lifted her juice glass as if to salute Josie. "There's a girl named Josie who is more fun than a magic show." She set her juice glass down and changed hands with the phone. "Yes, mother. I am safe. I am careful. Nothing dangerous." She hesitated for a moment. "I love you too, Mom. Did you want to talk to Monya?" She handed the phone over to her grandmother. "Monya, Josie and I are going out to the workshop now, okay?"

Monya smiled, nodded her head and started conversing with her daughter.

Brittany and Josie spun and turned, giggled and jostled each other as they went out the kitchen door. They stopped on the west veranda of the house, leaned against the rail and looked out toward the workshop and the pond. Brittany hopped down the three stairs to the cobblestone path and motioned for Josie to follow her.

"Let's get to it. It's my turn to mow. You can take the four wheeler and go down to the cow pens and make sure the animals have all been fed," Brittany said.

"Sounds like a deal to me," Josie said.

As the girls walked into the shop, they saw Potsy working at a bench in the far corner. The girls went over to see what was going on.

"What kind of project is this?" Brittany asked.

"I'm reloading shotgun shells. You've seen me do this before."

Brittany looked closer at the box of BBs Potsy was loading into the shells. "Hey, these aren't lead shot like my dad uses." She held a handful of the BBs over the box and let them pour out between her fingers. "This shot looks like gold with brown spots and it feels heavier than lead."

"Exactly right," said Potsy. "This shot was created special, in the Elfin workshops. They are tiny balls of black walnut wood covered in gold. Shamus tells me we can use them against any dark thing that comes from the Under World, except the Banshee."

Josie placed a hand on top of the boxes of empty shell casings. "You sure have a lot."

He smiled. "There are only five cases here. I'm just setting them up like Shamus suggested. He thought I might do better with a shotgun than with a bow and arrow. These have only half the powder and about a third of the shot load of regular shells."

Brittany smiled as she crossed the large shop floor to the riding mower. "Good luck with that. Come on Josie, lets hit the trail." She cranked the tiny tractor over as Josie raised the roll-up door.

"I'll be right behind you," said Josie.

Whispering Oaks - The Curse

The Nenuphar Wizard sat in his motel room at the table across from the soldier. "I think it's time for us to find new headquarters. Some place where we can come and go without being noticed," Mr. Emongaton said.

"Didn't you tell me that the old Indian had been killed by the Banshee before she was sent back to the Under World?" Robearus asked.

Mr. Emongaton jumped to his feet. "Yes, Bob. And that is where we shall go. We will move to his house. We can come and go from there without being seen."

Potsy eased his truck up to the stop sign on the street across from the Riverfront Motel. The motel was old, but it was in the process of being renovated. A year before the O'Hern family had moved down from Capital City and taken over the property after the death of Mr. O'Hern senior. It looked as though the remodel was almost done. There was new stucco, windows, paint and a new asphalt parking lot with bright yellow stripes in front of every room. Everything was refurbished except a couple of rooms and the sign which was small and leaned almost sideways over the street. He could see the entire motel parking lot from where he was. He looked close at the parking stalls in front of each room.

"What?" he said aloud. Looking hard at the parking stall in front of room six. There was a white car with an out of state plate parked there. *That's not Mr. Emongaton's car. Where can he be?*

He pulled across the street and stopped in front of the motel office. Leaving his truck he opened the new glass office door and went inside. A small bald man with a pipe in his mouth sat at a desk behind the counter. The man rose as Potsy entered. "Howdy, Bud. What can I do for you?" It was Mr. O'Hern himself. He had inherited the motel from his father who received it from his father.

"You sure have done a lot with the old place," said Potsy as he looked around at the new furnishings and paintings on the wall.

"I really didn't have to do much. Pop kept it in pretty good shape for all the fishermen that come down here. I've got a new sign on order. It's supposed to be up before Western Days."

Potsy leaned against the hardwood counter. "I was looking for Mr. Emongaton. I think he's in room six, is that right?"

The small man fingered a large card file lying under the counter. "Oh, yes. The man from State University. That man is a strange individual if you ask me.

"He checked out yesterday. Said something about having new accommodations. It seems someone died and left him a nice place."

Potsy placed a hand on the counter. "Oh, so he left and he's not coming back. Is that right?"

"He seemed pretty happy to be leaving. He was always complaining about the sound the construction workers were making. You know, he wouldn't even let maid service into his room. The room he was in, room six, was the last room to get remodeled.

"He said there was enough room at his new digs for both himself, his nephew and maybe a few more guests. He didn't indicate that he'd be coming back."

Mr. O'Hern picked up a pad and pencil. "If you'd like, Bud, I'll make a note and tell him you were looking for him if he does come back."

"Oh, no, that's all right. I'll run across him sooner or later and it's not really important. This visit was more social than business. Thanks anyway." He turned, pushed the door open and left the office.

As Potsy got into his truck he wondered. *Now, where has that scoundrel gone off to?*

154

Whispering Oaks - The Curse

Brittany and Josie were down at the chicken coop gathering eggs when they heard the sound of a vehicle on the gravel road crossing the pond dam. Brittany bounced outside and looked. "Oh my gosh!" she shrieked. "It's my parents' Suburban®!" Josie rushed to her side and watched as the large red vehicle came to a stop in front of the house.

Brittany grabbed Josie's hands and danced around in a circle. She spoke as if she were not sure whether to be happy or sad. "It's my folks. This is NOT cool." She abruptly stopped being jovial. "We can't have all these people coming in here. What about the safety of the Elfins? Everyone will be asking question. They're going to rain on my perfect summer."

As the girls watched, all four doors of the truck opened and out stepped Jon, Brittany's father, Chris, her mother, Little Jake, her brother and at the other door. . . Brittany's head shot forward and her eyes focused again. The red headed girl stepping from the vehicle was her favorite cousin, Taya.

"Oh my gosh!" Brittany exclaimed. "That's my cousin Taya."

Brittany turned to Josie. "You finish up here and I'll go up to the house and find out what's happening." Brittany picked up the egg basket. "I'll take the eggs to the house and be surprised. I'll be back shortly."

Taya saw Brittany coming up the road from the chicken coop and ran to her. She gave her a big hug, picking her off the ground and spinning around with her. "I'm so glad to see you, cuzzy!" Taya exclaimed.

"Yes, this is great," Brittany said as Taya eased her back onto her feet.

The two girls walked up the path toward the house. Monya was now out on the porch greeting everyone with hugs and kisses.

As the girls reached the house, Brittany ran inside with the egg basket and set it on the kitchen counter. Monya was right behind her.

As Chris, Jon and Taya entered the kitchen, Chris was speaking. "I'm sorry for the lack of notice. I was going to tell you we were nearly here this morning when we called from the road. I didn't want to ruin the surprise for Brittany. We can't stay long. Jon has business in Kansas City. Taya's schedule changed. She didn't have to work as a counselor at summer camp, so her parents said she could come with us. We thought we'd drop her off and she can spend some time with Brittany."

"That's great. She can stay as long as she likes," said Monya. "Taya is certainly welcome for the summer."

"Jon, Little Jake and I will only be here for tonight and we'll be on our way after breakfast," Chris said.

Brittany ran to her mother, embraced and kissed her. "Mom, this is a wonderful surprise."

Monya pointed down the hall. "The large guest room is right down the hall to the left. You'll find a private bath there, too. Little Jake, you'll be in the room across from your folks."

Brittany kissed her grandmother on the cheek. She picked up another empty basket in the kitchen and took Taya's arm. "Come on cousin. I'm going to show you how to gather eggs."

The girls went out the door laughing. Monya filled a pot and began to boil water for sweet tea.

As the girls approached the chicken coop, Taya pushed the door back and entered. Brittany could see a look of surprise on her face in the dim light as the door closed behind her.

"Taya, you remember our cousin, Josie don't you?" Brittany said. "She's been at school in England and is here to spend the summer with Potsy and Monya. I think it will be great fun to have two cousins here."

Josie placed her hand to her face and giggled. "It's great to see you."

Taya reached her hand out and Josie took it. "Howdy Josie," she said, laughter in her voice. "You probably remember me. I'm glad to be he . . . . " She never finished her statement. She had a blank stare in her eyes as Josie smiled and clasped her hand between both of hers.

Josie looked at Brittany, nodded and smiled.

"Let's finish and go to the house," said Brittany. She picked up the basket of eggs and nodded toward the door. "Josie, looks like you found a few more. Let's go feed the calves."

Josie picked up the pitchfork, broke the twine on a bale of hay and pitched two chunks over the fence into the calf pens. "That's done. Shall we go in?"

"Yes," Brittany said. "Monya is making sweet tea. That will be good."

As they walked up the road from the chicken coop, Brittany spun and started walking backward in front of her cousins. She pointed at Taya, "It sure is great to have you here."

Chapter 19

Visitors

The family sat around the kitchen table, each with a tall glass of sweet iced tea before them.

"I hope you enjoy the tea. I make it with sugar substitute. Potsy has to watch his blood sugar, you know," said Monya.

The front door opened and Potsy's voice could be heard coming toward the kitchen. "Hello, everyone. I'm home." He smiled as he entered the kitchen. "Chris, Jon, this is a surprise. What are you doing here?"

Chris jumped to her feet and ran into her father's arms. "Daddy, it's so great to see you. Jon has business in Kansas City and we thought we'd drop off Taya for the summer. We thought we'd save her parents the price of a plane ticket."

Jon extended his right hand in greeting to his father-in-law.

Potsy kissed his daughter on the cheek, shook Jon's hand and slid silently into his chair at the head of the table. Taya jumped from her chair and raced around the table, giving her grandfather a hug and kissing his cheek. "Aren't you glad to see me, too?"

Potsy hugged Taya, "Yes. I'm delighted to see you." He glanced at the rest of the people at the table. Leaning on his elbow he spoke to his son-in-law. "Good to see you, Jon. Little Jake, how is my favorite grandson? Brittany, how was your day? And," he squinted, "Josie, how is your day going?"

It wasn't long before the surprised mood of Potsy's arrival passed and normal conversation returned to the table.

Potsy looked at his daughter and then across at Jon. "I'm sorry I seem confused, but we've had some trying times around here lately, and I don't know if I should leave you in the dark or tell you the whole story. After all, you are our family and we don't want you upset with us."

He took a long drink from his glass and turned to Brittany. "We need to step into Monya's office and call Shamus."

Brittany smiled. "I'm with you, Potsy."

Both Potsy and Brittany pushed their chairs back and began to stand. "I'm afraid we're at a critical juncture here," Potsy said.

Brittany placed her hands flat on the table. "Potsy, do you want to call him with the family. . ." She never got a chance to finish her question. There was a *poof* and Shamus stood beside Potsy.

"No need to call me," Shamus said. "I've been watching since the sentries alerted me that your family arrived."

"I'm sorry, Shamus," Potsy said, "but we don't know how to handle this problem, other than with the truth. These are our children and grandchildren and we cannot lie to them."

"It is all right. I have spoken to the High Council and they are aware of the situation and have approved their knowledge of our existence."

Chris, Jon, Little Jake and Taya sat with eyes wide and their mouths open.

"Mom, Dad, this is Shamus," Brittany explained. "He's Chief Guardian of the Elfin city. Elfins live in the Inner World and we live in the Outer World. Nenuphars are from the dark side and they live in the Under World." She pointed to Josie. "This girl is not our cousin from England. She is an Elfin Wish Fairy and she's been my companion and very good friend since I got here."

Whispering Oaks - The Curse

All of the visitors stared at Brittany. She could see the puzzlement in their faces. "Whispering Oaks," she continued, "and all of its inhabitants are currently in a battle with the Nenuphar - the creatures of the Under World. We are on the side of the Elfins."

Little Jake, Brittany's younger brother, was now getting his excitement under control. "Cool!"

Chris took Jon's left arm between her hands. "Are these Nenuphars dangerous? I don't want our daughter mixed up in anything dangerous."

Jon, ever the businessman, looked across the table at his daughter. "And, exactly why is it we need to know about this war? We're leaving in the morning, and if there's some kind of confrontation going on, you're leaving with us."

Brittany looked at her father, tears welling up in her eyes. "I'm sorry, Dad. I started this war and I have to see it through."

Shamus leaned forward and scratched at the tip of his left ear. "Potsy, we need to give a full explanation."

Potsy started the story with Brittany's arrival and tried not to leave out any important parts. There were some items omitted, but Shamus quickly filled in the blanks.

Shamus looked at the people around the table. "There's something you should be aware of. The Nenuphars can assume the shape of any living creature. They prefer the dark creatures, but if they assume the shape of a human, you can tell by the shape of their chin. It's longer and more narrow than what you are used to and their skin is pink. Their eyes are gray, almost a shiny gray and most of the time, they wear powder blue colored sunglasses. With those glasses they can see an Elfin that has become invisible to the human eye. Some times they assume the identity of what you would call *fat* people to avoid being recognized by their sharp chins and long noses. About their pink skin. Many of the ones who are experienced in the Outer World will wear makeup, but there is no mistaking their eyes." Shamus stepped back. "There is one more thing we need to do before we go any further. I've explained to all of you about the blue springs of the Inner World and you have given permission to be duplicated. Would you all please come with me."

Everyone followed Shamus around the end of the table and up the hall. As they reached the front door, it opened, and eight substitute figures walked in past the family.

Little Jake's eyes popped open wide as a boy his age, wearing his face and the same clothes filed past him. "Mom! Did you see that?" He grabbed his mother's arm. "That boy is me!"

"Hold hands," said Shamus and tapped his cane on the floor twice. There was a soft *poof* and the family was standing in the great hall of the Inner World.

Brittany looked at her Potsy as he ran his fingers through his hair; it was thick and full. His paunch was gone. He was now about the same age as her Dad and Mom. She looked at Monya, who was now a slender young woman with rich auburn hair.

Monya couldn't resist an urge, she jumped into Potsy's arms and kissed him. "Jacob Bud Ellis, I love you," she said as he held her tight and lifted her from the floor.

Brittany took her mother's hand and tilted her head toward her grand parents. "They always do that."

"Follow me, please," Shamus said. He led the group to the dressing room doors beside the blue water pool. "Potsy, you and Monya, Brittany and Josie don't need to bathe, but you can accompany the others and explain what is happening." He pointed the males through one door and the females through another. "I'll be here when you come out. Be sure to dive under the water and get wet all over."

In a few minutes the group emerged from their respective dressing rooms. Jon seemed energized by the dip in the pool and walked around looking up like a youngster in a museum. Brittany watched her father as he looked around at the high cathedral ceilings.

Brittany took hold of the sleeve of Shamus's jacket as he watched Jon. "He's just a little curious."

"Would you like to see more of the city?" Shamus asked Jon. "Come with me." He led the family down the hall through a large wooden door, out onto a great balcony.

Gasps escaped from every mouth as they took in the view.

Brittany leaned against the handrail. "It's as if we're looking at a great city at night from the top of a mountain."

"Good eye," Shamus said. "That is exactly what you are looking at. The great city extends for what you would call thirty-four miles. And it is night here. Our sun and moon cycles are the exact opposite of yours."

"How can that be?" Jon asked.

Shamus looked at the young man and smiled. "What would you expect in a magic land that existed in a different dimension?"

"Holy cow!" Little Jake said, pressing close to his mother's side. "That's a big town."

"Yes, it is," Shamus said. "It is about the size of one of your metropolitan areas."

"A thriving city beneath an oak tree," said Potsy.

"How can that be?" asked Jon. "I mean, I thought there was just dirt under those oak trees."

Shamus placed his hand on his chin. "You are very astute. We are not underground in the sense of the words as you mean them. We are actually in a different dimension. The oak trees are simply our 'touch stone' if you will, our portal in and out of the two dimensions. Moving between dimensions is to us like ocean travel is to you. We need a port to leave from and arrive at."

With the bunk beds in Brittany's room there was plenty of room for the girls and they settled down for their first night together.

"Taya, it's great to have you with us," said Josie, extending her hand for a mind-match. "Let me fill you in on what we've been up to this summer." In a few seconds Taya had been brought up to speed on the adventures of her cousins from their point of view.

For the next hour, as the girls lay in the dark, Brittany and Josie discussed their experiences of the previous weeks with Taya.

Brittany said, "There's a boy at Torgilson's store. . ."

"I know," Taya interrupted, "he's kinda your honey. That is, if Josie's mind match is accurate."

"I think it's time we all went to sleep," said Brittany, reaching her night stand and flipping off the light. She rolled over in bed and covered up her head.

The family was enjoying a hearty breakfast of bacon, eggs, hash browned potatoes and pancakes. Potsy passed the strawberry jam to Jon. "The one important thing you need to remember. If you have occasion to shake hands with a Nenuphar or allow him to touch your bare skin, he can make a mind match with you."

"Don't forget," said Brittany, "They can also make a mind match by touching something you're holding."

"I thought our swim in the blue pool was supposed to protect us from any mind probe," Jon blurted.

Brittany sat back in her chair and spoke softly. "Dad, the effects of the blue water wears off. What Potsy is trying to tell you is, *IF* a very powerful Nenuphar lays a hand on you, you must be ready. You must immediately start thinking of the Great Wall of China. In your mind, put him on one side and you stay on the other. He will have to remove every stone to get to your thoughts."

After breakfast Jon, Chris and Little Jake loaded luggage into their vehicle and crossed over the pond dam road into the village on their way to Kansas City.

Jon eased his heavy vehicle around the long slow turns of the narrow two lane blacktop road that led out of the village to the freeway. He could feel the quiet surge of the engine, like the horses under the hood could not wait to get out on the four-lane so they could run flat out.

He followed a sharp curve in the road and as he topped a slight rise his eyes gathered a tragic sight. There before him was a three car pile up. Two cars had hit head-on. The third had plowed under the car coming from the freeway. There were two bodies lying on the grass near the pavement. An ambulance and a tow truck were on the scene. Medical personnel were tending to the injured men on the road. A deputy sheriff held up his left hand indicating that Jon should stop.

What kind of accident is this? Jon thought. *A three car crash. Squad cars, an ambulance, a wrecker, liquid spilling across the road, engines steaming, bodies here and there... and we're the first car in line to wait for the cleanup? Look at their sunglasses. I'm used to dark black or mirror reflective lenses, but powder blue? And all three cops are wearing them.*

A short, but very rotund deputy walked to the side of Jon's truck. "It'll only be a few minutes and you folks will be on your way," he said through the whiskers of a heavy mustache.

Jon rolled his window down just an inch or two.

"You folks visiting hereabouts?"

"Yes," Jon replied.

The fat man with a name badge that read, 'ROBEARUS', stepped close to Jon's car. "Who you folk visiting?"

"We've been by to see the Jacob Ellis family."

"Bud Ellis? Are you kin to Bud?"

"We are. I'm his son-in-law and this is his daughter, Chris."

"By golly." The fat man shook all over as he laughed. "Any kin of Bud Ellis is a friend of mine. I'd like to shake your hand."

Jon reached for the button to lower his window, but felt one of Chris' long fingernails bite into his other hand. "Uh," he said, jerking upright in his seat. "I'm sorry, I'd shake your hand, but my window is on the fritz. It'll only roll down so far."

Jon pointed to the road ahead. "Looks like the road is clear. Do

165

you mind if we go?"

The deputy frowned, looked around as the wrecker pulled the last car off the roadway. "Drive safely," he said as he motioned for the Standish vehicle to move out.

Jon stepped on the gas, made the slow turn onto the freeway ramp and entered the main roadway. As his truck idled up to freeway speed he turned to Chris. "Get Potsy on the cell phone and tell him about this guy. He might be a Nenuphar."

Chris reached the phone in her purse and pressed the speed dial. "Mom, is Dad there?"

Jon waved his hand. "If he's not there, give the information to Monya."

He looked in his rear view mirror as he continued. "I can't believe it. We sat at that accident site for five minutes and not a single car pulled up behind us. If that's an area with so little traffic that we didn't see any, why do they need three sheriff's patrol cruisers?"

Chapter 20

New Help

Potsy looked at the note Monya had left on the kitchen table. *Chris called. Said she thinks they ran into Nenuphars as they were about to go onto the freeway north of town. She said there was a three car pile up. The deputy sheriff that stopped them was fat with the name 'Robearus' on his name tag. Three deputies were there, all were wearing powder blue sunglasses. One deputy wanted to shake hands with Jon, but he didn't roll his window down.*

The girls and I have gone over to Parson Kelly's house to the meeting for planning the county's fair and Western Days next week. Love, Monya.

Potsy picked up the phone and began to dial.

"Sheriff's Office. This is Brandi, may I help you?"

"Brandi, Bud Ellis. Is Sheriff Fitzpatrick available?"

"I'm sorry, Bud. The Sheriff is over at Parson Kelly's house for the Western Days meeting. Is it an emergency?"

"No. No, I just had a quick question for him. Come to think of it, you could probably answer my question."

"I'd be happy to if I can. I answer most of the common questions folks have."

"Okay, good. Do you know anything about a three car pile up

167

near the freeway on-ramp north of town this morning?"

"Oh my gosh!" Brandi exclaimed. "Is it real bad? I'll get a hold of the Sheriff and get him right over there."

"Wait! Wait! Wait! There is no accident."

"You know, you can get in trouble for calling in false information don't you, Bud?"

"Yes. And I wouldn't want that to happen."

"This call hasn't made much sense. What is it you want, anyway?"

"Has there been any accidents reported today?"

"Ha! That's a laugh. The last accident we had was two weeks ago when old Grandma Murphy's car jumped the curb in front of the beauty parlor and she tore a fender off on the fire hydrant."

"That's all I wanted to know."

"Well, Mr. Ellis, is there anything else I can do for you?"

"As a matter of fact, when Sheriff Fitzpatrick calls in from the meeting at Parson Kelly's, would you have him drop past my place?"

"I'll get him on the radio and ask him."

"Thanks. It is important. Good-bye."

Jeff Fitzpatrick had been Sheriff of the county for nine years. Before that he had been Chief of Detectives for the police force in Kansas City. He had been involved in a shoot-out that ended his career in the city. The criminal's bullet struck his left knee, it was several months before he could walk and resulted in a distinct limp. The old injury was a constant source of pain and on a bad day his limp was very pronounced. He had come to town at the invitation of his cousin, Arthur Torgilson, taking his department's medical retirement. He was sure he was out of law enforcement for good.

In a very short time he had won the friendship and trust of

the entire county. He was a big man, at over six feet four inches tall, with thinning brown hair that had started to turn gray at the temple. He had a smile for everyone he met.

He was likeable, knowledgeable and most important, he was honest. Several folks had the opinion that if his name had been Smith, Brown or Jones, he would not have stood a chance of being elected sheriff.

Based in a town with a population of eight hundred people in a county just over twice that, he was involved in all facets of county government and civic activities. He knew most of the residents by name. He always said, "Policing is easier if you know all the suspects before something happens."

That is what he was doing at the Kelly residence today. He wanted to make sure there was adequate parking. He wanted to know which carnival company was being selected for this year's fair. Some carnivals had bad reputations for hiring just anybody and when they came to town, the crime rate went up. It seemed that everything that wasn't nailed down was stolen.

"Lots-A-Fun Carnivals has been selected for this year's fair," Parson Kelly said. "They were here last year and everyone enjoyed themselves. We'll set them up right here." He pointed to an area of the map on the large table. "That's where we had them last year. There's parking to the front and show barns to the back of them. Do you see any problems with that Sheriff?"

"That'll be great," Sheriff Fitzpatrick said. "I'll tell Chief O'Neil and between himself, his two patrolmen, and me and my two deputies, we should be fine. I'll get with the Chief when he gets back from Capital City and we can set up the handicap parking and special permit areas."

Sheriff Fitzpatrick shook Parson Kelly's hand. "I've got to be leaving now. If there's anything you need, please call the office."

"Thanks for coming," Parson Kelly said. He opened the door and the Sheriff walked down the steps.

When he reached his car, he flipped on his two-way radio and called his office. "Brandi, you got anything going on?"

"Yes, Sheriff. Do you have time to go over to Jacob Ellis's house and see him?"

"I do. Did he say what it was about?"

"He called and said something about an accident out by the freeway, but he didn't make a lot of sense to me."

"No problem, I'll go by and see him. Car one out."

When he got through reloading shells, Potsy had several pounds of BBs left. He put them into six small zip-type plastic bags and set them aside. He stacked the five cases of 12 gauge shotgun shells on a shelf near his reloading machine. Hearing a vehicle roll up on the gravel outside his shop, he opened the door.

The Sheriff got out and closed the door of his cruiser. "Hello, Bud. How's it going?"

"Things are fine right now," answered Potsy. "Would you care for a cup of coffee, a soft drink, or a cup of tea?"

"I can't turn down a cup of your coffee." Sheriff Fitzpatrick entered the shop, hung his hat on a familiar rack next to the door and sat on a tall stool.

Potsy poured two cups of coffee, set one in front of the sheriff and sat down across from him.

"What can I do for you, Bud?" Sheriff Fitzpatrick asked after taking a sip of his coffee.

Potsy placed the note Monya had left him in front of the sheriff. "I thought you should have a look at this. Do you know of any accidents today?"

Sheriff Fitzpatrick had a frown and a scrunched up face as a look of confusion came over him. He tipped his head slightly, his eyes nearly closed as he turned to look at Potsy. "This is a joke, right? What's this, *ran into Nenuphars,* did they hit somebody?"

"No, I'm sorry to say. It's not a joke. Nenuphars are a very bad bunch. And, no, they didn't hit anyone."

"And what is this Deputy Robearson, a fat man? You've seen my deputies. Flannery and Kavenaugh are definitely not fat. And three squad cars, I only have two besides mine."

The sheriff took a last drink of his coffee, stood and pulled his hat from the rack. "Would you like to take a ride with me? I've got to see the scene of this accident."

"I thought you'd never ask."

As they walked toward the door the sheriff spoke over his shoulder. "I reviewed the accident reports for the entire state this morning and none had more than two cars involved."

The two men took opposite sides of the road and walked up and down for several hundred feet. Soon Sheriff Fitzpatrick came over to where Potsy stood.

"Guess what, Bud?"

"There are no signs of vehicles being crashed, on or off this roadway?" Potsy said.

"That's it. Is your son-in-law subject to hallucinations?"

"Even if he were, there were three people in that car and they all saw the same thing."

Sheriff Fitzpatrick opened the door of his police cruiser. "Come on, Bud. I'll drop you off at your place."

As the car rolled up to the front of the workshop, Potsy turned to the sheriff. "Jeff, have you got time to come in for a minute? There's a couple of things I need to tell you."

Sheriff Fitzpatrick put his car into park and turned to Potsy. "I can't right now, I have to go back to the office and sign a few reports, but I can come back in a couple of hours." The Sheriff looked at his wrist watch. "How about two this afternoon?"

"That'll be fine," Potsy said as he left the car. "See you then." He closed the door and went into the shop as the cruiser pulled away.

Potsy sat down at his workbench. "Shamus Mactavish O'Riley please step forward."

Poof. There stood Shamus. "Yes, my friend. What can I do for you?"

"I'm worried," Potsy said. "There's going to be a fair in town in a few days and I can't think of a way to make sure the Nenuphars don't get into the village and maybe onto the property."

"At the moment, our perimeters are strong and the Nenuphars will have to work hard to get a foothold on Whispering Oaks."

"They might try something though. We need to alert our sheriff of the dangers, just in case they plan to infiltrate the population." Potsy handed Shamus the note that Monya had written.

"Yes. This is the work of the Nenuphars. You might be right. Perhaps we should move to the offensive. For the moment, the Nenuphar Wizard has nothing but suspicions. He needs a mind meld with a human that knows of us."

Potsy rubbed his forehead. "I've asked the sheriff to come back here in a couple of hours. He's a suspicious man and it may be hard to convince him to help us or even be extra alert if we can't explain our situation to him."

Shamus looked around the workshop. "I need to discuss this with the Council, but when I come back, we'll have a plan. Mr. *Not a Gnome* has come to town pretending to research the paranormal. Perhaps we can make that work against him. I think we shall have to involve your sheriff in our plans." *Poof*, he was gone.

It was just over two hours later that Potsy heard the crunch of gravel under tires, an approaching vehicle outside of his shop. He was about to walk to the door when it swung open.

"Potsy, are you in here?" Brittany asked as three teenage girls poured into the shop.

"I am. Come on in and join me," Potsy said. "Would you girls care for a cold drink? It is kinda warm out there."

"Yes," came the answer in unison.

"Potsy, these Western Days are going to be a blast," Brittany said. She moved to the small refrigerator and opened it. Retrieving three diet sodas she returned to her stool at the bench.

She pushed drinks toward the other girls and turned to face Potsy. "So, what's happening, Potsy?"

Potsy slid the note Monya had written toward the girls. "Are you aware of this?"

"Oh, ya," Taya said. "Monya told us all about it."

"Guess what, Potsy?" Brittany said. "Taya, Josie and I have volunteered to run a booth at the fair. It's for the children's hospital in Capital City. It's a dart booth. If a person buys four darts for a dollar, they get a different level of prize for every balloon they break. If they break four balloons, they get a teddy bear."

"That's great. I'm glad to hear you girls are going to volunteer," said Potsy. "The most important thing is that you stay together. Never be separated. If you want to go on a ride and you all three won't fit, go on it one at a time and the other two stay together and watch the rider, understand?"

A knock came on the door. Potsy placed a finger to his lips signalling quiet. Brittany stepped to the door and opened it. A large man in a dark blue suit filled the doorway. He wore dark sunglasses and carried a cane. "I'm Detective Shamus Mactavish, are you going to invite me in?"

Potsy could not see the man from where he stood, but he did recognize the voice. "Shamus, by all means, come in."

Brittany stepped back to let the big man by. "Shamus. Is that you?" she whispered as he passed.

"Yes. It's me. You were expecting Davy Crockett, maybe?" he quipped. Shamus sat down at the bench with his friends. "How long before the Sheriff gets here?"

"It shouldn't be too long," Potsy said. "He should be along within the next five minutes."

"Great. Brittany if you'd be so kind as to pour me a cup of coffee, I'll lay out my plan so that we can be ready when the Sheriff gets here. The Council has authorized his knowledge."

Chapter 21

The Sheriff

There was an impatient knock on the workshop door. Potsy opened it to find Sheriff Fitzpatrick standing outside. As the sheriff entered, he stopped, stuck his head back out and looked around. The black squirrel in the great oak tree chattered a greeting. Potsy waved as if to salute the squirrel.

The sheriff found a stool next to Shamus. He sat to one side of the seat, his crippled leg remaining straight, his left foot on the floor. It appeared that this was a bad day for his leg.

"Okay, Bud, I'm here. What was it you had to tell me?" Sheriff Fitzpatrick looked around at the girls and finally at the dapper looking fellow sitting next to him, wearing a black bowler hat. "If this is an inconvenient time, I can come back."

"No. No," said Potsy. "I want you to meet these people. These are my granddaughters, Brittany and Taya and this is my grand-niece, Josie. They are here to spend the summer with me." He now pointed to the man in the three piece suit. "This is Shamus Mactavish of the National Defense Service.Everybody, this is Sheriff Jeff Fitzpatrick," he said, gesturing toward the new arrival.

Shamus pulled a black folder about the size of a man's wallet from his inside coat pocket and flipped it open to display a badge made of gold and silver.

"Shamus, that's an interesting name. As I remember, it means detective. I've been around law enforcement for a lot of years, but I can't recall any National Defense Service," said Sheriff Fitzpatrick.

Before the sheriff could go any further, Shamus reached his hand toward him. "You have now. I'm glad to make your acquaintance."

Sheriff Fitzpatrick reflexively extended his right hand.

The lawman's eye brows raised and his eyes popped wide for just a second. He looked like a person who had just been zinged by static electricity.

When Shamus released his grip, the officer took off his Stetson® hat and dropped it on the table in front of him. "Bud, could I have a cup of your famous coffee?"

Potsy looked at Brittany, tipped his head and moved just his eyes and brows. She caught his meaning and went to prepare a cup of fresh coffee. "What do you think, Shamus?" he said to the man in the three piece suit.

"He's honest. A man of extremely high integrity, but he has great doubts about the supernatural and unusual. He told his office girl that the story you told him about the note and the accident was the biggest line of bull anyone ever tried to feed him."

Sheriff Fitzpatrick jerked upright, his body rigid as he looked at Shamus. "How did you know that? Have you got a bug in my office? What's going on here?"

"Relax Jeff," Potsy said. "What do you know about Elfins?"

"That's the little people, right?" The Sheriff moved his elbow so Brittany could set his coffee in front of him. "All I know is what that professor 'what's his name' told me when he came to town to investigate the disappearance of Torgilson's lion."

The sheriff now relaxed and took a drink of his coffee. "Great, as usual," he said, wiping his lips with the back of his hand. "I think Torgilson had that lion hauled out of here and he's responsible for all the uproar that's going on in this community. He's just trying to make money off of people. The curse of Whispering Oaks, bull!"

"One thing for sure," said Potsy. "It'll be hard for you to protect the Elfins from the Nenuphars if you don't believe in them."

"Bud, you're asking me to believe in something I've never seen. Something I know nothing about."

"Tell me," said Potsy. "What would it take to make you believe in the Elfins?" He pointed at Josie. "What if I told you that this girl is an Elfin Wish Fairy and Shamus there, is an Elfin Guardian? He's kinda' the Sheriff in his town."

"Yea, right," sneered Sheriff Fitzpatrick, "and I'm the pitcher for the New York Yankees."

Shamus waved his hand over Jeff's hat which was right in front of him. *Poof.* There before him was a pile of silver dollars as large as his hat.

Jeff looked down, an expression of amazement came over his face as he ran his hands through the money. "Wow! That's some parlor trick." He picked up a few of the coins and let them dribble between his fingers.

Poof. Shamus snapped his fingers and the sheriff was holding his hat.

"How did you do that? There for a second you really had me going."

"That, my friend, is what we call magic. Are you ready to believe in Elfins now?"

The sheriff laughed. "Not quite. I was at a show in Capital City last year where a magician made a car disappear."

Shamus picked up his cane, which was lying against his stool. "Would you please stand, Sheriff Fitzpatrick?"

Fitzpatrick rose from his stool and stepped back a foot or so. He moved his bad leg forward and back to ensure his balance.

WHACK! Shamus's cane struck the sheriff's left leg at the knee and the man dropped to the floor in a heap. He sprang to his feet ready to fight.

"Hey! What's the big idea? You could have hurt me. Hitting me like that could put me out of commission for days." He rubbed his left leg and pulled up his trouser cuff to inspect for a bruise or a red mark. His long rough twisted scar was gone. He rubbed his hand over the smooth skin.

"Oh my gosh! There's no pain! I'm not crippled anymore!" He walked up and down the length of the shop. He raised his legs as if to run in place and returned to his stool. "That's amazing. How did you do that?"

"Ever hear of Elfin magic?"

"Are you willing to believe us now, Sheriff?" Josie asked.

Sheriff Fitzpatrick took a deep breath and sat back down. "I certainly am, young woman."

"Good," said Shamus. "Give me your hand. I will give you selected information that I believe is important for you to be able to help us in this situation."

The sheriff took Shamus's right hand, blinked and sat up straight. As Shamus released his hand, he spoke again.

"Sheriff, cup your hands. I'm going to pour water into them. Wash your hands and face, don't forget your neck and wash behind your ears. When you're done with that, wash your hair." Shamus pulled a small vial from his vest pocket, removed the cork and dumped the contents into the sheriff's cupped hands.

As the water came closer to the sheriff's face it seemed to grow larger in volume, from a handful to a basin, perhaps even a bucket of water. The beads of the blue water seemed to leap from his hands, covering his entire head. It flushed over and under his wrist watch and raced up the sleeves of his shirt covering his entire body almost instantly.

When the sheriff finished splashing water on his face, neck and hair, all of his clothing was sopping wet. His shoes looked as if they might start dripping at any moment. He looked around at the floor under his seat as if to make sure he had not spilled too much, but the floor was dry. The workbench in front of him was also dry. A vapor rose from his body and he was dry.

Potsy walked to the back of the shop and picked up two of the five cases of 12 gauge shotgun shells. He set them on the table and pushed them across to Sheriff Fitzpatrick. "Here's a present for

178

you. They have one third the powder of a regular load and about a fourth of the buckshot, but they are designed for special prey. When you shoot one, you'll find there is no kick. It's like firing an air rifle. The range is only about a hundred feet.

"The Nenuphars have decided to move their battle into the human realm. We don't know what they might try to do. You must make sure your deputies and the police carry these with them at all times. But, you cannot tell anyone about the Elfins.

"If anyone pulls a weapon on you that you don't think would normally do so, or if you are being attacked by an apparition or unusual critter, blast them with one of these special loads. They'll work. I can promise you that one of our regular lead or steel loads could not stop such an adversary."

Sheriff Fitzpatrick opened a box of the new ammunition that Potsy had given him. The shells were a bright purple instead of the dull red that he was used to. "They look kind of cute. I'll get Chief of Police O'Neil over to my office and give him one of these. If the Nenuphars try anything during Western Days, we'll be ready for 'em."

Brittany picked up one of the full cases, Josie the other. "We'll help you out with these Sheriff," she said as Taya opened the door and held it.

As the girls were about to reenter the shop, Shamus called to them. "Girls, there's a large box with handles on it out there, can you bring it in?"

"No problem," said Brittany. The girls picked up the case by its handles, brought it in and set it on the table beside Shamus.

The Sheriff's cruiser pulled away as the shop door closed behind Taya, who had been holding it.

"Potsy, would you ask Monya to come out here, please?" said Shamus.

Brittany was closest to the intercom system, so she pushed the button and spoke. "Monya. Would you please come to the shop?"

Monya's voice came from the speaker. "Be right there."

Shamus flipped the latch on the box and began to open it as

Monya came in and took a seat at the work bench. "In keeping with the Western Days theme, our engineering department has been working overtime to create this new weapon." He pulled a lever action rifle that looked very much like an old fashioned Winchester® out of the case. The guns were made of plastic and were covered with a spot pattern of colors, pink, white and brown, a little wider, but not as long or as heavy the real thing. The barrel and interior parts of the guns were metal, painted brown with splotches of pink and white.

"You see." He pointed at the stock of the gun in his hand. "You load seven shots through this hole in the stock and then replace the tube to push the ammunition up into the magazine." He loaded one round to demonstrate. He pulled the lever, the cartridge was in the chamber and the hammer was back. He held the hammer with his hand and let it forward softly. He then pulled the lever down and the shell ejected.

"Those look like Little Jake's BB gun. They look even smaller," said Brittany.

"True," said Shamus. "As Potsy told the sheriff, when they're fired they kick like an air rifle and they don't make much noise. You'll notice one more handy feature, they all come with a strap so they can be slung over your shoulder or across your back."

"Wow," said Potsy. "They look like authentic replicas except for the colors. I doubt that anyone would question you kids if you carry them across your backs."

"Sure," said Monya. "You girls can wear neckerchiefs, jeans, shirts and boots. You'll look like real cowgirls, and we'll top it all off with a red flannel hat with a white neck string."

Shamus held up an ammunition belt. "Here is a final accent for your wardrobe."

"Oh, Potsy, do we have to?" Brittany pleaded.

"It would be a good idea if you all looked as near alike as possible," said Potsy.

Taya raised her hand. "I'll braid everyone's hair."

At that moment, the door burst open. Phillip was in the

doorway dressed in a black helmet and breast plate, carrying a bow with a quiver of arrows slung over his back.

"Master Shamus!" he yelled. "An oak tree has fallen over the fence in the southwest quadrant and a pack of black wolves is pouring onto the property. The Nenuphars are here!"

Chapter 22

Battle

Everyone grabbed a gun and began loading in ammunition. Potsy raised the roll-up door and jumped onto his all-terrain vehicle.

"I'll go down the perimeter trail and get to the breech in the defensive wall as fast as I can," he said as he pushed the gear lever forward and pressed the thumb throttle to engage the engine.

"Wait for me!" Brittany hollered, leaping onto the seat behind her grandfather, her gun slung across her back.

The four wheeler sped down the road past the cow pens and onto the trail that led along the fence line. The heavy foliage of the great oak trees darkened the trail as they raced along. Standing water on the road caused mud to fly up under the machine as large hunks were cast into the air by the spinning tires.

Potsy's gun, which he had across this lap, jiggled up and down violently. As they slowed near the southwest corner of the property, Brittany pulled her rifle from her shoulder and held it in front of her.

"Potsy!" Brittany screamed, pointing at two wolves on the trail ahead of them.

He jammed on the brakes and slid the ATV sideways. Brittany lowered her gun, pressing the butt against her right hip. She squeezed off a shot without aiming. The gold coated walnut BBs of the 12 gauge round reached the end of the barrel and spread. Both wolves were hit in the face and shoulders as they pounced. They seemed to explode like a digitized picture on a computer, flying into dust and mist, which evaporated into the breeze.

Both Brittany and Potsy were surprised by the disappearance of their attackers, even though they knew and expected what they saw. He swung the ATV back onto the trail and started moving slowly down the shadowed pathway.

They came around a bend in the trail and saw the tree across the fence. On the trail in front of them stood a huge white wolf -- its gray eyes half closed, its great mouth dripped saliva as it snarled at the intruders. The tree behind the great dog was not large, only six or seven inches in diameter, but it had been a tall tree, the log was about sixty feet long. It looked as if it had been blown over. Its foliage was on the ground on one side of the fence and its roots on the other. The fence was pressed down and the invisible barrier placed by the Elfins was shorted out and shut down in that section. Wolves were jumping to the tree on the root end and crossing the fence. Four or five were already jumping to the ground on the Whispering Oaks side of the fence.

Potsy turned off the ATV and leaped from it on the left side. Brittany came off right behind him.

Raising his gun toward the white wolf, it ducked under a log out of sight as quickly as his gun came up. The wolves that had been jumping onto the log were now streaming to the ground on the Whispering Oaks side, away from Potsy. He aimed at one about to leap down and pulled the trigger. The one behind it vaporized at almost the same instant; Brittany had fired.

There was growling and snorting in the deep undergrowth in a semicircle around the all-terrain vehicle. Potsy pointed. "Let's get up on the four-wheeler so we can see better."

The twosome climbed onto the seat, Potsy standing near the front and Brittany on the flat bed where hay was normally hauled.

They were surrounded on the front and sides with the fence-line behind them.

"One on the right!" She shouted, firing a volley into the brush. Black mist rose through the undergrowth from the spot where she had shot.

"They're attacking!" Potsy yelled. "Keep firing as long as you can."

The fourth of July never had so much noise. Gunshot blasts, growling, snarling animals and the last yelps of those that had been hit by buckshot. The air smelled of gun powder and a strange garlic odor that rose from where the wolves had stood when they were shot.

Brittany held her gun down and jacked the lever twice. "Potsy, I'm out of shells!"

He pulled the lever down on his rifle. "Looks like I'm out too."

There was a cackling, laughing noise from the underbrush in front of them. "That's what I've waited for," said a strange voice. Then there was a vicious snarl.

Potsy looked down to see the white wolf springing from the ground. The animal was a big as the four-wheeler. His yawning mouth open, his fangs glistening as he pounced.

Potsy raised his gun, a hand on either end and shoved it between the jaws of the great beast as it descended upon him. The creature's paws pounded his chest and he felt his feet kicking out from under him as his balance was lost. He pushed up as hard as he could, forcing the gun into the back of the great beast's jaws.

BOOM! Brittany heard another shot from behind her just as Potsy landed in the mud. The enormous beast was still airborne above him as it was struck by gold coated walnut pellets. The wolf shivered and separated like a digitized picture and floated away as mist in the air.

Potsy's breath was knocked out of him and he blacked out as he struck the ground.

Brittany looked around to see Monya standing behind the

steering wheel of the large field tractor. Taya and Josie were on either side of the driver, their gun barrels smoking. They had fired at the same time, both hitting the white wolf as it forced Potsy to the ground.

Potsy lay on the ground, his eyes closed, his rifle across his chest. The front of his shirt was ripped and his chest was scratched. The scratches were deep and blood oozed forth.

"Stop the bleeding, first," yelled Monya as Josie knelt next to him, touched her *sparkler* and placed her hand on his chest. Brittany and Monya ran to Potsy's side. Taya sprang to the seat of the four-wheeler, her gun at the ready.

Potsy coughed and sputtered for a second or two and sat up. "Wow. What just happened?" he asked.

"If it hadn't been for Monya thinking to drive the big tractor out here, we'd both be done for," said Brittany.

He sat up and kissed his wife on the cheek. "Thanks, honey."

He scrambled to his feet and walked to the back of the field tractor. "Let's see if I left my chain saw in the tool chest." Opening the lid of the large metal box mounted on the side of the tractor, he drew out a chain saw. "We must cut up this tree so no part of it can be used by the Nenuphars to gain access to Whispering Oaks."

The roar of the chain saw resounded through the forest as he carved up the small oak tree that had fallen across the fence. The girls reloaded guns as he cut branches into small sticks and the trunk of the tree into small logs, just right for the fireplace. When all the debris had been cleared from the Whispering Oaks side, he slipped across the fence and cut the remaining portion of the small tree into fireplace logs.

He walked the fence line on the other side for some distance as the family rode along parallel to him on the four-wheeler and tractor, keeping watch.

"The logging operation of a few years ago has eliminated most of the trees that would be large enough to be used as a bridge by the Nenuphar," he said.

A large black crow swept from the sky near him as he was about to climb back over the fence. Brittany pulled her rifle up and fired at the bird as it got closer. *POOF*! There was a spraying of feathers, a black cloud, and the big bird vaporized.

"Another Nenuphar bites the dust!" she shouted.

Putting his chain saw back into the tool box on the field tractor, Potsy laughed. He smiled as he came back to the four-wheeler. "This battle is over, and it looks like we won."

He looked around. "I haven't seen Shamus or any of his guardians out here while we've been battling the Nenuphars," he said as he slid onto the seat behind Brittany. "Let's head for home."

Brittany patted Potsy's arm and pointed skyward. A huge black hawk made a slow turn in the sky above them and disappeared over the tree tops toward home.

The field tractor reached the workshop first and was parked outside as the four-wheeler rolled into the shop. Potsy slid off and pulled the garage door down. He saw Shamus sitting at the workbench with Monya and the other girls as he came up.

"Shamus, your little plastic rifle invention worked very well against the wolves, but I kind of expected to see you and some of your guardians out there in the fight."

"To be honest, I had a terrible time holding back the guardians. There is a reason. I have tried to analyze the run-ins with the Nenuphars from the point of view of the Dark Wizard," said Shamus. "He strongly suspects that we are here, but he has no proof. Every time he comes up against Whispering Oaks, he finds himself matching wits with a man, a woman and three girls. All humans."

"Are you telling me that he doesn't know that *Elfins* live at Whispering Oaks?" Potsy asked.

"That's right," said Shamus. "I suspect he'll either give up or become more violent in the very near future. Which ever route he decides to take, we must be alert and ready at a moment's notice to respond."

Chapter 23

News

*P*otsy finished cutting boards for an oak cabinet he was building for one of the ladies in the village. The big table saw whined to a stop as the door opened and the three girls walked in.

Brittany gave her grandfather a hug and a kiss on the cheek. "Wow," she said. "Mrs. O'Hara is going to love this when it's done."

Josie sat down at the workbench. "Potsy, all the yard work and feeding is done. How about rewarding your troops with a hamburger at Torgilson's?"

He wiped his hands and looked around at the smiling faces. "Sure, why not? We have church tomorrow and Western Days starts on Monday. Next week promises to be a busy one for you girls. I was talking to the sheriff on the phone this morning and he said the old hotel, both motels and the RV park are all booked full. Folks are coming to town from as far away as Capital City for this fair and rodeo celebration.

"I can't wait," said Josie. "I've never seen a rodeo."

Brittany reached over and took Josie's hand in hers. "You remember, cuzzy. You are *just a girl* for this show."

"And what does that mean?" Josie asked.

"That means you shouldn't use magic to influence the outcome of a contest," Potsy said. "All of the competitors must win or lose on their own talent."

"Yes," said Taya. "You'll be hearing people wish for this guy or that guy to win. You must not give into their wishes."

Josie lowered her head slightly and drew a circle on the workbench with her finger. "Okay. I promise I won't."

"That's settled. Let's go get those hamburgers," said Potsy.

"Wait, wait!" Brittany said. "Give us a second to change and do our hair. This is the Saturday before Western Days and I think we should get into character and spread the atmosphere."

As the little family entered Torgilson's store, Brittany looked around and noticed the place was fairly busy. Mrs. Torgilson had two additional checkout operators working up front on the registers. The girl behind the deli counter on the far side of the store was filling the cooler case with all kinds of salads and sandwiches. There were customers shopping in almost every aisle.

"Wow! This place is turning into a regular *supermarket*," she said, grabbing her grandfather's arm.

"Look," said Josie. "There are plenty of stools open at the soda fountain. Let's go."

The girls looked like triplets as they slid onto their bar stools. Each wore denim trousers, cowboy boots, blue and white checked shirts with a red bandana and a red felt cowboy hat with white piping around the edge. A heavy white neck string held the hats which were resting on their backs. Their hair was tight to their heads with loose bangs and long braids. Each had a colorful plastic western gun replica strapped on her back.

Jinx was standing behind the grill and half waved to the new arrivals. "I know, burger deluxes with diet soda. Is that right?" He pulled out his pad and started to jot down the order as he walked toward the group. "Wait a minute," he said, "I don't know this lovely lady." He shifted his pencil to the hand holding the pad and extended his hand to Taya. "How do you do. My name is Marion, but you can call me Jinx, everyone else does." He looked at Josie as he released Taya's hand. "Come to think of it, I never shook your hand when we first met."

Josie took the extended hand. Jinx's eyes blinked as she spoke. "I'm glad to meet you."

Brittany was sitting between Taya and Josie and instantly recognized the blink and the temporary far away look in his eyes. She elbowed Josie. "Do you have to do that with everybody you meet?"

Josie flushed and lowered her head. She was obviously embarrassed. "I'm sorry. It's just a habit I've picked up. I'll try to refrain in the future."

Jinx stepped back half a step. "Taya, would you like the same as everyone else?"

"I would," she said, smiling.

Jinx finished writing down the order as he walked back to the grill, put on four burger patties, dumped four orders of potatoes into the deep fryer and started to draw four glasses of diet soda over ice.

Brittany could see Josie's flushed face was turning a deeper pink. "Okay, what gives? What secret information have you uncovered? You made a mind match with Jinx, now give."

Josie turned to her. "I don't think I'm supposed to tell. It's kind of personal."

Jinx arrived carrying sodas. "Brittany," he said as he set the drinks before each patron. "You know there's going to be a dance next Saturday night to close out the Western Days celebration." He stepped back, fidgeting with the string on his apron. "I was wondering. Would you be my date for the dance?"

Brittany looked at Josie, raising her right eyebrow. "I see," she said. She looked directly at Jinx. "I mean, I'd love to."

Jinx smiled and went back to the grill to finish the family's order. Brittany thought there was a little skip in his step as he walked away.

"Josie. Is that the personal information you didn't want to tell me?" she asked.

Josie had a shy little smile on her face as she nodded in the affirmative and took a sip from the straw in her soda.

A young man, about nineteen, dressed in working cowboy clothes had come in and sat down beside Taya. "My name is Lance O'Banyon." He extended his hand to Taya. "If that's how you get a date for the dance, I'd like you to consider going with me."

Taya giggled and took the young man's hand. "Wherever my cousins Brittany and Josie are, that's where you'll find me. If you're there, I'll dance with you."

Josie reached across Taya and Brittany to Lance and took his hand. "Hi, I'm Josie and this is Brittany."

Brittany watched as the young fellow's eyes blinked and got that now familiar far away look. She put her left hand to her face and drummed the counter with the fingernails of her right hand. "Some people never learn," she whispered in Josie's ear.

When the meal was concluded, Potsy paid the check, left a tip and followed the girls as they exited the store.

As Brittany reached the front checkout, she saw several copies of the **_Weekly Gazette_** lying on the end of the counter. She picked one up and handed the girl behind the counter fifty cents.

The headline read, _Rodeo, Fair and Carnival in Town Next Week_. As she climbed into the van, she folded the paper up so she could read the lead article that outlined the entire celebration and all the things that a visitor to the village could enjoy.

The van had just crossed the pond dam when Brittany suddenly exclaimed. "Oh my gosh! Look, Potsy." From her seat in the back she shoved the newspaper over her grandfather's shoulder and under his nose.

"Brittany! I'm trying to drive here, if you don't mind!" He clawed at the newspaper, trying to get it out from in front of his

192

face as he applied the brakes.

"Potsy, you have to look at this," she said, excitedly pushing the newspaper back into her grandfather's line of sight.

He shifted the van into park and jerked the paper out of her hand. He pulled it down in front of him to get a full view. "Okay. The rodeo is coming to town. We know that."

"No, no. The next article down. Read it," she said.

He refocused on the page for a second. Then he saw it. _Local merchant admits to creating lion disappearance scheme to popularize our community._ He leaned back in his seat and continued to read aloud. "Local merchant, Arthur Torgilson, admitted yesterday, that he had ordered the bronze life-size statue of the lion months before from the Markuson Foundry in Capital City. The delivery was held up until late at night because of production and transportation problems. On the night that it arrived he turned the lion over to the San Diego Wild Life Park. He was quoted as saying: 'When people in the village made such a big deal out of it, I just couldn't bring myself to disclose the truth. I just hope my friends and family will forgive me -- especially the Ellis family whose farm, Whispering Oaks, has been under great scrutiny as the story of the Curse of Whispering Oaks has spread throughout the region.'"

He handed the newspaper to Taya, who was sitting in the passenger seat and shifted the van into gear. "Now, we need to find out where that story came from," he said as he drove the last few hundred feet up the driveway to his parking space by the shop.

The girls got out of the van and went into the house to show the newspaper to Monya. Potsy went into his shop and picked up the telephone.

"Sheriff's Office, this is Brandi, may I help you?" came a clear crisp voice.

"Brandi, is Sheriff Fitzpatrick there? It's Bud Ellis."

"One moment, Bud."

"Jeff," Potsy said, "there's an article in the . . . ."

The Sheriff's voice cut him off. "Bud, I'll meet you at your shop in fifteen minutes."

Chapter 24

The Story

Sheriff Fitzpatrick sat at the workbench across from Potsy. He rubbed his fingers up and down the side of his coffee mug as Potsy unfolded the newspaper holding it in front of him.

"Have you seen this article in the *Gazette*?"

Sheriff Fitzpatrick raised his eyebrows. "Yes, I have." He leaned forward as if to get a better look. "As a matter of fact, I guess I'm responsible for it."

"How's that?"

"The other day, when I left here, I loaded six of the purple shells you gave me into my shotgun. I drove down River Road to where it comes off the freeway. I wasn't looking for anything. I was just headed back to the office. There were two Highway Patrol cars parked at the intersection of River Road and the freeway off ramp. These patrolmen had cones out. I pulled over at the big curve behind some trees and watched from cover for a minute or two. A car came off the freeway and stopped at the cones. I recognized the driver. It was Sara Kavenaugh, my deputy's wife. I saw a large dumpy patrolman walk up to her. He was carrying a clipboard. He appeared to ask for her driver's license, but he didn't take it from her. She held it out the window, he took hold of it, and just as quickly let go. He motioned her to drive on.

"I watched from hiding for a few minutes. These jaspers were wearing powder blue sunglasses. Whoever heard of a cop wearing anything powder blue?"

"Holy Christmas goose! What was going on?" Potsy interrupted.

Sheriff Fitzpatrick took a sip of his coffee. "You know how suspicious I am. When Mrs. Kavenaugh came down the road and turned around the bend where I was, I waved her down. She pulled over, out of sight of the patrolmen.

"I asked her what had happened. She said the man that stopped her, said they were checking driver's licenses to make sure they were current. When the man took hold of her license, she received a static electricity shock.

"Right then, I knew something was going on. I jumped in my car and rolled up nose to nose with the first Highway Patrol cruiser. I took my shotgun with me when I got out. I demanded to know what they were doing in my jurisdiction without my knowledge. The one closest to me went for his gun, so I thought I'd put a little buckshot in his leg to get his attention -- It was remarkable. He and his car, more or less, exploded. There wasn't a boom like an explosion, more like a loud *poof*. It was like a picture being torn into a thousand little square pieces, the color went out of him and then a black mist blew away in the breeze.

"The second joker got off a shot at me. When I shot him, he, his cruiser and their cones exploded into dust just like the first guy. They really surprised me with their hostile reaction. One thing I do know for sure, they were shooting real bullets. Come outside and look at the hood of my car."

Potsy slid from his stool and followed the sheriff. There in the hood of the sheriff's cruiser was a bullet hole. Potsy touched it. "It's real all right."

The men went back into the shop and sat down at their coffee mugs. "So, Jeff, how did the newspaper article come about?"

"I went directly to Torgilson's store and picked up my cousin, Arthur. I told him I knew he had perpetrated this entire hoax and that he is such a rummy and drunk he didn't remember getting rid of his lion and probably didn't remember getting the statue delivered. I took him over to Sean Younger's office at the *Weekly Gazette* and helped him tell the whole story to Sean and Old man Younger."

Potsy took the last sip from his mug and set it down softly. "What if some nosey party wants to track down documentation to verify this story of yours?"

"No problem." The sheriff leaned forward as if to give up a secret. "Jimmy Markuson, the foundry owner in Capital City. He's my cousin on the other side." He unbuttoned the flap on his left shirt pocket and removed two folded pieces of paper. He peeled the top one back and placed his right forefinger on the second one. "I was on the phone most of the day yesterday, getting this invoice." He slid the papers across the bench to Potsy.

The first page was an invoice from Markuson Foundry for one large casting of an African Lion and plaque, the second page was on Wild Animal Park stationery. A pick up order for one male lion, dated and signed by a park employee -- the time of the pickup was 11:10 PM. The foundry invoice was stamped: PAID.

Sheriff Fitzpatrick stood next to the workbench. "I'm on my way over to Arthur's store to give him this documentation when we finish here. He'll have it for his records if that nosey party you refer to comes around. I figure the newspaper story and this paperwork will eliminate our Nenuphar problem for good."

Potsy folded the papers and handed them back. "I sure hope you're right, Jeff. The problem is finding out where that wizard is, so we can keep an eye on him and make sure he leaves."

The sheriff pocketed the papers and turned to the door. He spoke over his shoulder as he left the shop. "No problem, Bud. As soon as Western Days are over, my deputies and I will go through this county with a fine toothed comb and find him."

Chapter 25

Celebration

*T*he girls came pouring through the door of the woodshop laughing and giggling. They were dressed in their western outfits.

"Potsy," Brittany said, slipping up to her grandfather's side and kissing him on the cheek. "We need a ride over to the fair grounds. We're going to be running the booth for the Children's Hospital. Mrs. Kelly said she'd have it all set up for us and she wanted us there by ten."

Potsy looked at his lovely granddaughters. "Wow! You're the finest looking bunch of cowgirls I ever did see." He touched the barrel of the rifle hanging over Brittany's back. "These guns look fake or like cool replicas. Don't take them off unless you have to use them. And whatever you do, don't let any of your friends handle them."

"Potsy," Taya said. She turned her head down slightly and raised her right eyebrow. It was her *I'm over five years old!* look. "We were there when these were handed out, and remember, we've had occasion to use them. We know they're dangerous and we won't let them fall into the wrong hands."

"Thank you, darlin'," said Potsy. "You just saved me a half an hour of explanation."

"So, Potsy." Taya moved close to her grandfather. "Do you have time to run us over to the fairgrounds?"

"Here," said Potsy, pulling out his van keys and handing them to Taya. "You have your license. Take the van and Monya and I'll use the truck."

"Thanks," she said. "We'll be careful."

Mrs. Kelly stood next to the Children's Hospital booth as the girls walked up. "Oh, there you are. You look like an ad for Western Days. That's great. I've put a couple of stools in the front of the booth at the outer edges. We don't want you getting hit by a dart, so don't walk back to pull them out until they've all been thrown."

All three girls answered in unison. "Yes, ma'am."

Mrs. Kelly opened a panel at the side of the booth. "Okay. Get in there and get ready to go to work. I'll have someone here to relieve you at six o'clock." She reached in her pocket and brought out three tickets. "I've got a ticket to the rodeo for each one of you. It starts at seven, you know. You'll have time to grab a snack or go on a couple of rides before it starts."

Again, in unison. "Thank you, ma'am."

The day passed quickly and Jinx showed up about four in the afternoon. He was carrying four small bags from Torgilson's soda fountain. As he approached the front of the booth he set one in front of each girl and kept one.

"Hey. What's this?" Brittany asked.

Jinx opened his bag and brought out a can of diet soda. "I was hungry after working all day, and I thought you might appreciate your *favorite* about now."

Brittany opened her bag, raised it to her face and breathed in the smell of the burger deluxe and fries. "This is great Jinx! Thank you," she said as she pulled an ice cold can of soda from her bag and opened it. "We were just about to make a run across the midway to the hot dog stand. We were thinking it was getting on toward lunch time."

"I must be just in time then," said Jinx as he hoisted himself up onto the end of the front counter next to Brittany.

The midway was crowded with people entering and leaving the big exhibit barns. Lots of folks, particularly young couples, were stopping at the balloon booth, trying to win a teddy bear.

Jinx took a bite of his burger and spoke to Brittany as Josie helped a young couple with their darts. "Rumor has it that your grandma has one of her famous peach pies in the baking competition, is that right?"

"Yep. Right there in the first barn," said Brittany. "We haven't been in to see if she's won a ribbon yet. We get off at six o'clock. We thought we'd go in after that."

"As soon as I finish my lunch, I think I'll wander around and look at the exhibits and rides. There are three of you here, why don't you let the girls watch the booth, and you come with me?"

Brittany flushed red. "I'd love to, but we promised Potsy we would stick together while we're at the fair. Do you have a rodeo ticket? We thought we'd go when we get done here."

Jinx took the last quick bite of his hamburger and hopped down to the ground. "No, I don't, but I'll have one by the time you all get through here." He wadded up his lunch sack without touching his fries and tossed it in a nearby trash receptacle. "Now, don't wander off, I'll be back in a couple of hours," he said. A big smile crossed his face as he walked toward the midway and the ticket booths.

Josie finished awarding a teddy bear to a young couple as Taya edged up beside Brittany. "Now, that guy looks like a happy camper. What did you say to him?"

Brittany took a deep breath. "I think I asked him to join us at the rodeo when we're done here."

"You think. That sounds a little bogus to me," Taya said. "I thought we were going to go on a couple of rides."

"We'll have time for that, cuzzy. We might even hit an exhibit or two before we head for the arena grandstands."

"Sounds like fun to me," said Josie as she retrieved the darts and replaced the broken balloons on the back wall of the stand.

Another young couple was at the booth, the young man trying to win a teddy bear for his date. The three girls were in the front corner where Brittany was sitting.

Taya tapped Brittany on the shoulder and lowered her voice. "Hotties at seven o'clock."

Brittany shifted her eyes, without changing the direction she was facing. Across the midway and just to the left of their booth, three young men stood, the crowds passing around them. Their backs were to the girls and Brittany could only see the sides of their faces as they were concentrating on the people riding the tilt-o-whirl. The young men were long and lean. They were all about the same height, nearly six feet tall, dark black hair that was swept back on the sides. They wore form fitting black jeans with black sleeveless tee shirts. A white imprint of a longhorn bull skull was emblazoned on the backs of their tees.

"Oh my gosh!" Josie said in a low, but excited tone. "Ne-nuphars!" She gripped Brittany's arm just above the elbow.

Brittany patted her hand. "Take it easy and keep an eye on them. If they're wearing those powder-blue sunglasses when they turn around, we'll get excited."

Taya stood very still. Her full concentration on the young men.

"Say. I want a dollar's worth of darts," said a young man leaning against the front of the booth.

All of the girls jerked to attention. "Yes. Yes. We can help you," said Taya as all of the girls rushed toward him, almost falling over each other. Taya got to him first and handed up four darts onto the counter. She pulled the dollar bill from his hand, stuffed it into her apron and backed away.

"Is there anything else," Brittany asked as she and Josie arrived.

"No thanks. Just get out'a my way and let me toss," he said.

"Sure, sure," said Taya as the girls retired to Brittany's corner.

Josie suddenly stopped and stood rigid as Brittany walked into the back of her. "They're gone," she said.

The girls looked up and down the midway and down the aisles of booths as far as they could see. The three black clad men were nowhere to be seen.

Brittany turned to the other girls. "I think those characters looked a lot like that nephew of Mr. Emongaton's that came to Whispering Oaks when we were swimming."

"Yeah," said Josie. "Whatever became of him? I don't think we've seen him since that day."

"I don't know," said Brittany. "We'll have to ask Jinx when he comes back."

The girls went back to work, but kept a constant vigil, looking hard at anyone wearing black, keeping a lookout for those ominous powder blue sunglasses.

Brittany stood close to Taya as she looked toward the midway. "I'll sure be glad to see Jinx when he comes back."

"I'll bet you will," Taya said.

Chapter 26

Rodeo

Jinx strolled up the midway, turning this way and that, making sure he had not missed any of the exciting things that were going on. He passed booth after booth that were games of chance. The ring toss, the ball toss and a dozen others. All offered prizes, but he knew that few were strictly skill and none were stacked to the patron's advantage.

Jinx found the large booth marked 'RODEO' and got into line. He had not been there long when he felt a hand on his back. He looked over his shoulder to see a young man about his own age dressed completely in black. His hair slicked back. His black tee shirt was sleeveless and there was a white print on the front. The skull of a longhorn bull was printed across his chest. Jinx's eyes gazed into the familiar face under the large white cowboy hat.

"It's me. Lance O'Banyon. I've been into your soda fountain several times. You make great sandwiches."

"Yes," said Jinx. "I just didn't fully recognize you. You're not sitting across the counter from me."

Lance laughed. "Are you trying to buy a rodeo ticket?"

"Yes," said Jinx. "I'm going to go with Brittany, Taya and Josie when they get done at their booth."

"You say Taya is going to be with you?"

"Yep. All the girls are going to be there. Are you going to be in tonight's show?"

Lance pulled Jinx out of line. "Yes, I'll be in the show and I've got something special for you." He reached into his pocket. "It's like a backstage pass at a concert." He held out a ticket and four plastic passes with strings on them. "Here is a ticket for you and here are four arena passes. You don't have to sit in the bleachers, you can come right down and stand among the cowboys, right next to the bucking chutes if you'd like."

"I didn't know you had anything going with Taya. When did this happen?"

Lance blushed. "We met at your lunch counter. We haven't had a real date." Lance raised a finger to his cheek. "You might say, she's my best girl."

Jinx could feel the smile flying across his face. He took the passes and stuffed them into his trouser pocket. "Fantastic, and I'm sure the girls will be there with me."

"That's great," said Lance. "I have to leave now to get ready and I may not see you until after my ride. I'm the second rider in the bull competition."

"Bull rider?" Jinx queried. "Is that the reason for the shirt?"

"Yes. The promoter figures that it stirs up public interest before the show. He thinks folks will stop us and ask us questions. That's a laugh. I haven't been stopped or asked about the shirt by anyone but you. We don't have to wear these getups when we ride though. Thank goodness."

Jinx watched as Lance walked away. He looked down at the passes in his left hand. "Cool!" he said out loud as he passed through the crowd and headed back toward the balloon booth.

Brittany watched as Mrs. Kelly walked up the midway accompanied by two girls from church, a plump girl with dishwater blond hair and a pretty girl with dark hair.

Mrs. Kelly entered the booth, opening the cash box. "Oh, my goodness. You girls have had a very busy day," she said. "Girls, this is Cynthia and Marla, I'm sure you've seen them at church. Cynthia, Marla, this is Brittany," she pointed at each girl, "Taya and Josie. They're Bud and Carol Ellis's grandchildren."

"Glad to meet you," said the girls in unison.

Mrs. Kelly quickly transferred the days receipts to her deposit bag and inventoried the prizes and balloons available for Cynthia and Marla. "Well, that's it. You girls are free to go. Have a good time. We'll see you tomorrow at the same time."

The girls stepped outside the booth and waited for Jinx to show up.

"How about we go over to the Ferris wheel and take a ride while we're waiting for him," Taya said.

"Sure," said Brittany, "we can see the booth and the midway from there. He won't get past us."

"Let's go for it," said Josie.

As the Ferris wheel operator was opening the gate in front of Taya, so she could step out, Jinx came jogging up.

"Did you get your rodeo ticket?" Brittany asked.

"Better than that," he said. "I ran into Taya's friend, Lance O'Banyon. He's a bull rider and he gave me these." He held out the yellow arena pass that was already strung around his neck as he pulled the other three from his pocket. "We'll be able to stand right behind the bucking chutes and see all the action close up."

"Let's go," said Jinx as he handed out the arena passes.

Finding an open vantage point behind the chutes, the group could smell the sweat from the bulls and hear their snorts and occasional bellows as the wranglers moved them into the bucking stalls. They nervously stomped up and down in place, raising dust in the chutes. The air hung heavy with tingling sights and smells.

Brittany could see the high round shoulder of one huge bull as he waited. A large black fly landed on the animal's side. The instantaneous flexing of a muscle under the bovine's hide sent the bug on its way.

The youngsters stood on the rail and looked out on the turned up sand of the arena. The roar of the crowd energized them. Brittany felt more than alive. A feeling she had never had before. Adrenaline rushed through her veins and she felt very alert. She had to scream and yell "Yahoo!" to let the excitement out.

"And now, ladies and gentlemen," the arena announcer called, "our first rider of the day, James Walker from Cheyenne, Wyoming, coming out of chute number one on Old Thunder. The cowboy has to stay on his bull for eight seconds to qualify for prize money." A loud horn blared and the chute gate opened.

A Jersey colored bull with curled horns came busting from the chute and twisted to its left and continued to spin until the rider was unseated and thrown to the ground. The bull turned to gore the cowboy, but a rodeo clown with a large red handkerchief stepped in front and distracted the bull. The rider scrambled to his feet and climbed the gate of the chute next to him as the bull was ushered out of the arena by two cowboys on horseback.

The announcer's voice broke the air. "No money for Mr. Walker today. Maybe tomorrow. And now ladies and gentlemen, if you'll take a look at chute number two, we have Lance O'Banyon from Billings, Montana, on Tornado. Lance is a real cowboy whose been getting a lot of good rides this season. It wouldn't surprise me if he finishes the year in the top money."

The youngsters pressed against the rail as the gate to the chute slammed open, aided by the horns of the huge black bull that came exploding out. Clouds of dust rolled up as the giant beast bucked and spun, trying to dislodge its rider. The big bull lunged high into the air and came down hard. The eight second whistle blew and

208

the rider looked for an opportunity to dismount and get away from the raging animal. The bull tossed his head and lurched sideways. As he did, Lance lost his hold on the rope and fell face first to the ground. The angry bull spun around and got his horns under the cowboy, launching him high in the air over his back.

One of the cowboys on horseback got a rope around the animal's head, wrapped a loop around the pommel of his saddle and pulled back hard, dragging the beast away from the downed bull rider. The bull broke free, pulling the lariat from the saddle and ran into the corral.

An emergency medical team rushed out into the arena with a stretcher, picked Lance up and brought him to the area behind the chutes where the kids were standing.

The emergency crew set the stretcher on the ground, waiting for the arrival of the doctor before proceeding to a waiting ambulance. Taya ran to the young cowboy's side and took a limp hand in both of hers. Lance was really beaten up, bleeding from his head and left shoulder. Taya broke into tears.

Josie moved to the other side of the stretcher.

"Oh, Josie, he's hurt real bad," Taya cried out.

Josie looked at Taya for a long moment and then took the bull rider's other hand between hers. The crowd of people around the stretcher suddenly looked upward as if to pray. A blue aura buzzed around Josie's clasped hands. Lance shivered, jerked and stirred awake. His eyes bright.

The arriving doctor pushed Josie aside, shining a flashlight into the rider's eyes. "How are you feeling, young fella?" he asked.

Lance sat up and turned his head from side to side. "Knocked out I guess, but, I think I'm fine."

The clown handed the rider his hat and pulled him to his feet. "Let's show the folks that you're all right."

Lance accompanied the clown back into the arena where he took off his hat, waved it and bowed at the waist. The crowd roared, applauded and whistled. The cowboy that had been so brutally battered was fine.

Taya hugged Josie and danced up and down. "Thank you, thank you, thank you."

Josie tipped her head down shyly and said, "You're welcome, cuzzy."

Lance came back to where his little group of friends was still standing and put his arm around Taya's waist from behind. "I sure appreciate you all being close at hand. That was a mighty nasty ride there at the end."

The girls giggled and smiled. "We were happy to be here," said Josie.

Turning his head, he spoke to Taya. "You know, I'm mighty dirty. You all can stay here and watch the show while I go take a shower and get cleaned up."

In less than half an hour, Lance was back with his friends, his arm around his favorite girl. "I'm hungry," he said. "Who would like to join me for a steak at the Village Restaurant? I'm buying."

"Don't you want to wait and see the results of the other rides?" Jinx asked.

"Nope. I got my eight seconds. I know I'm in the money."

The little group went to the parking lot where Jinx had parked his grandfather's Suburban®. "Hop in everybody," he said. "Next stop, a steak dinner."

Chapter 27

Ribbons & Buckles

*T*he late afternoon sun beat down on the fairgrounds as the puffy white clouds that had shaded the area drifted to the east. The crowds of people along the midway and the children waiting in line to enjoy the rides didn't notice.

All the refreshment stands were busy. Popcorn, cotton candy, candied apples, sugar cinnamon pretzels, hot dogs, hamburgers and ice cold sodas were being carried and eaten by the throngs as they moved in and out of the exhibition barns.

It was the last day of the Western Days celebration and this would be the last day of the rodeo. The champion cowboys would be announced and ribbons would be awarded to the prize winning exhibitors in every category of the fair.

Brittany noticed what appeared to be storm clouds, gathering to the south. The unnatural presentation was heavy and dark. She poked Taya with a long finger. "I don't claim to be a weather man, but doesn't it seem a little strange for a storm to be brewing to the south if the prevailing winds are from the west?"

Her question went unanswered as Mrs. Kelly came to the door of the booth, opened the gate and allowed Cynthia and Marla to enter. She spoke to Brittany, Josie and Taya who were now exiting the

211

booth. "You girls will be happy to know that this has been the most successful booth we have ever done for the Children's Hospital. This is a great year." Mrs. Kelly gave each girl a hug. "Speaking of great years, you girls should run over to the exhibit barn and watch the ribbon presentations."

Brittany opened the door to the booth. "Come on, gang. Let's go see how Monya did in the pie baking category."

Josie and Taya followed Brittany into the exhibition barn and found a chair near the back as the panel of six judges took their chairs on stage. Mrs. Torgilson came to the podium and spoke into the microphone.

"I'm sure everyone is aware of the fact that this is our best attended fair ever. I've been here a lot of years, and I've never seen anything like this." She leaned forward extending her right arm. "Right now, I'd like to introduce your judges." The judges rose beside their chairs as she opened her right hand. "And to present the awards, here is Doc Watson. Most of you know Doc."

Applause and cheers from the crowd filled the barn as Doc stepped to the podium. "Thank you, Mrs. Torgilson."

Brittany heard a rustling noise in the chair to her left that had been empty when the girls sat down. Her head snapped around. "Mom! What are you doing here? When did you get here?"

"Your Dad's business concluded early, so we made a beeline back here as quickly as we could. Would you like some popcorn?" She pushed the large bag in front of Brittany.

"Oh, no thanks, I just. . ." said Brittany as Josie reached in front of her and took the bag.

"Aunt Chris, I love popcorn almost as much as I love salad," said Josie. She held the family size container and began to shovel handfuls into her open mouth.

"So, where's your grandmother?" Chris asked.

"We haven't seen her, but she must be here somewhere," Brittany said. "Where's Dad and Little Jake?"

"They're out on the rides. You know Little Jake when he finds a carnival. He goes nuts." Chris raised her index finger to her lips.

Whispering Oaks - The Curse

Doc Watson was about to award a ribbon in a new category.

"A lady known in the village for her fantastic peach pies. This blue ribbon goes to Carol Ellis," said Doc Watson.

Monya stood from her chair near the front row and went up on stage to receive her blue ribbon. Chris, Brittany and the girls stood to applaud as the crowd roared their approval. Chris pulled Brittany out into the aisle. "You and the girls wait outside, I'll go get Monya and Potsy."

As the girls exited the barn, they met Jinx and Lance on their way in. "Hey, we were just looking for you girls," said Jinx. "We went past your booth and Cynthia said you were inside watching your grandmother get a blue ribbon."

Brittany jumped up and down as she took both of Jinx's hands in hers. "I don't know how she knew it, but she was right. My Monya just got the peach pie blue ribbon."

"Guess what else?" Taya asked. "They're going to name the number one bull rider tonight." She took Lance's right arm and snuggled next to him. "Yes, indeed." She looked up into his big brown eyes. "And I'll bet we can all guess who's going to get that award."

Lance looked down at Taya. "You know what my old daddy always says, he says don't count your chickens before they hatch."

Jinx patted Lance on the shoulder. "I'm sure your daddy is right, but we know who should be the winner of the bull riding buckle."

"I'll second that motion," said Potsy as he ambled up to the group, his new boots covered with dust.

"Thank you, Mr. Ellis," said Lance, extending his right hand.

Chris and Monya came up behind Potsy. Monya was waving her blue ribbon. "Let's not forget about me!" she said as she took Lance's outstretched hand.

"I have to get ready to ride in about half an hour, but we still have time to go over to the cafe on the midway and have a soda in the shade."

"That's a great idea," said Potsy. "I'm buying."

213

The small group withdrew to the Midway Cafe where Potsy ordered diet sodas, enough for all. Potsy carried the tray over to the large picnic table. Everyone was seated under a giant umbrella, out of the sun. As he set the tray down, Brittany spoke. "This is great, Potsy. Thanks."

"You all deserve it. I heard what a great job you did over at Mrs. Kelly's booth. I'm really proud of you."

Brittany sat up straight. "Not to change the subject, but, Jinx, whatever became of that nephew of Mr. Emongaton's that you used to pal around with?"

"His name was Bob, right?" Josie said.

"His name was Sai Robearus, but everyone called him Bob," said Jinx. "His uncle came by the store, I think it was the Monday after we came over to swim. He said Bob had to leave on a family emergency and he wouldn't be back. I was really busy so I don't remember the exact reason. Seems someone was killed in a hunting accident." A look of momentary confusion crossed his face. "Folks hereabouts don't hunt wolves, do they?"

"I never heard of it," said Potsy.

The moment Jinx said Robearus, Chris dug her fingernails into Potsy's lower arm. Potsy patted Chris' hand. "It's all right, sister, everything will be fine. I think a recent hunting accident took care of all your fears."

Brittany looked up and down the table, "How about we all head out to the bleachers and watch the last rodeo?"

"I can get arena passes for everyone, if you like," said Lance.

"No thank you," said Brittany. "Being that close makes enjoying the rodeo a little tense, if you don't mind."

The family found Jon and Little Jake at the shooting gallery, where Little Jake had just won a teddy bear and a stuffed squirrel.

Whispering Oaks - The Curse

The teddy bear was almost as large as he was. He had to wrestle it back and forth to get it into the open space on the bleacher beside him. Brittany held his little red and brown squirrel with glass eyes, so Little Jake could handle his hotdogs and soda.

"Don't forget," said Little Jake. "When I get done with my hot-dog, you can give back my squirrel."

"No sweat, Bro," said Brittany. "I was just thinking that he looks a lot like a little friend of mine at Whispering Oaks."

Potsy found his seat and wedged in between Brittany and Little Jake.

"I suppose your squirrel friend has a name," said Little Jake.

"Yes. His name is Phillip."

"Phillip? What happened? Did the squirrel name himself?"

"As a matter of fact," Josie barged in. "Phillip is black, Brittany. He was named after a very brave knight from the old kingdom far across the sea."

"Oh my gosh," laughed Little Jake. "This squirrel is your friend, but she knows all about him too. Is that right? A squirrel named after a knight. That's wild. "

Josie turned her head slightly, looking down her sharp little pixy nose at Jake. Her eyes half closed. "Jake, I think you should hold your tongue in areas where you have no knowledge."

Jon reached over and patted Little Jake on the knee. "I think that's a great idea, son. The show is about to start. Maybe the girls will introduce you to Phillip later."

The rodeo started with the bull riding event and as soon as Lance had finished his ride, he swung from the back of the bull onto a pickup cowboy's horse. He slid to the ground on the other side of the horse as the rodeo clowns hustled the large bull into the corral.

"Ladies and gentlemen," said the ring announcer. "I'd like to draw your attention to the center of the arena. This young man, Lance O'Banyon of Billings, Montana, is our new first place bull rider and winner of the Silver Buckle Award. Congratulations, Lance!"

The crowd went wild with yelling, whistling and applause.

Lance tipped his hat and walked through the gate into the back area under the announcer's box.

In a few minutes, Lance appeared in the aisle next to the family's seats. He was wearing a very large silver buckle on his belt with the picture of a cowboy astride a spinning bull.

"That is a beautiful buckle," said Jon.

"I'll say," said Potsy. "How does it feel to be a champion?"

"It's just great, Mr. Ellis," said Lance. "I was wondering. Could I take Taya to the dance after the rodeo is over?"

"You certainly may, Lance." Potsy looked around. "We do have one, sort of strange, family rule. All of the girls must go and the entire group must stay together."

"If it's okay with you, Mr. Standish," Jinx leaned over to see Jon's face. "I'd like Brittany to be my date for the dance."

Jon rubbed his face with his left hand. "Jinx. The answer for you is the same as the answer for Lance. The same rule applies. The entire group has to stay together."

"Thank you, sir," said Jinx. "That's fine with me."

"That ain't fine with me," bellowed Little Jake. "I ain't goin' to no stupid dance."

"Okay, okay," said Potsy. "When the rodeo is over, I'll take you home and come back for the girls later."

Chapter 28

Ultimatum

Mr. Emongaton, leaned forward on his chair as the black candle in the lantern on the table began to hiss. Black smoke billowed from the lantern forming a tall shape on the other side of the table.

The wizard dropped to his knees, his hands clasped together as if he were praying, his head bent low. "My Lord Gunarius! This is an unexpected pleasure. How may I serve you?"

The ominous figure extended his right hand. "Stand, Drayfus. I am here to check on your progress. His Great Majesty is getting quite concerned. We have read your reports of how close you are to capturing an Elfin city, but we have heard many rumors that you are being outwitted by a human child. The rumors say that you have lost over half of your command. His Great Majesty has taken note of the fact that all the reports were issued by you. There has been no one else in your chain of command to substantiate your reports."

"Flagrant rumors, my Lord. This is a very difficult case, but I promise, I shall have excellent results within a very short time," said Drayfus as he rose to his feet.

"Short time?" The ghoulish figure mocked the wizard. "You have been at this for thirty days. You have done nothing but expend our resources. Where is your second in command? I want to speak to Robearus."

The wizard lowered his head. "I am sorry, my Lord. Robearus was destroyed."

"Destroyed? One of the greatest soldiers of the Circle was destroyed? When? By whom? I must know, *NOW!*" The specter's voice roared and the rafters of the cabin shook. Dust and dirt fell to the floor.

"He was lost last week. . ." The wizard hesitated.

"Go on! Go on!" Gunarius commanded. "Who did this deed? Did he clash with a whole troop of Elfins?"

"It was the local sheriff that destroyed him," said the wizard softly.

As the wizard's voice got softer, the voice of the specter grew louder and harsher. "Are you telling me that a mere mortal has done this thing? Did you kill the mortal within minutes of his evil deed?"

"No, my Lord. We have not been able to get near the sheriff. He, like many of the human population here, seem to be charmed."

"How many Elfins have you captured?"

"None, sire."

"None? That's ridiculous. How many Elfins have you seen?"

"None, sire. But there is a place here called Whispering Oaks. I believe the gateway to the Elfin city is on that property. I suspect they are under the protection of the humans."

"You believe! You suspect! You have no proof?"

"Sire, there was a large lion that disappeared from a place called Torgilson's Store. It was replaced by a large bronze statue. I believe that was Elfin magic. There was even the signature sign of the shamrock left behind."

"I've heard all of those stories, Drayfus. Who is acting as your second in command on this mission?"

"Tayshus is here now, sire."

The specter waved a large left hand. "Get him for me. I want to talk to him."

"Yes, sire. As you wish."

The Nenuphar Wizard stepped out the door and soon a small-ish black-robed gnome came in. He bowed at the waist. "You sent for me, my Lord?"

"Tayshus, how long have you been on this assignment?"

"About a week, sire."

"Have you heard of, or seen any Elfins in this area?"

"No, sire."

"What do you know of the humans in this village?"

The gnome reached into a pocket inside his cloak and pulled out a newspaper. "I only know what I read about them, sire." He handed the paper to the specter, folded open to the article about Torgilson admitting to replacing the lion. "There are a lot of people of Irish decent and there seems to be a great deal of superstition here, but at the same time, there is a Bible in nearly every home."

"Thank you, Tayshus. You have been of great help."

"Sire, I hope I have not done or said anything to get Master Drayfus into trouble."

"Never fear. If Drayfus finds trouble, it is of his own making. Go back to your duties and send Drayfus to me."

The old wood door opened and closed. Drayfus stood before the slits of light that passed through.

"Drayfus. Tell me your plan to capture the Elfin city and how long it will take."

"Sire, I would like a hundred of our best changeling troops. The majority of the population of this village is at a fair near the center of town. I shall send Gargoyles, Griffins and Dragons after them. We shall kill them all and uproot every tree in the area until we find the Elfin city."

"You would kill a thousand innocents?" The specter smiled. "We haven't done such a thing since we made the world think it was covered with plague centuries ago."

"This area is frequented by fierce storms called tornados. When we finish, it will look like a great storm has struck and moved on. These storms are known for their violence and destruction."

The specter walked to the other side of the table. "You shall have one constraint, Drayfus. You will accomplish your mission by noon tomorrow or you will be judged.

"You have already caused the thirty-year destruction of the Banshee, the deaths of an untold number of soldiers and you don't even have proof that Elfins are here. It appears to His Great Majesty that you are being tested by humans. If you fail, you will have to pay."

The specter raised his hand and became smoke that moved into the lantern on the table. The smoke swirled and disappeared through the flame of the candle.

The wizard threw the cabin door open. "Tayshus, get in here! Bring all the officers."

When the officers were gathered, Drayfus explained his plan. "First, you four." He pointed to his left. "You will bring me Bud Ellis. He claims title to Whispering Oaks and I think he is the link between the humans and the Elfins. I sent a dozen troops onto his property and he destroyed them. Kill anyone who gets in your way, but bring him to me."

He waved his hand. "Now, go!"

Chapter 29

The Dance

The loudspeakers over the rodeo arena crackled. "Ladies and gentlemen, that was the last award of the evening. Your Western Days Rodeo has drawn to an close. We do want to invite all of you over to Exhibit Barn A, the one with blue doors, for the Western Days Dance. After the dance, we'll be having lots of great fireworks, so be sure to stick around for that."

The crowd roared with applause and cheers of approval.

Brittany, who was sitting on the end of the bleacher, turned to the others. "It's dance time, let's get started."

When the group reached the floor of the exhibit hall, Potsy pulled the pink, brown and white plastic gun from over his shoulder and passed it to Jon. He then handed over the ammunition belt that had been around his waist. "Please keep in mind that despite what it looks like, this is a real gun and it can be dangerous. I'm going to leave this with you and run Little Jake over to the house."

Brittany watched as her grandfather and little brother crossed in and out of the gathering crowd on their way to the parking lot.

Chris came up, waving small slips of paper. "Look, gang, I've got dance tickets." She gave everyone in the group an entry pass as they headed for the dance hall.

Monya took Chris's arm. "I'll see you kids later. I would have gone with Potsy and Little Jake, but I'm on the dance committee." She turned and slipped away through the crowd toward the bandstand.

The side of the dance hall had been opened up and a beautiful veranda was set up outside, decorated with flowers, foliage, bales of hay, small white tables and chairs and lots of hanging Chinese lanterns. On the second floor was a small snack bar, but, again, the veranda opened to the outside, creating a small romantic area with tables for two.

Brittany lead Jinx by the hand to the second floor veranda. Taya and Lance were already there, seated at a table. As they passed the snack bar, Brittany gave Monya a big wave. She was at her station, dressed in a red and white checked apron, selling hotdogs and sodas. Like the girls, Monya had the barrel of her gun sticking up an inch or two, just over her left shoulder.

Brittany pulled Jinx along behind her to the rail of the veranda and pointed up at the sky. "Now, isn't this a beautiful night?"

"I'll say it is," said Jinx, spinning around and sticking out his right elbow. "May I have this dance, ma'am?"

Brittany took his arm. "Lead on, sir. I'm with you."

The young couple went downstairs to the main dance floor and joined the party.

As the band played a slow dance tune, Jinx fidgeted with his right hand trying to figure out if it should be outside the gun or between the gun and his partner. He found comfort, placing his hand on Brittany's back with the gun to the outside. After the second dance, he said. "You know, it would be easier to dance if you didn't have your cowboy hat on, and you might think about taking that gun and ammo belt off. Costumes are great, but you girls are a little extreme."

Brittany walked to a nearby empty table, took off her hat and laid it on a chair. She pulled her rifle over her head and started to lay it on the table. "No. I'd better not. Some yahoo might come along and think it's a plaything and kill someone." She stuck her arm through the sling and replaced the rifle on her back.

"Why does your grandfather make you wear that silly rifle, anyway?" Jinx asked.

"It's a little complicated," said Brittany. "It would be best if I didn't tell you about it."

"I thought we were friends," said Jinx. "What's the big secret about you girls and Monya carrying guns? I see Sheriff Fitzpatrick, his deputies and the cops are all carrying shotguns. What's the deal? At first, like everyone else, I thought it was costume, but now, I'm not sure."

Brittany put her finger to her lips to shush Jinx. "Let's go up stairs to the veranda. I've got something to tell you."

As Brittany and Jinx reached the outside rail, Taya and Lance arrived.

"Hey Brittany, are you guys having any fun? It looks to me like you two make a fine couple." Taya said.

Josie walked up to the group, a carrot in each hand. "My goodness. This celebration is fun. The food is superb." She stood next to the rail looking out to the south and the full moon that glowed over the landscape like a great orange plate.

Brittany turned toward her cousin. "Josie, do you think it would be all right to tell the boys, Lance and Jinx I mean, why we're carrying these guns?"

Josie dropped one of her carrots and pointed out at the moon. "Nenuphars!" she exclaimed.

"Yes. That's exactly why. . . ." Brittany didn't finish. Her eyes followed Joie's finger and she saw ominous silhouettes against the moon. Large creatures of all descriptions were flying in from the south. Without thinking, she jerked the gun from her back and levered a live round into the chamber. The entire group stood with their gaze fixed on the moon and the approaching silhouettes.

Brittany leaned against the rail and yelled down to Sheriff Fitzpatrick, who was near the barn entrance. "Sheriff! Look at the moon!"

Sheriff Fitzpatrick looked up and grabbed the small hand-held microphone mounted on his shoulder and spoke into it.

A moment later, the loud speaker on the patrol cruiser at the main gate came to life. "This is an emergency order from the sheriff. Everyone outdoors must go immediately into Exhibit Barn A. Again! Go into Exhibit Barn A. Carnival personnel, turn off your rides. Turn off all lights except the spotlight truck where the light is pointed toward the sky. Turn off all music. Everyone, move as quietly as you can to Exhibit Barn A."

Carnival machines ground to a halt and lights turned off. A giant griffin, a creature of Greek mythology, was coming in close to the midway. Its head was that of an eagle, with the body and long tail of a lion, but the front feet were eagle talons. The griffin swooped near the Ferris wheel and picked up the operator as he tried to run away. The path that the griffin flew brought it almost directly over the heads of the group. Brittany heard the slow heavy beating of the creature's huge wings in the darkness. She twisted, raised her gun and fired. The griffin exploded with a *poof* and disintegrated into the darkness as the Ferris wheel operator fell to the deck next to the group. He moaned as he clutched at his chest where the eagle talons had cut into him.

Josie shook Lance's shoulder and handed him her gun and ammo belt. "Here, take these. I must see to the injured."

Brittany watched as Josie helped the injured man to his feet, her hand on his shoulder. She could see a light blue glow on the man's shoulder and chest as the look of pain left his face.

Lance spun back toward the rail and shot at an approaching gargoyle tossing spears at the group as it approached. **WHOOSH!** The creature blew into blackness. "Kinda like shooting clay pigeons in Montana," shouted Lance above the ruckus.

Monya came to the rail and fired at an approaching griffin.

"What's going on here?" Jinx yelled as he ducked below the railing to avoid an incoming spear.

Monya turned toward him, shoving her rifle into his hands. "Keep firing at them," she said. "I have to find Chris and Jon!"

Jinx aimed at an approaching dragon and pulled the trigger as

Monya ducked and ran into the building.

"Brittany, what's happening?" Jinx hollered.

"Nenuphars!" Brittany yelled over the chaos. "I'll explain later -- keep shooting!"

Taya ran to Lance's side, gun in hand. Two more Griffins swooped overhead. Lance and Taya backed against each other and continued shooting. Dark smoke exploded over them.

Brittany looked down from the balcony rail. The sheriff and his three deputies were firing at the swarming beasts. The creatures circled and one by one, swooped low attempting destruction on anyone or anything on the ground. The people who were still running toward the barn shrieked in panic, creating more chaos. The sheriff pointed some disoriented people toward the barn.

"Go quickly! Get inside and bolt the doors!" Deputy Flannery ran behind the crowd, giving them cover, firing occasionally toward the sky. He grabbed the edge of the large door as the people ran inside and closed it with a loud BANG.

"We need more light!" Brittany yelled.

Josie, who had returned to the rail tried to pass the message to the sheriff, but the noise was just too great for the sheriff to hear. She placed her hands to her temples and spoke in her mind, "Sheriff Fitzpatrick, give the order to set off the fireworks. All of them -- NOW!" The sheriff looked around for an instant, shook his head and reached the microphone of his shoulder radio.

In seconds the sky was lit up like day as a Roman Candle burst in the air and light flashed across the fairgrounds. A second rocket drove a lion creature off his attack course and he crashed into the Ferris wheel, where he was shot by Deputy Kavenaugh.

Everyone that had a gun, kept firing, reloading and firing again. The fireworks lit up the sky and the strange creatures kept flying in from the south. The crowd of fair patrons that had been enjoying themselves along the midway were now huddled in the exhibit hall as attacking creatures struck, breaking out windows, but they were too large to enter. They dug away at the shingles of the roof trying to get in. A nearby policeman and sheriff's deputy stood their ground to stop them.

As Brittany finished reloading her gun, she counted the shells on her belt and turned to Taya. "I only have nine rounds left."

Taya leaned back over the rail and blasted a gargoyle off the roof. "I'm in the same boat," she said, fingering her belt. "I think I have seven."

Jon now arrived from the dance area and opened fire at the incoming apparitions.

As the flying creatures became fewer and fewer, the remaining ones were concentrating on the balcony, swooping down over the heads of the teenagers.

Sheriff Fitzpatrick ran into the building and up the stairs onto the veranda. He opened fire on the beasts as soon as he arrived. His shoulder radio crackled, "Sheriff Fitzpatrick! It's Jake Standish! My Potsy. . ." The transmission broke up. "Come quick!"

Everyone who was nearby stopped what they were doing for a second to try to grasp what they had just heard. Jon, Chris and Monya ran to the sheriff, they had heard Little Jake's cry for help.

Sheriff Fitzpatrick radioed Deputy Kavenaugh. "Can you guys handle this situation from here? We have an emergency at Whispering Oaks."

The sheriff's radio crackled. "No problem. Good luck."

"Let's go!" Sheriff Fitzpatrick yelled. The group started down the stairs, rushing toward the parking lot.

Chapter 30

The Ride Home

Fireworks exploding over the fairgrounds lit up the scenery as Potsy drove his old van toward Whispering Oaks. "Jake, I don't quite understand why you didn't want to stay and see the fireworks display," he said as he turned off the blacktop to his country lane and headed across the pond dam.

"Come on, Potsy," Little Jake whined. "You've seen one fireworks display, you've seen 'em all. We just saw a huge show up in Kansas City. I'd rather go home and try out that new TV gaming system you put in the basement for us kids. Brittany and Taya both told me it's a blast."

As the van wound its way around the first curve, the headlights picked up a dark form on the road. There in the path of the van lay a body cloaked in back. It looked like a person had been hit by a car and left on the road.

Potsy slammed on the brakes. A cloud of dust rolled up from the wheels, almost blotting out the light from the head lamps. "Don't get in a hurry to run out there, we'll. . . ." He never got to finish his statement. Little Jake had already jumped from the van and slammed the door as he left. As the dust abated, Potsy could see Jake kneeling next to the figure on the roadway.

227

Fear seized Potsy as the figure on the road jumped to his feet, reaching out, grabbing Little Jake. The figure had Jake's body under the arms, holding him off the ground as he kicked and flailed around, trying to escape.

Potsy pushed his door open and stepped from the van. He heard Little Jake telling him something as he slammed his door.

"Potsy! Scream! They hate that."

Potsy felt a shock, perhaps a blow, on the back of his neck and the lights went out. A black curtain was drawn across his eyes and he felt his body sag and fall to the earth.

As the figure grabbed hold of Little Jake, he clutched the man's forearms under his cloak and dug in his fingernails. "Don't scream, please don't scream," the dark figure said, but his mouth wasn't moving. His mouth was making some kind of grunting noise.

Jake kicked the man in the stomach and poked at his eyes. He connected solidly with his feet, but his hands could not reach the man's face.

The voice came again. "Don't scream, you stupid child!"

Little Jake saw his grandfather fall to the ground. Two of the cloaked men were picking him up and dragging him around the side of the van.

Jake screamed as loud as his little voice would allow. He was now eleven and his voice was changing, but he still had that certain high pitched girly scream he could muster every now and then. "Eeee-yoooow-eeeeee," he screamed.

The dark figure started shaking. He released Little Jake and clapped his hands to his ears.

Little Jake dropped to the road running. He had no direction. He was headed down hill on the bank of the pond. The heels of his little cowboy boots dug into the soft mud as he tried to get purchase on the steep bank. His hands reached out and grabbed for anything to slow him down. His hands were filled with reeds along the bank and then -- splash! He was in the water. He raised to the surface and fought for air as he spun, turned and tried to discover where he was.

Then he remembered a story his grandfather had told him about Jim Bridger or one of those frontiersmen escaping from Indians. He lay down in the water on his back and stuck a reed in his mouth. He lay there in the water, trying to be as quiet and calm as possible.

Fireworks bursting over head cast enough light for him to make out the shadows of two figures bending low along the edge of the pond above him. They were talking, one occasionally yelling, but he could not make out the words.

He lay there quietly watching as the two cloaked figures climbed the bank and got into the van. It backed up and drove away.

After a few seconds, he sat up and took a deep breath of fresh air. *Breathing through a straw is definitely not for me*, he thought as he gasped. Standing up, he found his way up the bank and onto the road toward the house.

A few minutes of slogging up the road in wet boots put him on the porch of his grandfather's house. Automatic security lights clicked on as he crossed the porch. He reached for the door knob, which would not turn. "Locked!" he exclaimed in frustration. The ten key combination pad starred up at him in the brilliance of the security lights. *Oh, right! I know this,* he thought. *Potsy gave everyone in the family their own code, and I know mine. It's God Bless America, a space and my name.* Pressing the pad as quickly as he could, G B A - JAKE, he heard the large tumbler in the lock turn and he opened the door.

Once inside, he quickly found a telephone and dialed 911. "Sheriff's mobile relay, stand by. . . This is Sheriff Fitzpatrick, go ahead," a recorded voice on the other end of the line said.

"Sheriff Fitzpatrick! It's Jake Standish! They got My Potsy! Come quick!"

"Where are you?" Sheriff Fitzpatrick asked.

"Potsy's house."

"Stay there and stay inside. I'll be along as soon as I can get there." Jake could hear screaming in the background and two or three loud bangs like fireworks. The phone went dead.

Jake dropped the phone on the table and ran through the house toward his grandfather's bedroom. *Potsy keeps at least one gun handy for burglars. I'll find it and protect myself,* he thought.

He skidded down the hall to Potsy's bedroom, his wet boots failing to grip the hardwood floor. He clicked the light switch on and began to look around the room in obvious places his grandfather might keep a gun.

There was no gun to be seen. He flopped down in Potsy's large recliner to catch his breath and calm his nerves. His gaze suddenly fell on guns, half tucked behind the heavy window curtain in the corner of the room. *Guns! Not one, but four guns.*

He sprang to his feet and rushed to the guns, pulling one from behind the curtain. All were lever action. They looked like the ones he had seen the girls carrying on their backs. Jerking the lever, a shotgun round flipped out. *Purple! Holy Cow! Whoever heard of purple bullets?* He held his thumb on the hammer of the gun and let it forward slowly. *There's a live round under that hammer.* Examining the ejected shell, his fingers traced the sides and his thumbnail flicked the primer at the bottom of the shell. *They're real all right. Maybe Potsy is beginning to like purple in his old age.* Pulling the plunger out of the butt of the gun, he slipped the shell back into the magazine.

Little Jake hung the gun over his shoulder by its leather strap, flipped off the bedroom light and started for the kitchen. He heard the sound of a vehicle on the gravel driveway as he approached the living room. He jumped on the sofa, knees first, leaned forward and peered through the crack between the curtains. Blue and red flashing lights set in a narrow band on top of a Hummer® caught his eyes as he watched the vehicle pull close to the house and shut down. The driver got out, leaped to the porch in one step and shook the large knocker three times against the heavy door.

Whispering Oaks - The Curse

The man standing on the porch was tall, wearing a dark suit, a black bowler hat and carried a long cane with gold handle.

"Who are you?" Little Jake demanded.

"It's me, Shamus. You know me."

"I know Shamus and you're not him," said the exited youngster.

"Okay then. I'm a friend. I'm detective Mactavish of the National Defense Service. I heard on the radio that your grandfather needs help. Will you let me in?"

"You look too well dressed to be a detective to me. Let me see your badge and ID."

Shamus pulled out a leather folder, opened it and said, "If you'll open the door a little, I'll hand it to you."

The door opened tentatively until it reached the end of the heavy night chain, about an inch. Shamus handed his identification through the small opening. Jake took the folder and studied it, running his fingers over the heavy gold and silver badge.

"You know, we're wasting valuable time here," said Shamus.

The door opened wide and Shamus stepped inside. Jake handed his ID back to him.

"Tell me about your grandfather."

Jake closed the door and turned the bolt in the lock. "They were a bunch of ninjas," he said. "They took him." He went on to tell Shamus everything he could remember about the encounter with the abductors.

"The strange thing is, I could hear the one that grabbed me saying, please don't scream, even though his mouth was half open and he was growling and hissing like a cat. The weird thing was, when the van's headlights hit him in the face, his eyes seemed to glow a bright gray."

"He was trying for a mind match!" Shamus said. "Somewhere along the way, the Nenuphar that grabbed you, told you where they were taking your grandfather. You must think very hard, and tell me if you heard, or if in your mind, you saw images of the place they were taking your grandfather."

"Yes," said Jake. "I thought I heard him say something like Wayco House. I saw a desolate place in my mind."

"You must think hard. You must concentrate on the moment this fellow touched you," said Shamus.

Jake sank down on the sofa, his hands to his face. "The place I saw in my mind was gray, all gray. It was like a log cabin with a wood door, but when you go inside, one side is a stone wall."

Chapter 31

Interrogation

Potsy sat very still as the van rocked and chugged over the unkept, rutted, gavel road. The darkness was absolute. He couldn't be sure of where he was. He tried to sit up straight but the hand on his shoulder was worse than a mechanical restraint. A black bag or blindfold of some sort had been pulled over his head. He seemed to be frozen where he sat. He had no power of movement, but his senses of sight, smell, hearing and taste seemed to be working fine. He tried to move his head, to look outside. It was useless. He listened. There was no talking. His captors, if they were communicating, it was mentally. There were no words to be heard.

He sniffed the air for the smell of wild flowers, of pine trees, whatever he could catch on the breeze. The windows were all closed and the only smell was the fine red dust that filtered through the flexing cracks in the doors as the old van traveled down the rough road. The dirt and the Nenuphars smelled like the backwaters of a swamp on a warm day. A very subtle stale odor. Maybe it was the odor of a coal mine. It was a damp kind of odor.

The van rolled to a stop and the side door slid open. "Come with us human," said the Nenuphar that had been sitting next to him with his hand clasp on his shoulder. Potsy felt himself being

233

pulled up and forced to walk in front of his captor. The grip was so strong, he was being controlled like a puppet. The bag was pulled from his head.

When Potsy got out of the van he was able to see familiar surroundings. He was at Waycon's house in Black River Canyon.

The powerful Nenuphar practically lifted Potsy by the grip on his shoulder and shoved him through the open cabin doorway. "As you commanded, Master Drayfus," said the Nenuphar as he released Potsy to stand at a table in front of the Nenuphar Wizard.

"Well, Mr. Not A Gnome," said Potsy. "I can't say I'm delighted to see you. You have on a nice shiny cloak and your pointy ears are sticking up, but other than that, you're still the nasty little sack of slop I always knew you were."

A much taller guard standing next to Potsy, backhanded him with a large gloved hand covered with shiny silver studs. One of the studs caught just inside the hairline on his forehead and made a deep cut. Blood squirted out for a second as Potsy reflexively covered the area with his hands.

"It must be nice to have someone else to do your fighting for you, you skinny little runt," barked Potsy as the stinging on his forehead subsided.

"You misunderstand Mr. Ellis," said Drayfus. "As a Nenuphar Master, these Nenuphar are all extensions of me."

The guard drew his arm back to hit Potsy again. Potsy ducked and slammed his fist into the side of the man's face as hard as he could. The guard sprawled to the floor with a crash as a chair broke under his falling weight. Three other guards jumped onto Potsy and held him up straight.

"Enough!" commanded the wizard. "Put him in restraints."

Potsy was pulled across the room to a flat wall where chains hung with hand and leg irons attached. The guards quickly placed him into the irons. The guards then came to attention.

"Thank you," said the wizard. "Take up your posts outside and alert me as soon as the attack squadron returns."

"Now, Mr. Ellis, let's chat. I believe in a free exchange of ideas.

Whispering Oaks - The Curse

I have questions and you have questions."

"I'm not sure I want to chat with you," said Potsy.

"But I want to chat with you. Where did you learn to fight the Nenuphar?"

"I can read. You idiots have been making your way onto the pages of human literature for hundreds of years. You read a little, you learn a lot."

"You're trying to tell me that you read a book and figured out how to thwart every move I've made in the last month?"

"That's right. I also know humans have no value to you. They make poor slaves and you don't find them very easy to control. You can force them to destroy themselves or convince them to destroy each other, but beyond that, you are helpless."

"That is very good. It sounds like you have done your home-work." The wizard paced up and down, shaking the cane in his hand. He was getting very agitated. He suddenly stopped pacing and placed the gold hilt of his cane on Potsy's forehead, right on the spot where the skin had been torn open by the blow he had received. "You will now tell me where the Elfins are!"

Potsy could feel the nerves in his face going numb. *This guy is trying for a mind match with me. I must think of the great wall of China. How many stones are there? There must be billions and billions of them.* In his mind, Potsy's picture of the Great Wall of China was square in front of him. He could see rocks, pebbles and dust flying into the air on the other side.

The wizard began to shake. He withdrew his cane and slumped slightly. "What are you trying to do? You can't get away with this!"

Potsy felt the cane draw back and his face fell forward. His eyes were closed, but there were bands and bands of black and white bricks and stones appearing as shadows on the backs of his eyelids.

I've got to figure out a way to communicate with the family. What about the time Josie called me from the field? That was mental. Maybe I can I call her mentally and tell her where I am?

Blood dripped from Potsy's forehead, ran down his nose and made a hollow plop sound as it dropped into the dust of the floor. The cut on his head was open and bleeding. *Josie! Josie!* He screamed in his mind. *Josie, I'm at Waycon's house.*

The sheriff's car skidded to a stop in front of Potsy's house and everyone jumped out. Jon's Suburban pulled up next to the squad car and more people exited. As the family ran into the house, Little Jake ran to his mother. "Mom, they got Potsy," he cried as he tried to hide in his mother's arms. Little Jake grabbed the sheriff's hand as he passed. "Sheriff, you have to go after them. You have to get my Potsy back."

The group sat down at the table where Shamus was waiting. He explained all that the child had told him. He finished with, "Does anyone know were Wayco House is? A place of gray logs and piles of flat stones."

Brittany noticed Josie who was sitting across from her. She kept putting both hands to her head, like she was splashing water onto her face or she was trying to get water out of her eyes. She suddenly stopped and held very still.

"Waycon's house!" Josie screeched. "It's Potsy, he's communicating with me. He's still alive. He's at Waycon's house -- he says the Great Wall of China is breaking down, but it will hold for a while."

"It's time for us to act," said Sheriff Fitzpatrick.

"Wait just a minute," said Monya. "You can see all the approaches to Waycon's house a mile away. If we try to attack, Potsy will surely be killed."

The sheriff turned his head and spoke with rigid determination. "We can't let that happen."

Chapter 32

Rescue

Shamus stood next to the table. "You are all at the edge of human endurance. You will not be able to help Potsy if you don't get some rest to refresh your bodies."

"Rest, you mean take a nap, now?" Brittany asked.

"We can't do that," said Sheriff Fitzpatrick.

Monya leaned forward against the table, her face turned down. "I was ready to leave a minute ago, but after sitting here a moment, I feel exhausted."

"Think of the time we waste if we take a nap," said Brittany.

"Fold your arms before you on the table and put your heads down," said Shamus. He started to walk around the table. "As you hear my voice, you shall be comforted and fall into a deep restful sleep. Go now."

A chorus of snores rose from the table. Even Josie was floating in slumber land.

"When you hear the words 'time to wake up' you shall awake and feel strong and refreshed." Shamus continued to walk slowly around the table touching each person as he passed. "Very good," he said. "It is time to wake up."

237

"Say! That was fantastic," said Brittany, rubbing sleep from her eyes. "That's what I call a power nap."

Sheriff Fitzpatrick rubbed his eyes. "Wow! That was great. Now, back to the problem at hand. It is true that Waycon's house sits against a twenty foot high limestone cliff and from it, you can see the road approaches for a mile. Any dust stirred on the canyon rim across the way will alert the Nenuphars."

Monya took a pad and pencil from a sideboard and scratched a quick map of the area. "We need to get in there from behind, but if we are behind, we are above and that rock face can't be scaled easily."

"Here," said Brittany. She placed a finger near the top of the drawing. "This is the spot where Josie and I came out of the forest."

"That's perfect," said the Sheriff. "We can go cross country to the corner of the house and attack from above. The problem with an attack of any kind is the fact that there will be guards posted inside and out. If we shoot one outside, the shot will be heard."

Shamus took a chair next to the sheriff. "I may have the answer to that problem." He pointed his hand toward the hallway. "Phillip Mactavish, please step forward."

The guardian, Phillip, dressed in black with a shinning helmet and breast plate, stepped out of the shadows. He had a quiver of arrows slung over his shoulder and a small re-curve bow in his hand.

Shamus motioned for the guardian to step forward. As he did so, his size expanded until he was five feet six inches tall. "Phillip is the finest archer in the kingdom. He can easily eliminate the need for the use of guns."

Phillip bowed slightly, stepped back two feet and stood quietly.

Sheriff Fitzpatrick touched his chin. "Brittany, have you got any ropes and pulleys out there in your grandpa's workshop?"

Monya answered for her granddaughter. "There's a whole cabinet full of stuff. We were going to take the girls over to Irish Bluffs

238

for a day of repelling. We just never got around to it."

The sheriff laughed out loud as he pushed his chair back. "I can imagine."

While Sheriff Fitzpatrick and Brittany got the climbing gear from the workshop, Taya and Josie saddled a horse and brought it to the front of the building. The climbing gear was tied onto the saddle. The little band was ready.

Chris, Jinx and Lance stayed with Little Jake at Whispering Oaks and the rest of the family followed Phillip and Sheriff Fitzpatrick off through the forest.

As the group reached the perimeter fence, Sheriff Fitzpatrick opened a pair of pliers from his pocket knife tool. As he touched the wire, there was a blue spark and a guardian, dressed in armor like Phillip's, appeared right next to his hand. The guardian's short spear was raised above his head in the attack position.

"Hold!" Phillip commanded. "We have permission to cut this barrier, but we do ask that you stand watch here until we return."

"Aye, Master Phillip," was the reply and the guardian stood aside as the wire was cut.

The party passed through the opening in the fence and moved down the game trails until they reached the spot where moving any farther toward the cabin would expose them to the Nenuphar guards.

"The moon is about to set," said Sheriff Fitzpatrick. "As soon as it does, Brittany, Monya and I will take the horse and make a wide circle so as to stay out of sight and come up on the cliff above the house."

He pointed to Josie and Taya. "Phillip will stay with you girls until as many guards as possible have been disposed of. After that, you girls stay out of sight. You never can tell what might happen."

Phillip had crawled through the grass and watched the house

for a few moments. He was now back. "There are three guards out in the yard. There is one on the porch with the wizard. There must be no one inside with Potsy."

The wizard sat in the wooden chair he had seen the old Indian sit in. He motioned to the guard on the porch next to him. "Go in there and see if you can make a mind match with this human. I have tried, and I am sure his resistance is getting low. We will work in relays until we break him."

Without a word the Nenuphar entered the cabin and walked to Potsy who had fallen asleep, his head hanging down. His arms and legs spread apart in the irons attached to the wall.

"Wake up!" grunted the guard as he removed his glove and slapped Potsy's face. He immediately spread his fingers and took a tight grip on Potsy's forehead.

Potsy jumped behind the Great Wall of China in his mind.

The guard immediately released his grip. "So, you know that trick?"

Potsy turned his head sideways toward the door and pursed his lips. He let out a long breath through a whistle, "Whit - wheee -oooo! Wow, you guys are giving me a headache," he said as he looked toward his tormentor.

The guard's hands jerked upward and covered his ears.

That's it! Potsy thought. *That's what Little Jake was yelling about. I ain't much at screaming, but I sure can whistle.* He began to whistle.

The guard wretched, tumbled and rolled over on the floor, holding his ears. "Stop! Stop that horrible noise!" he pleaded as he struggled to his feet.

"Don't like that, huh?" Potsy said. "Have I got a tune for you? It has so many high notes, I can hardly whistle it."

240

Whispering Oaks - The Curse

The guard drew his large fist back to smash Potsy's face.

Potsy started whistling *"The Star Spangled Banner"* as quickly as he could.

The guard dropped to the floor like he had been struck in the stomach by an eight pound cannon ball. He squirmed and flopped about like a fish on a ditch bank and crawled into the wall twice. He finally reached the door and scrambled outside across the porch and down into the front yard. "No more! No more!" screamed the Nenuphar. Two other guards reached under his arms and dragged him to the other side of the yard while covering one ear with a free hand. Lord Drayfus had already retreated across the yard.

Now I know, thought Potsy, *why the Nenuphars only power over humans is to make them feel depression and despair. They can't do a thing when the human is whistling a happy tune. Maybe that's why folks say whistle, it'll make you feel better. It sure makes me feel better!*

The pains of the Nenuphar's tortures were ebbing and Potsy was starting to actually feel better. He whistled up every tune he knew, gave a complete show of bird calls, laughed loudly between songs and went back to whistling again.

They might kill me, but the Elfins will remain safe, thought Potsy. *In the meantime I will make it as hard on them as I can.*

Potsy could now see the rising sun pouring through the open doorway. Shadows cast on the floor showed him there were no Nenuphars nearby. He laughed aloud with great gusto, he felt jubilant even though his situation was anything but good.

Suddenly the doorway was filled with a Nenuphar guard. Two steps and the guard was to Potsy. He pulled down on Potsy's jaw with one hand and shoved a handful of dirt and sand into his mouth with the other.

The Nenuphar wizard now entered the room and closed the door. "Yes. We read books too," he said as he pulled up a chair in front of Potsy. "Kind of hard to whistle with a mouth full of dirt, isn't it?"

Potsy spit and sputtered and tried to clear his mouth, but it was impossible. He had no saliva with which to flush his mouth. He

241

flipped his head around trying to dislodge the dirt and rubbed his tongue on his shoulder as he tried to spit out the dirt.

"What's the matter, dust storm got your tongue?" The wizard laughed.

I'm exhausted, thought Potsy. *I can't imagine holding out very much longer, Great Wall or no.*

A knock came to the door. The guard opened it slightly. A voice from outside, "Master, there are two human girls running in and out of the forest to the north."

"Deal with it," Drayfus growled. "Take care of them! In the next ten minutes I shall have the secret of where the Elfin city is."

The two girls ran from the forest to the edge of the road, jumping up and down, making themselves very obvious and then ran back into the forest.

"Here comes two of 'em," said Taya. "We had better scurry down the hill so we'll be out of sight of the cabin."

The girls made a mad dash down the hill into the forest. Two wolves came over the top of the ridge right behind them. Taya and Josie stopped and stood before two large oak trees at the bottom of the hill. The wolves slowed and then shape shifted to their Nenuphar soldier forms. They each carried a long spear.

The first guard turned to the second, "Have you ever killed a human?" The second drew his spear back into throwing position. "Not since Henry was King of England."

Both of the Nenuphars got startled expressions on their faces as an arrow pierced through the heart of each one. Their eyes opened very wide and then closed as they became black dust scattered in the wind.

Phillip rose from the brush that had camouflaged him. "I must go and help the others." He left at a full run, going through the forest at a speed faster than a race horse.

In moments he stood next to Sheriff Fitzpatrick who was speaking to him. "Do you think you can hit that guard on the far side of the yard from here?" he whispered.

Phillip crouched low, knocking an arrow onto his bowstring. His black armor faded and turned to green. He now looked like one of Robin Hood's merry men. At the last moment, he stood erect and sent a walnut shaft flying through the air.

Sheriff Fitzpatrick and Brittany moved to the edge of the cliff and let their ropes down. They started to repel the twenty feet to the wood shake shingled roof of the cabin.

Sheriff Fitzpatrick arrived on the rooftop first. He unslung his rifle and took it in both hands. The old shingles refused to hold the weight of the big man. There was a loud crack as the roof gave way and he went plunging through.

The sheriff landed on his feet and fell forward. He saw the guard standing next to the door, a spear in his hand, arm cocked to the throwing position. *BOOM!* The sheriff's gun went off and the guard became black smoke drifting outside through the spaces between the slats of the door.

The gold tip of the wizard's cane glowed yellow as if charging. "You humans are so slow!" The wizard laughed. "I'll kill you and this man," he pointed at Potsy, "before you can cock that gun."

"But not before I can drop the hammer on this gun!" Brittany barked. The barrel of her rifle pointing at the wizard's head as she leaned down through the hole in the roof.

The glow on the end of the wizard's cane subsided. He began to back away. "Perhaps we can discuss this," he said as he edged around the table to the other side, near the lantern holding the black candle. His demeanor began to change. Frustration, anger and fear seemed to rake over him. "I don't know how you humans have beaten me, but I'll find out!" he shouted. His figure became black smoke being sucked into the lantern. There was a flash of light and the lantern and the wizard were gone.

Brittany slung her gun over her back, reached a rafter and

swung to the floor. "Now, that is what I'd call a great exit."

"Yes! Great and permanent, I hope," said Sheriff Fitzpatrick as he gained his feet.

The shackles that had held Potsy seemed to shatter and fall apart as the sheriff pried them open. Potsy fell forward, exhausted. "Water," was his only word.

Chapter 33

As You Were

As the little troop came through the fence line and started toward the house, Brittany noticed the guardian there was no longer wearing battle gear. He was simply dressed in his black suit and bowler hat with shiny green ribbon hat band. His spear was now a walking stick.

Potsy slid from the back of the horse as they reached the house. Josie had restored his health and strength before they left Waycon's cabin, but the group insisted that he ride as a sign of victory over the Nenuphars.

Monya had taken the van home by way of the road and she would be along in a few minutes.

Shamus stood on the porch in his guardian suit wearing his bowler hat. Potsy slipped from the saddle, taking Shamus's outstretched hand as he climbed the stairs. "Welcome home."
"Thank you my friend. Glad to be home," said Potsy.

Lance was waiting at the end of the porch and Taya rushed into his arms. "What a beautiful day this is turning out to be," she said.

"It sure is," said Lance. "The problem is, I have to go back to the fairgrounds to help my dad pack our trailer. We pull out in the morning. We're on our way to the big show in Denver."

As Brittany mounted the stairs, she looked for Jinx but he was

245

nowhere to be seen.

"Brittany," said Shamus. "The High Council has asked that you and Potsy come talk to them for a few minutes."

Brittany hugged up to her grandfather's arm. She looked into his face. "I think we'd be more than happy to come and visit with the Council."

Shamus's staff came down on the porch with a loud bang and the threesome were standing inside the gold circle in the inner chamber. Shamus lead the way as they passed through the great hallways and into the throne room.

"Here we are, Grand Master Enis." He bowed at the waist.

The Elfin leader gestured to chairs in front of the throne as he said, "Please be seated."

The Grand Master took his place on his throne, held his gold scepter high in the air as a salute to his two guests. "On behalf of the entire Elfin community, we would like to express our thanks for your friendship and your courage. Without your wonderful help, our entire civilization could have been destroyed.

"I know you understand that we can not have too many people in the Outer World knowing of our existence. Particularly since you know there are Nenuphars who will try to destroy our world."

Potsy sat up straight in his chair. "Grand Master Enis, is there anything we can do to ensure the security and safety of the Elfin world?"

Grand Master Enis leaned forward, his chin on his hands which were folded on the hilt of his scepter. "I have a great favor to ask. We know you are honorable humans and you will not give away any secrets. We know the memories of the experiences you have had are yours.

"What we ask, is that you give up all of your memories that have anything to do with Elfin magic or Elfin influence. We know you have friends in this city and among our population you are loved and revered as our champions."

Potsy looked at Brittany and raised his eyebrows. "What do you say, darlin'?"

Whispering Oaks - The Curse

A tear ran down Brittany's cheek as the full realization of the request came to her. She shook her head up and down just enough to let Potsy see her answer.

"Yes. For the safety of our friends we are willing to give up all of our memories. There are a couple things I would ask, Sheriff Fitzpatrick's leg. It has been cured by Elfin magic. Can he keep that? And what about the young cowboy that was so badly mauled by the bull?"

"Yes, those things may stay. It is settled then. Tonight as everyone sleeps a great storm shall come. In the morning the only memory will be that everyone had a wonderful time at the celebration. Every memory of Elfins, Elfin magic or Elfin influence will be erased from everyone's mind. *Anything* that happened as a result of or by happen chance, through Elfin association will be gone from your minds."

When Brittany and Potsy returned to the Outer World, Brittany took the keys to Potsy's van, drove to the edge of the property and walked to Torgilson's store. She ran into the soda fountain, set up on her favorite stool and spun around. Jinx came to her right away. She stood up, leaning over the counter, she hooked her hand behind Jinx's neck and pulled him to her. "I know this isn't the top of a Ferris wheel," she said, "but this will have to do." She kissed him hard on the mouth, jumped from her stool and ran out of the store. Tears flooded her eyes and she cried all the way home.

Back at her grandparents's house, Shamus and Josie were gone. Brittany lay in her bed and wept silently until a thunderstorm came up and restful sleep overtook her. At first she dreamed fitfully and then she heard, "And you shall be as you were."

Potsy sat at the breakfast table, drinking coffee and reading the latest copy of the *Gazette*. Brittany and Taya sat across from each other picking at their waffles.

"I think we ought to head over to Torgilson's for one last soda before we have to pack up and go home with the folks," said Brittany.

"Yeah - huh," said Taya. "Sounds like a winner to me."

Potsy moved as if by reflex and laid his van keys on the table. Taya picked them up and kissed her grandfather on the cheek. Brittany was not far behind with a kiss.

"I love you, Potsy," she said.

The girls also kissed their grandmother's cheek as they left.

As the girls reached the top step at Torgilson's store, a white pickup truck pulled in, a sign on the passenger door read: Lance O'Banyon, America's number one bull rider.

Taya placed her hands on her hips as the cowboy exited the truck and started up the stairs. She spoke to her younger cousin. "Now that's the kind of boy I'd like to meet."

The cowboy stopped before running into her and removed his hat. "Hi, I'm Lance, what's your name Red?"

"Taya, Taya Jefferson and this is my cousin, Brittany Standish." Taya kept talking as the group entered the store and walked to the soda fountain. "Brittany's from Salt Lake City and I'm from San Diego, she's fifteen and I'm seventeen."

"That's great," said Lance. "We'll be doing a rodeo in San Diego next year. Maybe you can come and see me ride if you haven't forgotten me by then."

"She'll remember," said Brittany. "Why don't you join us for a soda?"

The Standish Suburban was packed and the family all inside, the good-byes all said when a back window rolled down and Little Jake stuck his head out. "Potsy, next year, can it be my turn to come

248

and spend a month with you at Whispering Oaks?"

Potsy stepped back, raised the thumbs of both hands in a positive manner and said, "You betcha buddy. Maybe, together, we can solve the curse of Whispering Oaks."

Brittany leaned out her window and waved, calling to her grandfather. "Thanks for all the great fishing trips. I had a ball!"

In a jail cell, a dungeon unknown to anyone, a dark figure, arms folded, rocks back and forth on his cot. He mumbles the same thing over and over again. "There are Elfins at Whispering Oaks."

About the Author

Meredith Anderson was born in Osceola, Missouri, the seventh child of a share-crop farmer. He lost his father at the age of five and his mother remarried shortly there after. He did most of his growing up in Moab, Utah. He served in the US Navy during the Vietnam War and was honorably discharged from the USS Currrituck AV7 with the rate of Storekeeper Second Class. He graduated from Weber State University with a degree in Business Management.

Meredith lives with his wife of forty-five years in Osceola, Missouri.

He has been a member of the League of Utah Writers for many years and in 2007, he was president of that state-wide organization.

Meredith received the coveted Gold Quill Award for his novel MORE THAN A JOB, AN ADVENTURE. The book he wrote with his daughter Kristi Sandgren, CIVIL WAR, WOMEN OF COURAGE is very popular among young people who enjoy History.

All of Meredith's books can be found on Amazon.com.

Whispering Oaks 2,
Unexpected Adventures

Watch for Meredith's newest novel on Amazon.com. WHISPERING OAKS 2, Unexpected Adventures, will be out by March of 2012. It picks up two years later as sixteen year old, high school student, Brittany Standish accompanies her cousins Makayla and Taya to Lake Powell for spring break.

There is a serious accident on the highway and Brittany uses the *sparkler* she doesn't know she has. Shamus shows up, Robearus, brother of the Nenuphar soldier in book one, also shows up.

The action and adventure starts on page one and continues throughout the book.

All of Meredith's books can be found on Amazon.com.
MORE THAN A JOB, AN ADVENTURE
CIVIL WAR, WOMEN OF COURAGE
WHISPERING OAKS, THE CURSE
WHISPERING OAKS 2, UNEXPECTED ADVENTURES

Made in the USA
Charleston, SC
07 June 2012